THE
Triple
MOON

THE
Triple
MOON

MAIDEN

Jesse Piper

Copyright © 2022 by Jesse Piper.

Library of Congress Control Number:		2022902974
ISBN:	Hardcover	978-1-6698-8679-2
	Softcover	978-1-6698-8678-5
	eBook	978-1-6698-8677-8

All rights reserved. No part of this book may be reproduced or transmitted in any form or by any means, electronic or mechanical, including photocopying, recording, or by any information storage and retrieval system, without permission in writing from the copyright owner.

This is a work of fiction. Names, characters, places and incidents either are the product of the author's imagination or are used fictitiously, and any resemblance to any actual persons, living or dead, events, or locales is entirely coincidental.

Any people depicted in stock imagery provided by Getty Images are models, and such images are being used for illustrative purposes only.
Certain stock imagery © Getty Images.

Print information available on the last page.

Rev. date: 02/10/2022

To order additional copies of this book, contact:
Xlibris
AU TFN: 1 800 844 927 (Toll Free inside Australia)
AU Local: (02) 8310 8187 (+61 2 8310 8187 from outside Australia)
www.Xlibris.com.au
Orders@Xlibris.com.au
839173

CONTENTS

Chapter 1 Domus...1

Chapter 2 Covena..7

Chapter 3 Adrenal 25

Chapter 4 Sollicitus 35

Chapter 5 Puella 51

Chapter 6 Rigor Mortis 73

Chapter 7 Solstitium..85

Chapter 8 Silva 101

Chapter 9 Ignosce Me 117

Chapter 10 Conventus 133

Chapter 11 Exitium 149

Chapter 12 Ferox 157

Chapter 13 Suavium.. 185

Chapter 14 Porta Mortis... 195

Chapter 15 Subpoena 205

Chapter 16 Mors Omnibus..213

Chapter 17 Proelium Incipit 227

Chapter 18 Meminerunt Omnia Amantes.................................233

Chapter 19 Dolor In Ira..241

Chapter 20 Cum Laude 253

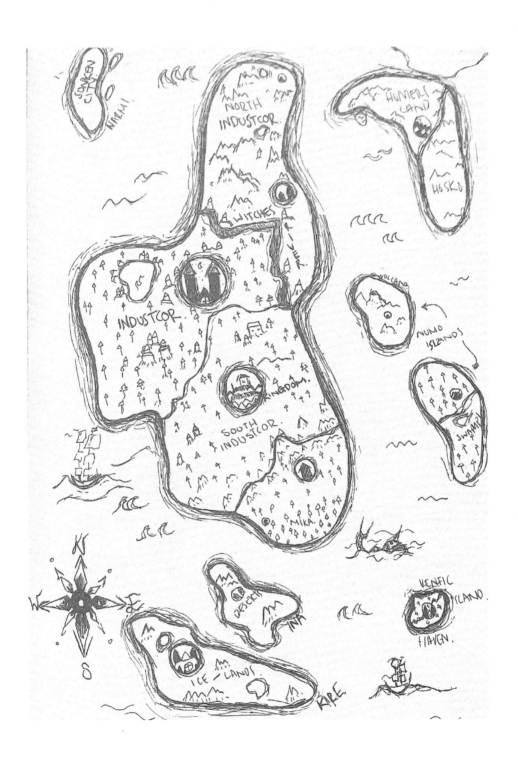

For Liv,
My best friend.

1

Domus

The crippling heat seared the skin, flames wild and scorching hot. As her heart hammered against her brattled ribs- she cried and sobbed for help in misbelief, in the hopes she would awaken from the too realistic night terror. The girl who gasped and choked for air through the fog of smoke, was unaware of the lack of help she would find- scratching her nails across the locked door enclosing her, her nails beginning to bleed at the vicious tendency of her begging.

"Please," She sobbed, the fire reaching closer. "Someone! MUM! ALDORA!" her voice tore at the violence of the screams. This was no game, no twisted night terror tormenting her mind. This was real, and the fire was going to consume her completely. In the beginning, she was sure this was just a tormented and insane dream, but the fire scorched her skin, and she couldn't seem to pinch herself awake.

With a terror-stricken peer behind her, she had already seen the monstrous destruction of fire. Her roof was beginning to cave, floorboards creaking in aghast. Her bed had already shrivelled away, but her heart hadn't.

Not yet.

"Fuck you." She cried, scorn seeping through her as hot as the ashes hitting her skin. This fire was ultimately her evilest enemy, a witch's worst enemy. Death came quicker with fire, all nine lives a witch would have would completely dimmish compared to any other attempt at death. Witches were not so easy to kill unless the fire was in their enemies' grasp.

Her sight was beginning to falter with the smoke that began to drown her, eyes watering painfully and her lips curling in an agitated scowl of defiance. It hurt to breathe, to move, the smoke choking and the fire grazing too close to the skin.

She shoved herself against the door, and despite the shaking of the house's flames- it stuck, budged. For once in her life, she cursed the sheer power of a witch's magic. Her mother's conjuring had made sure protection locks worked, but now her protection lock was not protecting her at all, it was locking her with her catastrophic demise.

"I'm not going to die," She choked, barely able to hear her voice, consumed by smoke, she screamed, black smoke choking down the witch's throat, the fire desiring to consume all her lives.

"I'm-"

She smashed her whole body against the door, body screaming and shrivelling in the pained process.

"Not."

Smash.

"Going."

Smash.

"To."

Smash.

"DIE!"

Smash.

"DIE!"

Smash.

"DIE!"

Smash.

She crumbled into the enchanted bedroom door as the roof began to collapse from above. She began to scream with wild, distorted agony as the fire began to chase. She wailed high and deafening, hands shoving against the door ferociously as smoke began to gust and swoop around her, fire catching. With a shattering scream, the enchantment fractured, the door shattering and flying off its hinges.

"I'm. Not. Going. To. Die." She hissed through heaving lungs, and blind- valueless brown eyes trying to navigate her way through her household as the fire began to spread, the roof stammering. Her ankles screamed like her lungs, eyes streaming with tears and her hair sticking to her sweat and the bloodied, blistering burns erupting along her body the longer she remained to find refuge inside her burning bedroom.

She forced herself through the blaze, not daring to look behind over her quivering shoulder, not daring to see the burnt down corridor or the burnt bodies of her fellow occultist family. She was sure by now she would only be the person to survive this massacre. The hunters had caught onto her family's haven, that was the only solution to why they were all burning to their demise.

She ploughed through with that very rallying cry; *You can make this.*

You can continue the bloodline.

You, The third child of the Amunet family of Witches, the last of the Amunet Family.

You, Arcane Amunet, the last of her blood.

I will not let them kill me too. Not now, and not with fire.

Sprinting through with fire at her heels, the entrance to the house was in clear view- a wide-open door glowing in the light of the crescent moon. However, there was no empty path. A still body laid lethargically and charred black by the entrance.

Her stomach dropped.

The stench made her taste a trace of bitterness on her tongue.

Arcane went to halt herself, her muscles faltering with fear, her heart plummeting down to her stomach. The figure despite being charred by fire; was distinctly one of her sister's bodies, twisted and mutilated with the bane to a witch's existence. Fire.

The girl slipped on the figure, twisting awkwardly to land herself furthest from the defunct body of her oldest sister. Her face was striped, layered with a char of burnt skin. Her body collapsed next to the figure as her face stared breathlessly at her sister's wide open and unfocused doe eyes. That was the only thing left of her face, those delicate eyes.

Tears began to stream down Arcane's hemic, soot-covered face, her heart wrenching, her lips quivering and her stomach twisting as she lurched up on her scalded and bleeding hands, retching the dinner she had only a few hours ago shared with her Sisters and mothers.

"No," She sobbed, choking for air as she dragged herself away from the collapsing abode-which once remained her dynasty of family witches. Now, it was just the memorial for a dead Coven.

"No, Please, no, no-" she continued to sob, stutters of shock slipping from her lips as blood from her bitten tongue dribbled from her mouth. She couldn't bear to look from her burnt hands to her withering and burning house. The only sound in her ears ringing and loud deafening cries that contrasted to the real silence around her. She could still hear her Sisters' cries, their sobs as they burned to death.

Arcane couldn't hear the grinding and twisting of a human figure before a hand gripped her hair, ripped her from her crawling stance, and onto her side across the dirt ground. She sputtered, beginning to scream and kick, aware that her lack of knowledge of magic would ultimately be her downfall.

"Quiet! Please Arcane!" A broken chortle of a dying voice parted her cries. She stilled, peering to the charring form of one of her siblings, barely moving as she lay twisted as if she had crawled to catch Arcane.

Arcane was still, her muscles contracting as she stared into Aldora's charred and missing eyes, the only visible image of her sister was the stale and pained movement of black and charred lips through the burned skin. She was at the brink of death.

"Aldora?" She sobbed. "You're, okay?"

Aldora, her last living sister upon the brink of death, quiet beside her sister's wheezing body could barely reply, her body unable to hold herself up as she lay numb in the dirt, the only comfort being her little sister, the sole survivor.

"No-" Heave. "I'm…...No…"

"Aldora?" Arcane sobbed, moving to grab her hand, but only able to find mutilated fingers.

"There. Sch-"

She struggled to continue, taking a sharp and strangely sounding breath of smoking air as they lay burnt and withering by the towering forest trees that hugged their previous home.

"There's...A Haven.... Ven...Ven-fic...An Island."

Arcane gaped with blinded eyes, unblinking as her sister did not pursue her intended words, but silently smiled through charred skin. It was barely a smile, but that strange, distorted smile only sank Arcane's traumatized heart. A solemn rise of the corner of the lips broke upon Aldora's face before she began to sag dully into the ground beneath them.

"Find it." She whispered; words that urged to be promised.

The light slowly left her eyes. Like the gleaming of stars as they are consumed by grey clouds.

"I love....I... *Love you*...Princess."

A bitter silence erupted within the forest's breeze.

"I love you too." She sobbed, heaving her blood sweat, and tears up above the crescent moon. She watched in utter despair- her organs twisting and her entire heart quivering, a dull ache consuming her as the moon parted a light onto her sister's dead body.

Arcane watched through blurring tears as the crescent moon took her soul to the other side of life itself. Her soul-wrenched from her limp, charred, and mangled body.

Arcane promised then, that she would kill every hunter that threatened her existence as a witch in this crumbling world.

Aldora deserved better.

She deserved better than death.

2

Covena

It took nine months. Nine blistering, and agonizingly empty nine months. Of travel, of pain, of suffering, of burying bodies, of running, hiding, killing- and burying more bodies, of trailing leads, of swimming across the ocean, of climbing, of sinking, of stealing and crying-no, not just crying, sobbing, vomiting, and bleeding.

Bleeding- from the nose, from the internal insides of her organs, from her broken toes becoming mangled in broken shoes, to the scabbing on her knees and the cuts seeping blood from her body.

Nine months of an endless search for salvation that Arcane herself was unsure whether sincere assurance of safety was provided. She peered up through a month of unwashed dirt containing mahogany hair. Gloomy eyes peering up at the preserved palace, towering and glistening in an ancient elegance. It looked empty, without light illuminating the palace windows, no sound aside from the whistling wind through her ears.

With wobbling knees, Arcane shuffled closer in busted shoes and a fractured ankle that recovered over time rather than through healing treatment. As she slipped past the stairs and by the towering entrance doors, she discerned the shrill of a spine chill seeping through her body, her body shivering inaudibly.

Abruptly a blast of sound hit her, shrill laughter and giggling, and the waft of sweet dandelion seeping through her nose. The thrilling chill released as she peered up at the towering and bright palace.

An enchantment.

A word.

For a second, her eyes welled- that was before she wiped them harshly away with her battered and dirtied sleeve. Arcane struggled to keep a contorted face as the laughter began to seep to her personally, relieving the alleviation of hearing sweet sounds and smelling soft scents. She hadn't heard such a soft and welcome sound since...Since too long. *I cannot even recall the last time I heard laughter.*

She took a soft breath of air, shaking the thrill from her body, and outstretched to bang the brass door knocker that was grasped in the hands of a lion's mouth. Three knocks, that's all Arcane pushed herself to do- too many knocks just makes me desperate. But...*I already look desperate. I haven't showered in months, having to find salvage of cleanliness in rivers and ponds. My shoes are barely wearable, and my white skirt is neither white nor wearable anymore- I am death itself, I am desperate.*

Arcane jolted back as the lion moved, roaring back in retaliation. Arcane scrambled back, choking on her gasp- almost falling and tumbling back down the stairs. She regained herself before she could and observed as the lion relaxed into its previous position. Its enlarged head smiled through the brass knocker in its mouth before the towing door swiftly opened for Arcane.

"Snide little cat," Arcane muttered insultingly at the Lion's humour.

Her faltering and exhausted form froze as a group of figures stood by the entrance, and as the afternoon sun spread light across the forest surrounding, it also pierced a soft light into the shaded entrance. Four figures stood bent and smiling by the door- young, childish figures. They all gleamed with teary smiles and wide arms before they began to gleefully gasp and scream-pulling Arcane into an enlarged and befriending group hug.

THE TRIPLE MOON | 9

"Hey!" A voice berated. "Hey! Stop!" It carried down deeper into the palace before the girls were torn away, and another smiling figure appeared. "Leave her alone, she needs a bath and some food before anything else!"

The abrupt sound, movement, and human interaction forced Arcane to stare, unsure how to react- unsure on whether this was real or not, she sensed herself curling inside, her fingers shaky, she feared blinking, of looking away.

She hadn't seen another witch in months.

It was surreal, almost like a dream.

As Arcane peered away from the small plump blonde girl arguing with the other uniformed teenagers and younger girls- at least ten years old. She shakily observed the pure elegant archaic palace, basked in soft chandelier lights and paint-covered halls, bright lights emitting from towering windows. The antique scent wafting through her nose, the inside of the palace prettily comforting. The outside, with the ward, forced people to see an abandoned palace, but now, inside- it was magnificently crafted for comfort.

"I'm so sorry about them!" The blonde gasped delicately. Arcane shook her sight away from ogling at the palace, observing the other students as they gleefully ran off through the halls, waving politely as they disappeared around a corner.

"I hope you understand...There's not much left of our kind, when girls arrive at our steps, it's profoundly relieving."

Arcane awkwardly nodded, rubbing her palm against her shoulder, finding a relieved smile tipping her lips. This girl was comforting, she was close to Arcane's age, with a generous smile that did not falter- even when looking at Arcane's awful figure.

"I get it. We come here for emancipation, for freedom."

The blonde smiled gleefully, and it was contagiously sweet.

"My name is Spring. I know, embarrassing..." Her soft cheeks went pink.

The name wasn't embarrassing at all, it was refreshing.

Quite welcoming.

"Arcane," She muttered with a small, awkward smile. "And don't be embarrassed, it's nice."

She only hummed, reaching out to grasp her bicep and trail her through the palace. She started to chat as she had never, going through basics, going through things that didn't even matter. Arcane let her wild rambling slide because she appeared to be in high spirits.

"I need to know, how does the enchanted ward work?"

"Oh," Spring scrunched her nose in thought, eyebrows furrowing. "I don't particularly know how Mistress Mori did it, but it never leaves, and it only gives entry to witches. This place is our homestead, a haven, only a witch can pass through, so don't fear, you're safe."

"Is it obvious?"

Spring furrowed her brows. "That you're scared? Yes, but that's okay, everyone fears when they first get here, your fear will disappear as soon as you realize how safe we are here. I promise. The girls are really friendly."

Arcane nodded as she mindfully peered out through the large windows that showcased the expanse of the towering forest wrapped around the palace.

"And who is this Mistress?"

"How else can we uphold this haven? There always must be a Mistress, they're life source goes into our protection. They're usually students, just like us. You would've had a Mistress in your last Coven, but ours is different, we are all young here."

"Can I meet them?"

Spring shook her head distantly. "Not many people meet her, she's quite busy, with there being so many students, she doesn't have time. She isn't anything important anyway."

"Oh-"

Spring immediately altered conversation as she skipped along.

"How did you know how to get here? You seem like you have no idea what's going on."

"It's a long story."

"Ah," Spring hummed. "It can wait for trust, then."

Arcane nodded, a soft yawn parting her lips.

THE TRIPLE MOON | 11

"I'll get you to a room," She smiled. "I have an extra room in mine, or you could have your own. It's completely your choice, we have plenty of rooms. That's why its…called a haven." She was nervous, not used to talking to strangers.

Arcane nodded, sucking in an exhausted breath.

"I don't mind."

"Well, you have to mind because unfortunately, I can't choose for you."

Arcane shrugged, her heart hammering as the recollection of panicking as she awoke alone every morning, day after day for nine months after the massacre resurfacing and causing a dreaded ache to fill. This abrupt fear shooting through her made her flinch, immediately making up her decision.

"I'd like to share a room."

Spring simpered with wide pearly teeth; a single front tooth twisted awkwardly.

"Amazing! I've never had a partner in my room before," She began to ramble on and on and on about the other students and what girls shared whose room and who she liked and didn't like, and then to how dirty her room was. She rambled on till she halted at a door, by the highest level, just past the stairs.

Arcane observed the array of doors along the halls, bigger than the other, more sophisticated.

"Warning," She peered up to Arcane with a wince. "I haven't cleaned."

Arcane shrugged. "I won't judge." She was being honest, she couldn't judge, could she? Her entire house was burnt to the crisp, and she hadn't slept on a bed in months. She was more than delighted to take any mattress, it was a blessing to sleep at all.

The room was large and shared two beds by the corners of the room, a window between the beds which Spring had visibly created a nest by the window to sit on with pillows and blankets. The room was barely dirty, but more overwhelmingly filled. She had layers and layers of witchery and enchantment books, melted candles, and white chalk markings all over the wooden floorboards.

"Its-"

"Disgusting," Spring huffed. "I know. I didn't even make my bed."

Arcane peered to her bed, the blankets were entangled and slipping to the floor, the pillow removed from its case. She shrugged, awkwardly smiling at the blonde who stood embarrassingly by her door.

"I was going to say it was homey."

Spring sweetly smiled in gratitude but was more than aware it wasn't.

"What were you trying to do, anyway?" Arcane quizzed, peering quizzically to the chalk markings.

"I was trying out a sweetening spell."

Arcane visibly furrowed her brows.

"Oh...You've barely been taught, have you?"

Arcane was going to retort with the dark trauma card, a type of joke that Spring wouldn't have laughed at. So instead, she zipped her lips shut, trying not to roll her eyes.

"I only know how to move objects. My Coven didn't practice magic because we were close to civilians, too dangerous I suppose."

Spring nodded. "Sorry, I sounded spoiled, didn't I? You're here now, at least. We learn how to control our magic too. You're in the right place if you want to learn magic. Sweetening spells is just something you use for people to like you more."

Arcane barely understood but opted to flop awkwardly and exhaustedly onto her new bed.

"Did it work?"

"I could barely use my magic, let alone get the spell to work." Spring huffed. She blinked as though she had only just realized something. "I'll wake you up for dinner. I'll find you a uniform, one of the girls will have a spare one. The spots under your eyes are.... pitch black."

Spring's uniform in question was a simple black blazer, a white blouse, and a burgundy red skirt, she added black tights for effect, a red bow by her collar to eccentricate her sweetness.

THE TRIPLE MOON | 13

She closed the door behind her, and even with the light bright and blinding-Arcane rolled onto her side and immediately fell unconscious at the delicateness of the pillow, careless to the patch of dirt she'd find on her bed when she'd wake, or the night terror that would trail her sleep.

The same night terror she had every night.

Fire, just fire.

Oh... And burning, screaming bodies.

Hands grasped onto Arcane's sleeping figure, tight and restrictive, and in such a shock she rebounded from her nightmare and lurched up from the bed. Her heart hammered within her chest, a blackness swelling within her. She was ready to reach for anything her fingers could find. She was ready to find anything that would kill whatever grabbed her. With a wild stare, Arcane peered up from matted hair to find Spring.

She had jolted back, hands flying away from Arcane defensively. Her pale brows were furrowed, her chubby figure skittish, unsure. Her eyes were wide, but the stare only appeared for a second before a soft, sympathetic smile tipped her lips.

"Sorry," she muttered. "I need to remember not all witches like physical touch…"

"No," Arcane cleared her hoarse throat, trying to pull the bits of forest life from her mangled hair. "It's fine."

"Well, it's almost time for dinner... I asked if you could sit with me."

"They let me?"

Spring shyly smiled, a glimmer of mischief in her eyes.

"I asked Nipuna, she's one the Mistress' closest hands," Spring began to blabber on about Nipuna; someone Arcane hadn't heard of. She was trying to glimpse an image of the person. "You might like her, she's not talkative though. She probably didn't even ask for us."

Arcane only shrugged, unsure as Spring continued rambling on. "But here's a pair of the uniform. We don't usually get new witches, with all the murder stuff- so I had to track down someone with extra clothes. You'll have to talk to Ohno, say thanks. She wasn't inclined to help."

She said it too lightheadedly for Arcane's liking, but with so many years of turmoil and trauma, sometimes witches turned to jokes to enlighten the mood.

"Wasn't inclined to help?" Arcane asked with furrowed brows as Spring pulled the taller, tanner girl to the shared bathroom. A small room with a single tub of hot water. Spring had made sure the water wasn't too hot, but hot enough to scrub the grime from Arcane. It looked bad, but Spring didn't say anything about the dirt and blood that covered her body, nor the wonky ankle that Spring had earlier watched Arcane struggle to remove the shoe from.

"Ohno is hostile. She also doesn't like me much. I like her though, she's good at witchcraft but she has no friends."

"Oh…" Arcane muttered, stripping from her clothes as the steam rolled off enticingly from the water. Sweat stuck to her clothes as she struggled to strip her long skirt off her legs.

"All these girls you talk about, they don't seem friendly at all."

"Nipuna is unfriendly because she's introverted. Ohno is just arrogant, though I don't mind her company most of the time."

"Isn't Ohno a surname?"

"Yep! She's Aika Ohno, but she doesn't like her name. We just call her Ohno."

"Interesting," Arcane muttered, shakingly removing her undergarments. Her dim eyes peered unsurely at Spring's teetering form by the door.

"I'll leave you be," She smiled, catching on.

Arcane found herself faltering, she didn't want to be alone.

"Talk to me through the door. Tell me about everyone."

Spring vividly beamed, white teeth glistening. "Okay! Well-"

As soon as the door shut, her voice became muffled. Arcane could hear well enough, though. She urgently slipped herself into the warm, steaming bath. She dunked herself beneath the water and came back out after a long second of silence beneath the heat. She watched the dirt and grime darken the clarity of the water.

THE TRIPLE MOON | 15

"I'll just talk about the girls we sit with for dinner, we see them the most-" She began going on and on about twins, but Arcane found herself fumbling with what Spring was saying as she began to feel a shot of fear through her ribs. These fears and flinching were always momentarily apparent, especially when Arcane was surviving alone, but now she was safe.

You're safe now.

Arcane.

Arcane?

You're safe here.

Arcane swallowed her trauma down, the images of her family often appearing at the worst of times. She could still smell the stench of burnt flesh, still feel the flames against her skin. Her hands shakily touched the scarring flesh of her right shoulder. From her collarbone to her bicep was itching, scarring burns.

People say injuries heal, but this injury never heals, and neither will the memories. Even when Arcane is beyond the age of the hundred digits, she will always remember.

Things like death do not simmer away easily.

They live within a person till their very demise.

"Arcane?"

"Oh," Arcane jolted, hands peeling away from her scarring side. "I'm done!"

"Come out, I'll comb through your hair!"

By the time Arcane looked presentable, and smelt presentable, the group would be appearing for dinner in the hall. Spring excitedly tied a red bow to the girl's wrist as they walked through the archaic halls, floorboards creaking with each step Arcane fumbled with her words as she stared, unable to fully take in the interior of the haven.

It was less of a haven and more of an ancient palace.

"It took me a very long time to get used to how beautiful it is here." Spring smiled, peering up at Arcane's curious eyes.

"How long have you been here for?"

"Since I was born. My Coven dropped me off at the door when I was maybe.... five years old? It was the smartest decision they ever made."

Arcane furrowed her brows. "Because you're safe here?"

"Exactly. Barely any of my Covens are still alive, the only ones alive live here. I promise Arcane, this is the safest place you can be. Hunters are glamoured to see an abandoned palace, Mistress provides a spell that compels them away."

"There's no other place like this?"

"Not that I know of, Ohno might know though."

As she exclaimed the name, the double doors peeled open automatically, leading the two to the dinner table. It was at least able to seat twenty people, and it seemed at least half of them sat in seats. A long table was situated in the middle of the room, the room chatted in quiet talk.

Heads turned quickly, aware of Arcane.

There was a thick silence, and Arcane struggled to relax with every single eyeball on her, analysing her from her toes to the tip of her head.

"That's the newbie?" A figure muttered from a chair further from the head chair, away from the entrance. She stood stiffly, and as Arcane joined the table of peering girls, she could see her features more closely. She had circular spectacles on the edge of her nose, her face a sickly paleness in contrast to her warm brown hair. A red bow twisted in her ponytail.

"Arcane, this is Ohno."

"I've heard things about you," Ohno peered through her spectacles, obviously reluctant.

Arcane wanted to say I hope they're good things, but that was not the case.

"Thank you for the uniform." Arcane awkwardly pulled her long sleeve blouse down over her fingers, hoping it wasn't translucent enough to see her scarring. She was overthinking, of course, she was, the uniform wasn't translucent at all.

THE TRIPLE MOON | 17

"We can't let people walk around without uniforms; it would just make us look cheap."

"No one cares about that, Ohno." Spring cut in.

"Still, the uniform is important in a small society like ours. It provides order and stability."

"Oh, by the moon, she likes to go on, doesn't she?" A figure cawed from across the table. Arcane watched Ohno scowl in distaste and peered towards the untamed laughter. Spring shivered distastefully by Arcane's side, but she couldn't seem to look away from the stranger to see Spring's facial reaction.

The figure was sitting awkwardly on the table, her legs stretching across the top and toppling over an empty glass. She was careless of her riding skirt, and the fact that if Arcane looked any lower, she'd very well see every part of her thighs, along with her red underwear. Arcane reddened and peered to her wild, fanged smile. It was far too mischievous for Arcane's liking.

"Takanashi Ito, but you can call me anything you like," she winked with abnormal eyes. Her right orb is brown while her left was a murky white. Blind, she was blind in her left eye, Arcane realized. She had a little scar vertically beneath and choppy, uneven hair that looked just as bad as Arcane's had once looked. She didn't adorn a red bow like the others, though. She seemed to lack a lot of things, including bloomers underneath her short skirt.

"Nice to meet you," Arcane didn't smile, but her eyes did. She tried to seem friendly, but Ito's character was catching her off guard. Ito leaned back against her chair; her blouse barely buttoned.

She hummed. "Finally, a witch with personality."

Ohno scoffed. "Hardly. She barely spoke."

"Silence speaks louder than words." Another voice aroused. Spring smiled wild and proud as she twisted away from the banter. Arcane was unsure why Spring was so excited, till she saw the towering figure of a woman. For a second, Arcane thought the figure was the one and only Mistress of the Coven.

But no, her hopes were too high.

"Nipuna!"

Nipuna barely reacted to Spring's outburst. She was taller than all the girls, and rather than wearing a skirt for uniform, she wore long black pants. Her dark skin gleamed against the white blouse; her hair chopped boyishly over her eyes.

"Take your seats," She muttered beady eyes peering at Arcane, before twisting away to her seat beside the head of the table. The head of the table, the Mistress' seat. Spring pulled Arcane beside her. Spring sits idly across from Nipuna, and Arcane found herself eye to eye with Takanashi Ito, more commonly known as the deranged witch with the tendency to stare.

She simpered cunningly.

"I never said she could sit with us." Nipuna drawled. Arcane furrowed her brows in confusion, peering to Spring- but was ignored.

"You didn't, I know," Spring nervously replied. "But I had to do what was best for her. She's with us."

More girls peeled inside the warmth of the dining room, finding their designated seats.

"I say we vote to determine her introduction to this group."

"We aren't a cult, Ohno." Spring denied. "Seriously, the designated dining rooms and levels are overrated anyway."

"Overrated?!" Ohno sneered. "Mistress Mori designated these rooms specifically for similar witchery levels and ages of maturity. Without set protocol and set stability, we will break under pressure. Without a hierarchy, society fails."

Across from Arcane, Ito mocked Ohno silently, scowling as she stabbed her napkin with a sharp steak knife. "Here she goes again," she muttered, only for Ohno to give her a searing glare through her spectacles.

"We aren't voting," Nipuna muttered distastefully. "I'll talk to Mistress Mori myself."

"Why can't we all?" A twin muttered from down the line, a replica sitting by herself, with her hair pulled into a bun on the other side. "Mistress has been away for long enough; we haven't seen her in weeks."

"Away?" Arcane questioned. As she did, food began to pile up on the table in bursts of black magic, a black mist filling the room as plates covered in divine foods littered the table. Arcane struggled to contain the shock on her face, jaw slackened.

Spring nudged her elbow softly with a shy warning to stay quiet as the table began to argue.

They played with their food as they spoke, Nipuna entirely ignorant to their words as she ate. It was clear she had no regard to their discomforts.

"The woman hasn't left her bloody study in weeks," One of the twins barked out, to which the other complied, mimicking her words. It was hard to tell them apart, they were identical aside from the way their mouths raised and dipped.

Ito rolled her mismatched eyes at the desperateness of the twins, a simpering fitting her lips as she listened to the argument across the table. She found joy in the chaos, and Arcane watched the excitement flicker in her eyes before she provoked, and only stirred the pot.

"She's probably dead."

Silence as the group tore their eyes to Takanashi Ito as she leaned back lethargically in her chair, stabbing at her meat.

"Ito!" Ohno snarled. "Don't you dare say that-"

"Come on, Nipuna's probably already buried her body-"

"Nipuna tell her to be quiet-"

"Maybe her bodies under your bed, *Aika*. Check your bed tonight!"

Ohno's eyes narrow viciously.

"Don't you dare call me that again?"

"A-"

"Quiet," Nipuna muttered, and with her drawl of detest, the group stilled, the stab of Ito's knife against her napkin being the only sound. "I'm sick of your entitlement on whether you all decide when or when not to see Mistress Mori. As you all eat divine meals and drink red wine, she's ensuring our safety is perfected."

"She needs to relax," one of the twins muttered, quieter, less crude than the other. "We've been safe here for years, it's not common she eats with us, and we need to stay accustomed to that."

Nipuna did not reply, and the silence ensured.

Arcane couldn't help asking questions.

"Is there a possibility I could see the Mistress?"

Ito scoffed.

"Only her little minions get to see a glimpse of her."

Nipuna side-eyed her attack.

"You're just jealous," Ohno smiled as she cut through her stuffed chicken.

The psychotic witch only cackled, high and shrill. "I'm not jealous. Trust, I'm one of them."

If Arcane could not see the Mistress herself, she'd have to figure out another way.

She could not live much longer without vengeance. She craved their deaths, slept dreaming of it- daydreamed of it. She knew such a large Coven of witches could revolt, if need be, but how exactly could Arcane start such a thing?

The death of her family made her realize their deaths were closer than expected.

The hunters grew stronger with each passing day, as the witches in hiding only diminished.

They didn't have much time, none of them did.

Lionesses don't hunt on their own.

Nor did the witches.

Nipuna rolled her eyes beneath her fringe, unable to peer at anyone but her food as everyone began to break away from their conversation. She wasn't the type to talk. Still, Arcane tried.

"It's really important that I see her,"

"Look," she muttered, "I would help if I could, but Mistress Mori doesn't let people come to her, she comes to them. You have to wait for her help, with whatever that may be." Nipuna looked doubtful at Arcane, almost as though she doubted the severity of why Arcane needed help.

THE TRIPLE MOON | 21

"Don't look at me like that," Arcane muttered, a searing ache of ire sinking through her. They wouldn't take her seriously; she knew that now.

"Like what?"

"Like you think my issue isn't important. Matter of fact this issue involves every single one of us."

Witches were going extinct; it was all their issues to overcome.

Hiding will no longer be an option once the hunters learn of the haven on Venfic island.

Nipuna didn't reply, nor did her face show any form of reaction. It never actually displayed any form of emotion, only the occasional irritation aimed at the psychotic Ito.

"How so?" Ohno quipped from further down the dining table.

"Why we're here," Arcane muttered, abruptly with the whole table gaping at her for an explanation. "We've been driven from our homelands, massacred by the millions throughout history. This has not changed and sooner or later they'll find us again."

"That's absurd," One of the twins muttered. "We're safe here. I'd rather stay here and be safe than even try to attempt to stop what's happening in the cities."

"What happens when they find us?" Arcane sneered shortly, finding less and less patience when it came to their neglect. They'd lived most of their lives in this safety, perhaps they had not seen what the world of witches had come to.

"Nothing will happen." Nipuna interrupted as she eyed Arcane sharply.

"How are we so certain?"

"Mistress Mori was born to protect her Coven; we are hidden from the world. What are you even implying?"

"I'm implying we build a rebellion, fight, not hide. We cannot live on this island forever. My Coven thought we could do the same thing and look at us now."

Look at us now.

Look at *me* now.

Just me.

The group glanced questionably at the latest Coven member, her cheeks glowed in mortification and ire, her entire body thrumming with irritation at the fact none of the witches agreed with her. She clenched her teeth, digging her nails into her palms in the hopes of holding herself back from lashing out. She peered at Ito, who smirked mischievously.

There was a thick, unsure silence until Takanashi Ito broke it.

"I would love to shed some blood."

Nipuna sneered at Takanashi Ito's comment, but Ito did not take this as a warning as she proceeded.

"The girl has a point-"

"Her names Arcane-" Spring interjected to which the woman was blatantly ignored.

"-We can't hide like little rabbits in our burrows, waiting for the snakes to devour us for dinner. We look weak. We cannot live like this forever. I say we bring this to Mori-"

"Mistress Mori," Nipuna and Ohno hissed simultaneously.

"-Oh, *please* as if you don't chide her name as if you are not a subordinate and a worshiper for her. You kiss her feet." She sneered through fanged teeth.

Ito aimed her words splittingly at Nipuna, to which she eyed her darkly, and motionless.

"Our Coven has remained here for hundreds of years without Hunter's finding us."

Ito scoffed. "We don't know that. Half of the witches who lived through the genocide hundreds of years ago are dead now."

Arcane watched as Nipuna and Ito began spitting at one another with curses, countering each other with flimsy points and factual evidence Arcane was unsure on whether was true or not.

"Why did you have to start this?" Spring whisperer beside Arcane, her eyes were wide as she peered up at her.

The girl furrowed her brows at the blonde.

"What do you mean?"

"That idea will only kill us Arcane, are you crazy?"

A swell of dread hit Arcane, her nerves freezing and a shock of chills seeping down her spine. It was humiliating hearing the one friend Arcane had, said she found the idea awful, disconcerting even.

Am I crazy?

Nausea overcame Arcane, her naturally bronzed skin becoming ashen, as though the life had drained from her. She twisted from her chair, her stomach rolling and twisting, she needed air, she needed to spew out the nonsense.

"May I be excused?" She eyed Nipuna, she only nodded her head stiffly, tall body unmoving as it glared along with her form, having broken from her argument with Ito.

"You may."

3

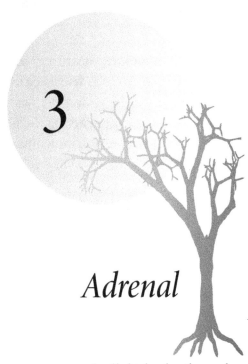

Adrenal

Arcane escaped the bedroom as soon as daylight broke through the forest's trees. She didn't want to see Spring, not right now, at least.

How dare she call me crazy?

If only she knew why I had asked.

Arcane wasn't so irritated as she was embarrassed. Her first start was at a new beginning, a new Coven, a Haven, and it had been ruined because she initiated a conversation that endangered the group's safety, even then apparently what she asked was crazy of her.

Lunatic, even.

"I'm not crazy, nor am I some lunatic," Arcane whispered beneath her breath, her eyes darting upon the books of the labyrinth of a library. Her fingers wiped the dust off the spines of the books as she observed the agelessness of the intricate pages.

"Only lunatic's talk to themselves."

Arcane whipped around, involuntary flinching at the breath that fanned her neck. She pressed herself against the bookshelf, as she came face to face with Takanashi Ito, the psycho witch with red panties.

Arcane should've heard her approach, should have but didn't. Ever since the fire she had been as vigilant as she could ever be. Because she was so wide-eyed, she didn't even sleep, the lingering vision of death keeping her on her feet. Her eyes were always peeled open, nose always ready, mind always prepared for the worst.

Acting in such a way allowed her to live so long in such a cruel world.

Often, Arcane even found herself scouting for exits. In the dining room, the only exit was the entrance, either that or the door that led to the kitchens, but Arcane wouldn't trust there would be an exit from the kitchen. There were no windows in the dining room. The exits in Spring's room were the entrance or the single opening window between the beds.

So how could she have missed Ito sneaking behind her?

Arcane furrowed her brows.

"How could I not hear you?"

Ito's fanged teeth peeked through her smirk; her bandage-covered arms crossed over her chest as her single eye gleamed. She stared at Arcane with a strange atrocity, unblinking.

"*Magic,* Little Dove."

"Don't call me that."

Ito only hummed teasingly as Arcane continued.

"And what sort of magic?"

"Witch magic."

Arcane huffed as Ito proceeded.

"Just say it."

"If it means making you pleased? No, I will not."

"Well, I guess I should take my leave," Ito went to turn, she unevenly cut hair swishing as she turned away. Arcane bolted, her fingers grabbing onto the sleeve of her blouse. As Arcane pulled her back, a mischievous smile appeared upon her face.

"Fine," Arcane muttered. "Could you please teach me?"

"Hm... I'd like you to plead for it, but I'm sure you are not *that* desperate." Arcane tried not to glow red at the cheeks, her stomach twisting. "You haven't been taught much...Have you?"

Arcane rolled her eyes. "No, I haven't."

"How strange, a witch who is magicless…"

"I'm not magicless," Arcane sneered. "My Coven never had time to teach me, my home wasn't on a hidden island, we couldn't risk using magic."

"That's why you want to see Mori."

"Mistress Mori," Arcane gulped, eyes wary of listeners. "Yes. I'm sick of running, and I want to learn more magic. I have the basics, moving things, and such."

"You've come to the wrong person,"

"What?" Arcane snapped. "What is that supposed to mean?"

She yawned like a feline, stretching her arms over her head. Arcane watched with narrowed eyes and red cheeks as the hem of her blouse lifted, showing her toned stomach beneath. Arcane's heart gradually hammered against her ribs at the closeness of Takanashi Ito.

"Mori is the strongest witch we have. She's the only one that could teach you well enough and the rebellion idea…"

"Spit it out already," Arcane muttered beneath her breath, trying to cover up the hotness of her cheeks as she rested herself against the bookshelf.

"It's a ravishing idea, but implausible. Say, I love the smell of dead hunters, but we got to find them first, even then, do we know where they are? Mori is the only person who would know."

"There seems to be a 'but' at the end of your sentence."

"Mori isn't friendly, nor does she let herself be seen unless she has to. But love, I always have brilliant ideas. We'll get her to come to us, then we can persuade her to think about our plan."

Arcane couldn't trust her word.

"Your idea?"

"Make the creature come out of its cave," She cackled beneath her breath, teeth gleaming. She snatched the book in Arcane's hand, snapping it shut. She inched close, breath caressing Arcane's cheek as she nestled the book into space upon the endless shelves. "The best way to get a creature from its cave is to starve it."

Ito was too close, a strange itching controlling Arcane's body, she tried to peel away from the hotness of her breath against her neck. Ito's long nails dragged beside her head, along the shelves as she drew and drew a masterly mischievous plan.

Arcane furrowed her brows. "We aren't going to physically starve her, that's implausible."

"She's already starved from contact. She used to leave her little cave, I would visit her, so would Nipuna."

"How long has she been gone?"

"Gone-No, No... Not gone, hidden, hiding-" she reiterated. "The little creature has been hiding inside her cave for weeks now. She hasn't even opened for Nipuna."

Her long nails softly dragged down Arcane's hot cheek. Arcane had a glimmer of ire in her wide eyes. Ito only simpered up into her stare, finding a sense of masochism dwelling beneath her skin, tickling her.

"How do you suppose we do this?" Arcane began to get tired of her frolicked games, but not of the way a gleam appeared in her eye; that was something she did not tire of, the emotion emitting from it was mischievously endless, and tireless to stare at. Arcane tried to swat her nails off her, to no use, Ito only slipped closer, lips pulling into a sinister grin.

"Her bedroom is on the highest floor, a few turns from our hall. We go close- so close, but not so close she suspects u-"

"How would she know?"

"Magic, my little Dove."

"Don't-" Arcane furiously huffed, crossing her arms as she shoved herself into the shelf. "Forget it." She huffed underneath her breath.

"Don't get so flustered, it only makes you more entertaining."

"Get on with the plan, Ito. I don't have all day."

"You do, actually," Arcane went to protest, but Ito placed her long nail down against Arcane's scowling lips. "We have all night, we can skip dinner, just for us."

"How do you expect to get Mori to talk to me? Mori is already derived from contact, now what do we do? Depriving her of contact will make her more willing to talk?" Arcane was beginning to question the girl's sanity, well, she always questioned it. The sinister idea always lingered in her mind. Some sort of strangeness to Ito, a masochistic sense when she looked into her mismatched eyes.

How...How did she lose that eye?

"Mori was born to protect us, that is her purpose by the founding witches, just like every one of her Sisters created. She has a timepiece upon all of us, a predicament pair of eyes, always watching. She senses our fears, she knows when we are in danger."

Arcane huffed, "I don't like this plan."

"I wonder...Does the idea excite you? She may be watching us, right now."

It barely took a second for Arcane to understand what Takanashi Ito implied.

"You want to endanger my life..."

"She comes every time."

"You know because?"

Ito simpered cunningly, attractively- insanely, fluttering her eyelashes as she bent closer, attempting to stand intimately close with Arcane, her nails drawing circles through her blouse, along her collar bone.

"It has worked every time I have been derived from her. Trust me."

"There is...Little to trust." Arcane narrowed her eyes, holding in a gulp of fear as Ito's eyes narrowed for a millisecond, before they relaxed, her previous face of fury only seemed to be a hallucination of anxiety.

"She will come. She has come to save me every time, always. I have never once truly questioned her ability to save my life, only the times I have not wanted her to come."

"What," Arcane furrowed her brows. "Are you going to stab me? Shoot me with flaming arrows? Throw me off the tip of the building? *Are you insane?*"

"Only sane during the hours of sleep, yes."

Arcane stared at her, stunned.

"Now, Let's go."

Ito gripped her hands against Arcane's blouse, ripping her from the shelves and out of the boundless library. Arcane could barely sink her heels to the floor before she was hurled down the hall.

The air was frosting, cold, and icy to inhale the more the darkness cascaded along the sky. A hot wisp of air parted Arcane's lips as they trembled. Her hands were firm against the rails, shaky and decrepit, Ito's figure suspiciously too close to her, a voice in her ear. Despite the uneasy closeness, she valued the warmth of her body.

Arcane gulped. "So… I just jump off?"

Ito smiled cunningly. "We jump off. I will come."

Arcane suspiciously peered to Ito, observing the unceasing gleam of a smile.

"What's in it for you, Takanashi Ito?"

A sharpness cut through her voice, a bristle inching down her spine as Ito only smiled wider.

"I am not sleeping, that's why."

"And you question why I don't trust you." Arcane narrowed her eyes.

"I would like to see Mori just as much as you. Maybe if I were to accompany you, she'll stay longer to scream at me, maybe hurt me in a way in which I will enjoy."

"Your profit for helping me is to be yelled at?"

Ito only simpered, wide with fanged teeth.

"Oh, the thrill of hatred, I love it."

Arcane couldn't bear to listen much longer, she hoisted herself onto the balconies railing, her knees bent, flexing to keep herself on top without faltering off the edge. With a teetering, quivering breath like the shaking of her hands, she peered down below her. The wind was hardly a soft shove, the ground a long dive down. Beneath stood the entrance, the place Arcane had only just stood upon, waiting for a welcoming into the sense of safety.

"I don't- I c-"

"You can do it and you will."

Tears strained to erupt, but she held them in, her stomach quelching as she peered down upon the lingering fall. If the woman with Arcane's life upon her hands did not save her, Arcane could imagine her body lifeless upon the steps of the haven, blood dried upon the morning, where one of the girls will find her body.

She could imagine the girls screaming but rather than praying to survive the fall, she rather prayed that the girl to find her would not be younger than a child, traumatized by death upon her doorstep, literally.

Arcane was too deep in the consciousness of fear to realize Ito had sidled beside her on the rails. She smiled like a cat, mischievously. Arcane narrowed her eyes, taking a sharp breath of distaste.

Arcane knew she had many lives to spare. Eight, to be exact. Even if she were to splatter against the stairs leading to the haven, she would recover within her own body, and awake like a cat- but then, only with seven lives remaining, and the rebirth of a dead body took months, years- at some lengths.

Seven lives were too little to have, especially when Arcane was so young.

"If I die-"

"Yes, yes. I promise that if you die, you can kill me yourself." Ito rolled her eyes.

"If I die, I'm taking one of your lives for myself, Ito."

Arcane tried to ignore what they implied, the strange imagination that maybe Arcane could steal one of Ito's lives. She had never done such a thing before; the idea was frightening. Only the worst of witches killed one another to steal their souls and with it their lives and magic.

It was a silent agreement, the witches were Sisters, and only a cruel monster would kill their sister.

She nestled it in the back of her head, content enough with the threat-despite Ito's lack of reaction.

She knew deep down she would never be able to kill Ito, no matter how hard she tried. That sort of cruelness of killing a sister was not a part of her.

"On the count of three-"

There was no count of three. Ito barked a laugh, cutting Arcane off abruptly- before her hand shoved the other witch harshly into the air, tumbling through the wind and off the balcony. A scream was short-lived, caught in Arcane's throat as her stomach flipped over and over, the ground inching closer and closer.

Through teary eyes, Arcane peered up to find Ito soaring above her, the wind clearing her hair from her scarred face. Staring at Ito forced the spiral of fear to halt, for a second of released fear as she stretched her arms out to sense the chilled wind against her heated skin.

Ito was surging above her, reaching for her hands, before a black mist enveloped her, and she disappeared. A scream of fear tried to break through her throat, parching through Arcane's lips, but nothing could do it. She was falling straight for the ground, too close to the ground, too close to the splatter of blood and the lack of a beating heart.

A sharp breath tore through her throat, tears streaming down her face. Though she blinked through the blur of salted tears; hands, as cold as snow enveloped her through the dark mist that hung around her in the air, as if the blackness was chasing her- or whatever controlled it was trailing.

A witch's breath fanned her face through the mist, their faint hold unfaltering as they fell through the air.

The sky flipped, and Arcane was no longer flying through the sky, no longer holding the figure through the mist. Her twisting stomach had halted as she peered to the sky, sharp, uncontrolled breath parting from her parched lips. The wetness of the grass pressed against her healing scars, soaking through her white blouse. She jolted up, twisted to the dark mist.

Only to find nothing but the lingering scent of a witch's magic.

"Fuck," Arcane snapped. "It didn't work."

A meter away Ito lay upon the wet grass, a figure in the form of a kitten stretching from a nap. She yawned loud, sharp fangs peeling from her lips as she peered dreamily into the night sky, observing the constellations.

Ito maniacally screamed before she stilled.

Arcane jolted up, through a mass of air-blown hair she peered to the tearlessly sobbing Ito, her skirt riding too high, her blouse half unbuttoned.

"I'm completely done for; my time is over."

"Why are you upset? She saved our lives; without her, we'd have one less of a life."

"Well next time-" Ito jolted up to meet Arcane's irritated sneer, she cried like a maniac, eye wild with ecstasy. "-Let me die! Let me splatter- no, let the blood splatter upon her very, pale, delicate face. Let her be the one to see my demise. Make it romantic!"

"You are insane, was her saving us not enough?" Arcane huffed.

"All I want is her attention, that's all I want. She used to give it to me too, but now, she doesn't value me like she used to. She saunters in her room day and night and no longer lets me in. Well, I'll find a way in I will," It was silent, only for a second as Arcane questioned Ito's sanity. "Guess what, little dove?"

"What..." It wasn't a question, Arcane didn't care at all.

The plan didn't work, Mistress Mori didn't even give her a second of her day, and it turns out Ito was more obsessed with her than she realized. Arcane wouldn't be surprised if she had a shrine of Mistress Mori, maybe even a strand of her hair, or maybe a vial of her blood.

"You're helping me."

Arcane rolled her eyes.

"I'm not helping you-"

"Help me, it helps you. Listen, we break into her room-"

"And let her kill us? She's the Mistress, the leader of our Coven. She could snap our necks with a single word, a single wrong move-"

"That's preposterous, you sound like you'd be mad."

"I would be! I don't want to die! It seems every second I spend in your presence I am quicker to lose another life."

Arcane stomped up from her lying position, finding the outside too cold, too vulnerable for her liking. She gave a stifling cold glare to Ito before she sauntered back to the haven. She was very aware of the simper, and the beady glare on her back as she departed.

"She would never kill us, only- severely dismantle us..."

Arcane couldn't bear to listen to the psychotic Takanashi any longer despite her obscure beauty, she was horrified to converse with. Her mind reeled with the strange ingenuity of life.

Arcane found herself back at her shared bedroom with Spring Lee. She dismantled the door with a flick of magic from her fingers- it was the only thing she could do, and she hated admitting it. It was shameful, to call herself a witch yet to know so little.

She watched the door open and close with a creek behind her. She slipped inside her room, finding Spring unconscious upon her bed. She peered to her sleeping form, hair was thrown across her pillow, blankets falling off the small bed. Arcane sensed the tingle of distaste at what Spring had said to her yesterday. Despite her grievances, she flicked her fingers, and the blankets rolled back onto the blonde witch's sleeping form.

"You're lucky I don't want you to freeze to death."

Peeling away, skipping over piles of books, and still lit candles. Arcane stripped herself of her sodden clothes, slipping into the covers. With a final flick of her fingers and the quivered- uncomfortable stare aimed at the candles, the fire blew out.

The scent of magic only lingered, like ash, dirt, and what the colour forest green would smell of.

4

Sollicitus

"Come on! Get up!" The voice sounded sweet like honey, chiming like her sister's voices as Arcane curled deeper into the blankets, having imagined her Sisters shaking her awake, aware that Arcane was always the one to sleep in, and never get out confines of her bed. They always came around the same time, almost every morning. Arcane remembers the ire she had when her Sisters woke her up, jumping on her bed, throwing broken pillows with falling feathers at her body as she hid underneath the cover...

Now, she wished that irritation was complacency.

Now, she never slept, let alone slept in. Her mind was consistently in the state of awareness, or at least the irrelevant fear of death leaning around every corner, watching, observing, and waiting for the right moment to strike her down.

Every night as she gawked to the rooftop above, she begged and hoped that if she were able to sleep- she would never wake, other days, she hoped to awaken back in her bed, at home, with her Sisters and mothers.

She wished that the voice chiding her to wake was her Sisters, cradled around her.

Like they used to.

36 | JESSE PIPER

But they would never wake her up again.

She peeled her eyes open, twisting off the aching of her scarred shoulder, unwrapping herself from the blankets shielding her head. She had barely slept, and at the wince of Spring's face, it was visible.

"Did you lose a life?" She tried to joke, but the wince on her face provided a sense of sympathy.

"Feels like it," Arcane croaked and yawned. She rubbed her eyes, hoping to mask the welling of tears at the short memory of her dead Sisters. Arcane observed as Spring breathlessly bounced across the room, leaping over the witchery items amongst the floor and into the bathroom.

"Let's go for a walk,"

Arcane only huffed stiffly.

"Where exactly?"

"Hmm," She began to talk through the bathroom door. "I'll give you a tour?"

Arcane didn't want to confess she had already given herself a tour yesterday.

"I'd like to see the courtyard," Arcane peered out the window, finding girls already outside the courtyard in the early afternoon light, hidden to the outside world by the Mistress' glamor. Some girls, half Arcane's age, skipping ropes, others lounging on picnic blankets around the courtyard's fountain, and by one of the large trees- Takanashi Ito sat.

She was carving writing into the tree with her knife, hazardously.

"Actually-" Arcane yelped, peeling away from the window as Ito sensed a stare, and looked up from her crouched position by the tree. "I heard there's a ballroom, can you show me that?"

"Sure! I also have somewhere else I'd like to show you, the greenhouse."

Arcane, after cleaning herself, and letting Spring brush the air-bound knots from her brunette hair, followed Spring out of their bedroom. Trailing behind, Arcane observed silently as girls skipped past, welcomely saying hi to Spring- some even wishing Arcane a 'good morning.' Some of the girls were around the same age, and as sweet and as welcoming as ever. Some younger, at least half Arcane's age, one in particular at least as young as five, toddled by, smiling.

"How many people live in this Coven?" Arcane asked, following the little child as she turned downstairs.

Spring hummed. "Many, sometimes I think too many. But- yes, I know. I can't think like that. Not when all these girls are being protected by the forces of the hunter's army. Honestly, I'd say there's a few hundred of us, give or take."

"Are you ever worried this place won't have enough room for witches like us?"

Spring shrugged. "That's the least of my worries. I value my life; I value my safety. I don't care if I have to share a room with tens of girls, as long as I'm not burned to death by hunters."

Arcane nodded. "Agreed."

"Even then, some of the women leave when they see fit, some have lived here for longer than me, some grown and willing to protect themselves, or even..."

"Or even?"

Spring cautiously looked to Arcane, unsure whether to talk. "Some of the women leave to rebel against the hunter's, they'll often say their farewells, and leave, others will just disappear in the night. Those know they aren't coming back."

"Why were you so compliant in telling me that?"

"I just don't want you to go off thinking you're a hero like them. They all believe they're helping, but they're just dying for some sense of reprisal."

"You don't know me like that."

Spring turned on Arcane, cheeks red, she faltered.

"But I want to! Can't you see? I want to be your friend, a friend you can rely on. I don't have many, and people like you are hard to come by. I'm just worried, that's all."

Arcane crossed her arms over her chest, unsure how to reply. She wasn't good at replying to affection. She was horrible with her Sisters too, and that made her regretful of how she never did tell them how much she loved them. It made her inwardly mope in bitterness and longing dread because she never questioned how long she had with them all.

"Thanks...." Arcane whispered. "But I don't understand what you mean."

Spring shrugged. "I don't know either, I just like your company. You're easy to talk to, and you aren't rude. Sometimes you can be a standoff, but I get that."

Arcane tried to hold back a smile.

"Thanks for being a friend I can turn to, Spring. You're very welcoming."

Spring smiled gleefully as they turned into the ballroom.

It was an enlarged, and endless room with an alluring chandelier, dangling with white crystals that glowed in the light. The roof was endlessly high, with stories higher than displayed each level of the palace, exits, and entrances came from every story above.

"It's..."

"Gorgeous, I know. It has an ancient feel to it, so luxurious."

Arcane stepped closer in, admiring the ballroom's comforting opulence. She peered closer to the middle of the ballroom, observing a group of witches sewing into ball gowns, magic twisting gowns into colours of jet black, silvers, azure, peacock, and sky blue. All mingled to create an imagery of the winter's moon. The moon the witches worshiped.

"Why is there a ballroom?"

"For the solstices, we like to celebrate."

Arcane guessed so, and Spring's declaration only reminded her that her family once celebrated the Solstices, but not like this- nothing like this- actually. Not so royal or fantastical, it was more homelike, a small cottage filled with Sisters, eating a feast of farmed foods and wine.

"My Coven never celebrated, from what I remember. They were the unfriendly sort through," Spring muttered, spinning around the dance floor, closer to the group. Arcane stumbled to follow her skipping walk without looking awkward.

"For the solstice, we like to do it differently to other Covens. We like to make it competitive."

"Damn right," A snobbish voice aroused from the group. Arcane peered close to find the twins, the girls who had snobbishly sat upon the table, side by side at dinner. One gave a soft, friendly smile, the other jabbed her in the side.

"My dress will stun; I'll win this winter solstice."

The other twin looked to Arcane, a sympathetic smile that pleaded her to ignore her unfriendly twin sister. They were both relatively small, little dimples by their cheeks, and soft monoid eyes-they would be mistaken for angels if not for the scowl on the other twin's face.

"It's good to see you Arcane, I hope you find comfort with your new family."

"Our family," Arcane corrected. "It's good to be a part of a Coven with you both."

The other twin rolled her eyes. Arcane didn't despise her for it though, she did the same thing on the regular, she just…. Disliked the attitude. It was another layer of negative to her own, too unfriendly. The strangeness of observing two people with completely different personalities in the same bodies caught her off guard.

"Miu's just stressed about the dress, try not to think she's being personal."

Miu was the unfriendly sister, then.

Arcane nodded, peering to the dresses thrown upon their crossed knees as magic moved to form dresses. The dresses were peculiar in shape but intricate in detail. Despite the similarity in figure and face, the girls were crafting completely different dresses.

They had a book to share beside them, open to display *Chapter Five, crafting the waistline.*

The friendly sister yet to be named proceeded to talk to the two as they stood above, observing the handiwork of their magic.

"Miu won the last competition for the summer solstice, she chose the prettiest orange! It was like a sunset."

40 | JESSE PIPER

Arcane furrowed her brows, observing as Spring awkwardly peered away as the twin started discussing the summer solstice. It seems the twins were aware of Spring's reaction.

"Don't be like that, Spring. Your dress was pretty too, it's not as embarrassing when it's only your Coven seeing."

Arcane went to ask, but Miu erupted into a high laugh, akin to Ito's cackle. "Oh Arcane, she didn't do her spell properly, and the dress was dismantled during the dances."

"Please," Spring begged, cheeks hot and red. "Don't remind me."

"It only makes it funnier knowing-"

"Shut up!" Spring whined, twisting away. "Let's go Arcane, they're being too rude."

Miu only laughed harder, and unfriendlier as the two parted ways.

"Ask her who she was dancing with, Arcane, please!"

"Don't be so mean, Miu-"

"Shut up"

"Please ignore them," Spring whispered, gripping her hands around Arcane's bicep as they walked. They scampered down the stairs, Spring aiming to lead the girl to the greenhouse with a redness blooming on her round cheeks.

She was uncomfortable by the way she avoided eye contact; her palms clammy. Arcane was aware of this and tried to change the conversation in the dire hope of it changing the grim mood.

"I know Miu is the ruder twin, but the sweet one...What is her name?"

"That's Sora Hino, she was born four minutes earlier. She's really lovely, but her sister doesn't like it when she is, especially when it's to other people," Spring took a shaky breath. "About the solstice thing..."

"You don't need to tell me. I can be another person who never saw or knew of what happened."

"No.... You should know," Spring tried to make herself laugh at the memory, but her cheeks only grew hotter, and a bright, painful red. "I made this nice dress; it was the first one I made myself. Some girls just get the tailored witches to make their dresses, but I wanted

THE TRIPLE MOON | 41

to try making one myself, with magic and all. It was the summer solstice, so it was a fine pink, and I had a little bow to look cute. I did look cute, until..."

Spring proceeded. "Until I asked Nipuna to dance with me."

"Oh.... Okay," Arcane only began to feel inwardly embarrassed already. Nipuna wasn't the friendliest of people, Nipuna's presence would only have made it worse. The girl could barely even imagine the lanky figure dancing. She was far too stiff for anything of the sort.

"My dress was dismantled; it completely began to fall apart. I missed a step in the process of making it, and..."

"I'm sorry," Arcane awkwardly winced, trying not to flinch at the story. Imagining herself in Spring's position only worsened the abashment.

"Don't be sorry!" Spring spurted out. "It was a while ago; I just hope Nipuna has forgotten."

"What did she do when it happened?"

Spring winced. "She just froze, gave me her coat then left."

Arcane didn't know what to say, *nice work...At least Nipuna gave you, her coat?* Nipuna did the bare minimum and disappeared. Arcane just hoped she felt terrible for leaving Spring like that. Arcane couldn't say anything- everything she tried to say seemed impolite, almost insensitive.

After the trek across the halls, they left the interior of the palace and found themselves outside in the cold, gale tossing their hair wildly and causing redness to brew upon their noses. It was so cold, it hurt to breathe in winter was close, and Arcane was aware of how freezing it would become.

"Look!" Spring burst, lurching the two towards the large greenhouse, the door was slightly ajar, and the two walked in with the swish of Arcane's finger. "How pretty is it?"

The greenhouse was magnificently comforting, vines entangled across every inch, and all along with the glass panels, a strange assortment of flowers bloomed, an array of warm and cold colours amongst the gardening room.

Spring had a face reflecting a sense of pride.

"I'm guessing you did this?"

"It's the only magic I'm good at," Spring shyly smiled. "Growing flowers and plants, that's the only thing that I can do; it was passed down to me by my parents."

"Be proud of that, this place is comforting." Arcane stumbled around the greenhouse, over pot plants and growing vines across the floor, her new shoes walked through the puddles of water without dampening her boots.

"I wish I was as good as you, plants aren't useful in this world."

I am barely a witch. I know nothing of magic. Spring," Arcane whispered, her fingers grazing a soft white flower, bursting with the dry sweetness of femininity. Arcane wiped her nose before she could sneeze. "Plants give you meaning in life, it can create contentment."

"I guess, but you wouldn't want to be a witch that's vocation is plants, would you?"

"No, I wouldn't. But I'm not searching for happiness, Spring, I'm searching for a sense of safety. Even then, I barely know much about magic and magic is the key to my safety."

"You know, that's a Chrysanthemum," Spring cut, rushing to the flower Arcane was admiring. "And I think you're lying, you're a natural."

"Moving things is all I can do, Spring. Nothing else."

"You could always see Ohno about that, learning if that's what you want."

Arcane thought it through. Ohno wasn't the friendliest, but most people here weren't. They were either delusional, rude, or rarely sweet. Ohno could help, Arcane could learn and leave for the hunters relatively quickly, but a lone wolf would never beat the hunters and their army, no matter how powerful. The other witches that had left and never came back or burned to the stake were proof of a loner's failed attempt, despite how powerful they were as witches.

Though, the recommendation was trailing within her mind- she had more important matters, more important people. Mistress Mori could teach her magic and build an army. Arcane could hit two birds with one stone if only she could figure out how to get to Mistress Mori. That included without, Ito.

"How well do you know Mistress Mori?"

Spring peered up from the chrysanthemum, unsure.

"Umm...Well, I've been here majority of my life, and I've seen her grow up-but we never played as kids. We aren't close if that's what you mean. Why are you so curious?"

"I just want to meet her, that's all. I want to put a name to a face."

Arcane lied through her teeth.

Spring shrugged. "She's quite small actually, surprisingly."

"Oh..."

"She also looks like a boy sometimes. The first few years of living here, I assumed she was just a mortal boy- I never talked to her, so I never heard her voice."

"Erg-"

This description wasn't very helpful.

"Not in a bad way, I sometimes wish I looked like her, she's very pretty. Her beauty, though, I don't think matches her personality. She's quite... a reclusive person, which is why not many people know her personally. I've grown up with her since I was five, it's strange I never truly became her friend."

A loud bang erupted from the entrance, the roof rattled, and a pot fell from the wooden truss of the roof, landing abruptly by their feet and shattering into little pieces. Spring squeaked, and Arcane's face hollowed out in distaste as Takanashi Ito appeared behind the blonde, knife in hand.

"Why do you have a knife? Get it away!" Spring snapped. "Are you crazy?"

"Don't answer that," Arcane muttered.

Ito only smiled mischievously, twisting around Spring to lean close to Arcane. Ito's eyes reached Arcane's, peering up with her mismatched eyes and her fanged simper. She leaned against the wooden table of assorted plants.

"Could I talk to Arcane privately?"

Spring stood her ground.

"Why would you even want to do that?"

"She's an acquaintance."

Spring scoffed, less guarded than she was, and faltering her stubbornness. She turned, and left, eyeing the two as she departed completely out of sight. She was less than willing to leave Arcane with the witch.

"Listen, last night was...."

"Utterly useless."

"But it was insanely unbelievable-"

"I'm not an adrenaline junky, Ito. I didn't get shoved off the top of the palace for fun. I did it to get Mistress Mori's attention. It didn't work, your plan didn't work. Realising she was deprived of people, of affection, and then jumping off a building now seems like a ridiculous idea. It was."

"Call me Takanashi," She smiled, stunningly, but still insanely. When Arcane peered closer, she realized her fanged teeth were not natural, but cut and scraped accusingly by Ito herself. It seemed she enjoyed damaging things, even herself...

"I don't think I want to call you anything that makes us remotely friend-like."

Ito smirked, her tongue lapsing across her lips as she cunningly eyed Arcane.

"Hmmm.... Stubborn. You're pissed at me."

"Because you didn't help me, you just helped yourself."

Ito shrugged. "What more do you want from little poor me...Huh?"

"Piss off," Arcane went to exit, but Ito's finger aggressively wrapped around her neck, shoving her against the table, hard enough for the plants to tumble off the side and break against the ground, the plant Arcane was just admiring shattering into pieces. Spring would not be happy. "You're *bloody* insane-"

"If I kill you, will she come find us? Will she intervene? Or will she let you bleed?"

"I'd-" Arcane choked under the pressure of her hands. Arcane could have very well shoved her off, but that was till the knife in her hand pressed sharply against her stomach. A hot flush hit Arcane, and she took a sharp breath to relax her pulsing heart, thrumming against her chest.

"Listen here my little dove. I'll help you again, but I want something in return."

"No."

Ito blinked, an iciness in her stare.

"I am holding a knife against you, said are you talking to me like that?"

"You don't frighten me. I won't work with you despite how hard you try. You're selfish, if you could you'd kill me nine times over, just to get your pathetic tendencies for attention quenched."

Ito stilled and her stillness made Arcane shiver at the sense of ice cubes trailing down her spine.

"Talk to me like that again, and I will kill you nine times over."

Arcane shoved her back, but she held still-even as Arcane spat in her face, saliva drooling down their lips.

"If you wanted to kiss me, you should've just said so."

Heat crept up amongst every inch of Arcane's body.

"You're a slimy git-"

"It's easier to work together, we will be powerful enough together."

"It isn't. We want completely different things. I cannot have you in my way at getting to her, for all I know, you have a final plan that involves using me."

Arcane flickered her finger against Ito's thigh, and the one-eyed ghoul of a witch was thrown against the greenhouse panels upon the wall. She heaved a sigh as the greenhouse rattled, rather in annoyance than pain as she laid still.

Arcane inched close, peering down upon her.

"It was fun working with you, Ito-But I would rather work for the sane, rather than the insane."

"This isn't over little dove," Ito cackled as Arcane began to take her leave. "You'll come back; I can see it in your eyes. We want the same person; we want the same thing."

"The only thing you see through that eye of yours is sex," Arcane smirked. "Too bad you're deprived of it, good luck getting to Mistress Mori, before I do...."

She slammed the green house doors behind her.

The aftermath of their conversation only led Ito to ogle and glare at her all of dinner. Her eyes never once left Arcane, even when Arcane indicated with a knife she'd slit her throat. That only worsened it, and Ito was a smiling stalker for the rest of the night. It seemed threats wouldn't lessen the stalking, and Ito was relentless for Arcane's attention, or maybe even her reaction.

It was as though the threats only thrilled her.

Ito rested back upon her chair, letting herself balance on the two back feet. Her skirt rode up, and Arcane teared her eyes away, cheeks hot as she gulped down the last of her food. Struggling not to choke on her food at the perverted nature of Takanashi Ito, sitting across from her.

She shoved her chair back, peering to the clock- ten o'clock, then to Nipuna.

"May I be excused?"

"Yes." She muttered without looking.

As Arcane left, she provided a menacing and ominous stare directly at Ito.

She only gleamed her edged teeth back.

Huffing, Arcane bitterly sauntered past her own bedroom, aiming to scout for the bedroom that housed the Mistress of the Coven. Arcane allowed herself to follow the trail of light along the hall. They were at the highest level of the Venfic Haven. It was most likely that with the Mistress being assigned to eat with this level, she would be on this story of the Haven. Following through the halls, Arcane found herself staring at the mist that parted from her lips, the cold air nibbling uncomfortably across her body.

She turned a corner, but with movement down the hall, she abruptly stilled before placing herself pressed into the wall. She peered, having to narrow her eyes to observe a small figure seemingly only having come from the same direction Arcane had come from.

Arcane was sure all the girls were still eating, no one had left the room before she had departed, and the stairs to the lower levels were much further away than the dining room. The person must have sauntered past not long after Arcane had left.

The figure walked around another corner, and Arcane struggled to silently run after her. She was small, yet nimble on her feet- as if she feared being seen. The brunette could barely catch a glimpse of her turning a corner.

Arcane was holding onto the glimmer of hope that it was Mistress Mori, because only the older and strongest of girls were supposed to be on this level. The small, almost useless fact of her being so short, with such a messy haircut was her only indication. Not only so, but the woman she followed despite being shorter than her, seemed older from her mannerisms.

The sort of century old mannerisms that Arcane had seen in her parents.

Turning another corner, Arcane stopped as the small figure leaned against the entrance of a door. It opened with an aged creak, and a towering woman walked out idly. Arcane could see the knots in the tall woman's hair from a mile away, her lanky fingers grasping the long skirt by her sides. She had a pale face, with wide eyes and dark eyebrows that framed her face.

"Don't look at me like that," The first girl whispered, voice throaty as tho9ugh it had been days since applied. Her words were loud enough to echo across the empty hall, a shiver running through Arcane's spine, the thrill of being caught only energized her to stay.

"Are you ready? We must be quick."

The tangled mess of a figure reached back into the room, a lantern alight with fire within her hands. It was too hard to see their facial features, even with the light upon their faces. Arcane flinched at the fires hot flickering, peering away over her shoulder at the strange sense flouting her, her scars sizzling at the flickering memory. It was so normalised for witches to use the very fire that could kill them, Arcane only realised now how bizarre it was.

Memories of fire made her shudder, and she clasped her eyes shut, taking the sight of the lantern away from her. Arcane twisted away from the corner, pressing her scarring shoulder to the coldness of the walls, struggling to breath.

This had not happened with the candles inside her room, so *why now? Why have these memories resurfaced now of all times?* Arcane fluttered her eyes back open, and eyes peered down upon her.

The sound of heels pressing against the floorboards forced Arcane to pull herself from her trance.

"You shouldn't be out walking as of now."

It was Nipuna. Arcane wasn't sure whether to be relieved with fortune- or reacting with unfortunate inconvenience in the fact it was Nipuna. She hadn't decided yet. She tried to soften her breath, like her thumping heart.

"Why not?" Arcane whispered, she suspiciously peered up at Nipuna as she placed her lanky fingers into the pocket of her uniformed pants. Arcane could barely see through the dark strands of hair that showed her narrow, bitter eyes.

Arcane only huffed, a burst of mist parting her thin lips.

"It's not safe at this time, nothing more. Now go back to your room."

"I live here, I think it's my every right to know what's infringing on my safety." She crossed her arms defiantly, observing as Nipuna peered down the hall where the other two witches once were. She sucked in her breath.

"I'll be infringing your safety in a minute-"

Arcane barely flinched, resting against the wall.

"I think I'm very safe walking these halls, there's no one out to murder me."

"Are you sure about that?" Nipuna muttered, bending down enough to face Arcane's burnished glare. Her arm resting against the wall.

"I would if you told me why I should be worried."

A long second, contemplation teetering in Nipuna's dark eyes.

"We have a missing girl." She stated after a long reluctant pause.

"And? Could they not have just left willingly?"

"No. You don't get it," Nipuna muttered, her huffed breath warming Arcane's trembling lips and her numbed nose. "She's eight pr nine years old- give or take, the young ones don't leave, they wouldn't even have the idea in those little minds of theirs."

"Oh…"

There was a grovelling sense of despair at the words. A child, missing, a witch at that. This wasn't good, because why on the earth would a child want to leave this place? *Leave their home and their safety?*

Nipuna pulled away, reluctance in her eyes. She was unwilling to talk, she seemed more unwelcoming the more she talked to Arcane.

"So, get back to your room, and don't even think about following me-"

Arcane rolled her eyes, irritated.

"Why would you think I'd follow you?"

"It's blatantly obvious."

"Before you go," Arcane burst, catching Nipuna as she began to leave. "Was that Mistress Mori? Around the corner?" She pointed down the hall urgently. Nipuna only ignored her, not even daring to give her a look as she left. Her feet padding across the floorboards.

Arcane only groaned.

"Fine, I'll figure it out myself."

5

Puella

The morning after was more silent than usual, and as Arcane peeled open the blinds and peered out into the courtyard, it was solemnly empty- desolate of life. Spring was nestled within her blankets like a cocoon, staring idly at Arcane, observing the way her eyebrows drew together in frustration.

"What's wrong?" Spring muttered, yawning softly.

"It's so quiet…"

"Perhaps it's a rainy day?"

Arcane shook her head.

"I don't think that's the case."

Because even if it was a rainy day, the younger girls would be dressed in their uniform, jumping in the puddles before being caught by Nipuna and forced to wash and change. Even then, Ito would still sit by that tree, even if it did rain, it was her private area she prioritised, and today she was not there.

Spring struggled to unwrap herself, furrowing her brows just like Arcane as she peered through the window. Somehow, her hair had barely been affected through her sleep, her blonde hair coiling in ringlets.

"Where are all the girls?"

A knock erupted by their door, and they jolted up, not prepared to associate with anyone with their morning fatigue. Spring was lucky enough to have a matching set of pyjamas, but Arcane, all she wore was a white singlet and shorts. As quickly as she could, she stretched for her blanket, wrapping it over her shoulders as Spring peeled open the door.

No one needed to see that ugly scar of hers, the one that distastefully reached along her shoulder- the scar of an enemy's fire.

Every time her fingers caressed across the ugly scar- a sense of dread and shame wafted through her.

Ohno appeared, dressed pristinely in her uniform, as always.

"I have a message from Mistress Mori."

Arcane jolted at the name, standing her toes against the coolness of the wooden floorboards as she drew herself to Ohno and Spring by the door, wrapped in her blanket. Spring gulped, visibly unsure, eyes wide.

She sensed an awful mood that came from this message.

"What sort of message?"

"We've been ordered to stay inside our rooms, and to only leave if requested and accepted by Mistress Mori herself. Nipuna said she is not even allowed to accept."

Spring furrowed her brows, panic clear in the way her cheeks bloomed hot pink, eyes wide as they peered up to Arcane.

"That doesn't sound good at all."

Arcane blanched, a chill thrumming through her nerves as she peeled away, twisting to stare out into the yard. Waiting for any activity. From her bedroom window, if she looked further enough over the palace buildings, she could see the lining of the forestry.

Spring began to stammer.

"Why? Why do we need to be isolated? This- This isn't right-"

"Mistress Mori sent little information out, Nipuna told me even less. You know how they are."

"Maybe there's a storm coming," Spring furrowed her brows, to which Ohno shrugged.

"That's implausible, if it was that bad, Mori would redirect it."

THE TRIPLE MOON | 53

Arcane kept her mouth shut, the less that knew the better. The unknown factors were better than the whole haven panicking. Whether Arcane knew or not, it was most likely they found the witch, whether she was alive or not, Arcane needed to know.

Ohno sauntered into the room, seating herself on Arcane's tangled bedsheets- her eyes judging the mess.

"I may as well stay here."

Spring shrugged. "We may as well have company, then."

"Yes. I would rather not be alone as of now. I've already finished my to be read list from the library, I need new recommendations, preferably some non-fiction readings on the development of animals."

Ohno pushed her glasses higher upon her nose as Spring began to reply. Despite their general conversation, Arcane couldn't find herself to listen, nor to concentrate on anything aside from the entrance of the forest, a place she had only trekked through to find her safety.

The forest sang to her, like a dull chant. If the girl was found anywhere, it would be there.

"Hey," Arcane muttered, unable to tear her eyes away.

The girls peered over, waiting.

"I left my notebook in the greenhouse yesterday."

There was no notebook, Arcane wasn't a writer, she didn't have a journal either.

"It'll be fine, just stay here-"

Arcane hesitantly unwrapped herself, moving to the bathroom to change. Instinctively covering her burn scar as she went. She spoke through the door, struggling to assure them.

"I'll be quick, don't worry about me. The notebook is important, I really can't afford to lose it."

Ohno coughed to gain attention, but Arcane didn't give her any.

"At least ask the Mistress."

"I'll only be gone for a few minutes."

"Perhaps living another day would be great, too-"

"Arcane you should stay, we can get your notebook later," Spring begged from the other side of the bathroom. "What if it's hunters, they could be on the island, they could've found us, that might be why- what if it's a storm and you get locked in the greenhouse?"

"It'll be fine, promise. I'll be gone and back in seconds."

Just let me go and see for myself.

Arcane immediately left their bedroom as quickly as she could, ignoring the two's protests as she buttoned her blouse and ignored the blazer by her bed.

The haven was just as desolate and empty as the courtyard. Arcane shivered at the coolness drifting along the halls, without the laughter of girls, there was neither an atmospheric warmth, nor a physical warmth.

Arcane kept her soles soft and silent against the wooden floorboards, her ears listening into any sound. There would be a chance someone was scouting the halls for people like Arcane, people who effortlessly and without question- broke the rules.

It seemed Arcane was more aware than the other person beginning to turn past her hall, and quick enough, she pulled herself into the corner, and observed as Nipuna stalked by. Her lanky limbs forced her into a stride, but her face twisted into an unsettled and disturbed frown.

Arcane released a long sigh of relief and followed where Nipuna had just left from. She scurried down the halls and slipped down the winding stairs before escaping through the entrance to the courtyard.

It was silent, aside from the wind chiming against Arcane's ears, and the soft sweeping of the courtyards swinging trees. As Arcane watched for eyes, she peered to her own bedroom window to find not anybody peering back. As silently as she could, Arcane slunk into the forestry past the front building without anyone noticing.

Through the silence of trees and slipping deeper the distant sound of a voice tempted her closer, her stomach twisting inside as she feverishly trailed the noise, twisting silently through the dark forestry. Nearing closer to the sound, Arcane found herself perched beside the roots of a tree, hidden from sight behind shrubs of bush land.

Two figures stood hidden from the light behind a hanging tree, seeming to have been within the forest for the entire night. They were the same two girls Arcane had seen in the halls last night. One still held a lantern, no longer alight, while the other stood eerily still, staring up through the tree. Arcane furrowed her brow, her stomach twisting in a sense of dread as she struggled to follow the girl's gaze.

"We need to cut her down." The female muttered, throaty and raw- almost as though the woman hadn't spoken in days, or at least; could not. The sound of her voice wavered an itching dread in Arcane.

Cut what down?

Arcane crawled forward despite her unease of not having been caught- but having seen what was hanging from the tree.

A crack echoed softly through the forestry around Arcane, almost not recognisable- but despite this, Arcane didn't care how much sound she made, not when she was looking at a child's dangling feet. Shakily, with trembling lips and watering eyes- and that disgusting, twisting fear within her stomach- she peered higher to find the charred, and hanging dead body of the little girl that went missing only a few days prior.

Arcane crawled back as silently as she could muster with shaking, quivering hands. She rested herself against the base of the tree, curling up through the bush and pecking through the hole as she watched the two girls communicate as though they were less than fazed by the little girl's hanging body.

Arcane had thought she was just as desensitized as them, but she wasn't- and she had to deal with that fact. Death was relatively new to her, and it would prevail within her life till her own death became of her. She would have to realize that being a witch meant living with the fear of death every day.

"Sybil," The shaggy haired witch muttered to the other. "You may leave, I can handle her."

The tall girl did not speak, peered to her questionable.

"You did well today, but it's safer for you at home."

The other girl-presumably Sybil- slumped her shoulders, and with strange gangling arms and legs, disappeared through the shrubs, silent. The strangeness of her silence caught the brunette off guard as she observed.

For the next half hour, Arcane recovered through her shock by observing the witch as she dismantled the girl's body from the rope with utter delicateness, before she snapped her fingers, and the shovel lying by her side automatically began digging the grave. It stood neatly below the hanging tree, and as the woman stood idly with the young girl's body in her arms, waiting for the hole to be dug, she peered through the shrubbery to where Arcane sat, staring with not a single drop of emotion in her face.

Arcane faltered but did not dare break away from where she hid.

"You know," she whispered. "You will get a cold without your blazer."

A shudder of adrenaline drained through Arcane's face as the woman's eyes peered back at her. The short woman did not smile, and she did not emit any warmth within those eyes. They were empty, and dark- her figure becoming overshadowed with the fog drifting in.

The woman did not speak as Arcane took a sharp breath and pulled herself out of the shrubbery with numbed ankles that made it harder to stand. Dread dripped down every section of her body as she observed the girl holding the child's dead body in her arms, her ankles almost collapsed, her heart sinking.

"Who are you?" Arcane breathed, air coming out as a puff of white mist.

"Perhaps, you should tell me who you are first."

The little girl's head had limped over the girl's arm, the dead child's eyes rolled and white, skin consumed with the scarring of fire with her mouth still wide open as though she were still screaming. Arcane struggled to breath, unable to tear away. Her face was in so much pain and agony- and as she tried to find features to the face, all she could see were the faces of her dead Sisters.

"Look at me, not her." The woman whispered; voice chaste.

Arcane peered to the woman's inky black eyes and observed the details of her face as Arcane stumbled a step closer. A sense of comfort overcame her, and she found herself unconsciously trailing closer. Arcane peered to the delicate scar beneath the woman's eye, miniature though deep- like a scar of a knife that had nicked the skin too close. Her lips were thin, and pale- alike to her sick face and sunken cheeks. Her eyes were naturally narrow, her facial features becoming familiar to which Arcane had seen only the night before.

"There's no point telling you who I am," Arcane breathed, assuage consuming her senses. She was not as scared of this woman as she was prior. "You know who I am. I know enough about your magic to know you watch us all."

Mistress Mori blinked; her face roughened as a glimpse of curiousness twisted through the purse of her lips before it dissipated as rapidly as it appeared. Arcane observed her eyes, hoping to see a flash of emotion in those eyes, but the more she waited- the less hopeful she became, there was no emotion in those eyes.

"Arcane Amunet," She tested the name, and it was sweet on the tongue- said swiftly as though rehearsed to perfection. "What are you doing here?"

"I saw you last night."

She raised a thin brow. "So, it was you watching me?"

"I-" Arcane faltered. "I just needed to find you."

"I know you did."

Arcane narrowed her eyes, furrowing her brows.

"I just need answers."

The shovel by their side stilled, wedging itself into the finished pile of dirt. Mistress Mori peered away, and it was the only time she had done so throughout the whole conversation. As Arcane solemnly observed her placing the child into the hole, she realized how much younger Mistress Mori was to what she assumed. Her face was youthful, though youth in a witch determined nothing. A woman could be three hundred years old and have the same face as what she was 100 years prior. There was truthfully, no telling.

"The answers you want, Arcane, I cannot provide for."

She delicately placed the girl into the hole before pulling away and turning back to Arcane's ruffled figure as the shovel began to move again, burying the poor child.

"I just..." Arcane took a shaky breath. "I need reassurance."

The Amunet girl peered hopeful, beggingly down at the shaggy haired woman.

She caved after a pregnant minute of staring.

"Fine," she huffed. "I know what you want, you know that. I shall invite you for conversation, and we can have a talk that is more private."

"Will you?" Arcane suspiciously eyed the woman.

"I don't like lying, Arcane. It will be tonight."

Arcane cocked her head questionably. She didn't trust it, even with her assertion.

"How can I trust your word?"

"Because you need reassurance," Mori muttered. "And I am the only one who can give it to you."

Arcane began to realize a breath of a humourless chuckle, finding her words intelligent as the women had twisted the words back- though she was no longer peering down at the girl, she was clouded in black mist, and as she blinked, she found herself standing outside the door of her shared room.

With an empty notebook she had never seen nor touched before in her life, within her hands.

A spine-chilling dread sunk through her.

Mistress Mori was always watching, she could hear everything, see everything.

Does the idea scare me?

Spring sat with her bed reclined her bed beside Ohno, seemingly discussing spells and conjuring as a large enchantment book and a few candles scattered the bedroom. There were chalk marks on their fingertips, as though they had attempted and later removed the incantation.

"I can't believe you!" Spring burst, wide eyes watching as Arcane stiffly sat by her bed, resting her back against the wall and struggling to remove the face of the little girl from her mind. The blood, the charred face, it wouldn't leave- her eyes- rolled and unmoving, stuck

THE TRIPLE MOON | 59

in time, stuck in death. It made Arcane realize how close to death she was, seeing it take another.

"Arcane!" Spring snapped her fingers from across the room, and the door Arcane had accidently left open slammed shut. As soon as the bang echoed, and Arcane broke from her subconscious, she observed the regretful frown on Spring's face.

"I-" Spring took a sharp breath, peering at the emotionless Ohno as she uninterestedly read through the aged incantation book. "I didn't mean to snap like that,"

Arcane waited, silent.

"I was just worried; you took so long."

Arcane's mind went blank with excuses.

She raised an eyebrow, struggling to act unfazed as she shrugged.

"I found my notebook, then I bumped into a friend," The word friend came out unsure. Mistress Mori was not a friend, but she liked to pretend the woman had some sort of relation with her, even if it was a plain lie.

Ohno raised her eyes from the book, edging her glasses off the tip of her nose as they slid down.

"Who?"

"Nipuna,"

"She was out?" Ohno looked down through their circular spectacles.

"Yeah...I saw a few women out."

"Who?"

"I... Couldn't put a face to a name even if you told me to."

"Welp," Spring shrugged. "It only matters that you're safe now."

Arcane nodded, struggling to relax into the hardened wall, her head peering up to the roof- half-heartedly listening into Ohno's explanations of spells and incantations. She went on for drooling time about spells, and after seconds of deliberating, Arcane spoke.

"Ohno, if I were to learn to use my magic better, what should I learn first?"

Ohno blinked, peering away from the book.

"You don't know how to use your magic?"

Arcane shamefully peered to her feet, observed the way her bare ankle twisted and rested strangely.

"I know how to move objects, I'm good at that."

Ohno rolled her eyes, aware Arcane would not answer her question.

"Object manipulation? Next you might want to study incantations- little spells you can place on people, or things. I'm teaching Spring if you want to join, she's struggling to learn lie detecting spells."

Arcane furrowed her brows, though willingly sat closer to the edge of her bed so she could hear better as Ohno taught.

"Why would you need to know that?"

Spring shrugged shakily, seemingly unsure herself.

"It's good to know anything."

Ohno ignored their conversation as she prevailed with going through the process, for hours they discussed and explained incantation and ways of using the magic of the witches. In between, she'd help the two try and use their magic, and somehow- to Arcane's surprise, she did well.

As the sun began to set over the horizon and shroud of towering trees of the forest, Arcane could effortlessly move objects, close windows, and use doors. She could tell when her magic sensed lies, through the prick against her neck. Not only so, but she had taught herself how to move water swiftly without spill and allow flowers to become healthy while close to death. They were small things with minor detail- but it was progress.

Arcane's head rested on her bed as she sat in between the layers of books on the floor. Through the afternoon, Arcane had silently blown out the candles across the room without even a flick of a finger or any addressing from the girls they hadn't seen at all, too consumed with their magic.

The lack of fire comforted her, made her feel safe.

Sometimes Arcane questioned why Spring relentlessly kept fire alight, she wanted to say something, anything- tell her how uncomfortable it made her, how much it made her skin crawl in the most uncomfortable places, and the way it made her sister's face appear in her vision, in the shadows and as she closed her eyes. Though Arcane would unlikely say anything, she didn't want to upset anyone. She'd pretend she was okay for a little longer.

As Arcane observed Spring as she struggled to make the plant in her pot grow any bigger, Mistress Mori's face gradually began to reappear in her mind, the nagging fear overcoming her system, her stomach twisting in anticipation. The woman said she'd bid her, but as the sun began to set, Arcane wasn't so sure she trusted her word.

"Ohno," Arcane called. "Have you met Mistress Mori?"

"Not this again," Spring chuckled half-heartedly, seeming done with the questions.

Ohno shrugged, closing her book shut futilely. She was clearly exhausted but not exhausted enough to break posture in front of others as she sat with her back strictly straightened, hands bunched together on her lap, patiently intrigued in conversation.

"I have."

"What was she like?"

Ohno pursed her lips in thought.

"Comforting, intelligent. She knows how to make someone feel safe. She's always been friendly to me. Most of us aged into our teen hood together, she was born here, a few years older than us so she's always been around, just not in our age group." Arcane assumed Ohno was finished, but she narrowed her eyes distractedly and began to scowl. "So, when Ito doesn't use the respectful terms of Mistress Mori- it infuriates me, The Mistress does not deserve that disrespect."

"She's definitely an Odd one...Ito..."

Ohno rolled her eyes. "Ito Takanashi is obsessed, not just odd. She's a lunatic."

"She's always been like that," Spring muttered. "I heard her Coven were infamous for their strangeness, must run in the family."

"I presume Ito and The Mistress Mori had some sort of close relation?"

Spring shrugged, clearly oblivious. "Not that I know of."

"That's something I know nothing of, and something I never want to know of," Ohno dusted her ruffled skirt as the chaste knock of the door went off. Arcane stilled, watching silently as Ohno sauntered to the door as she continued. "Ito and the Mistress' relationship is something no one knows of."

"I wouldn't be surprised if Ito was just lying the whole time." Spring muttered.

As Ohno pulled the door open, the girl's observed the lanky figure of a woman, she was silent as she stood eerily- and as Arcane stared into the drooping eyes of this woman, she realized this was her bid. The woman was the same as she had seen with Mistress Mori.

She was eerily lanky, with knobbly knees and hunched shoulders as she held up a lantern in her hands- held in a deathly grip. The women peered down; observation unwavering as the woman stared at Arcane past Ohno's figure.

The woman had small pink lips, and wide eyes that looked as though she had slept for eternity and only now woken up from slumber. Spring hopped up in enthusiasm, anxiously wiping any access chalk or dust from her clothes.

"Sybil! Aren't you supposed to be preparing dinner?"

Sybil stood silently, though tipped a smile then allowed heat to reach the woman's cheeks.

Ohno turned to Arcane, aware Sybil would not look away from the said woman, she looked expectantly, almost as though Arcane was aware she would come. Arcane perched up, realization adorning her brows.

"Sybil, this is Arcane. Arcane, this is Sybil- She's the chef here, controls the kitchens."

Sybil was silent as Arcane nodded her head in acknowledgement.

"She's mute," Ohno muttered beneath her breath. "But she works thoroughly for Mistress Mori- as a groundskeeper, kind of..."

At the words, Sybil's lips turned into a smile that showed a lack of teeth.

"Why are you here, Sybil?"

At the words, the girl straightened, attaching her lantern to her skirt, and gripping Arcane tightly from outside the door. Her eyes glimmered as she effortlessly pulled Arcane out, and with a single finger, pointed to Arcane.

"Oh!" Spring gasped. "You need Arcane? Why?!"

Ohno gave Spring an exaggerated look, rather unimpressed.

"Did you really just ask a question she is incapable of answering?"

Arcane's heart hammered in her chest as the woman carelessly shut the door as they argued, holding tight as she walked her down the hall. Though she emitted a strange aura, her gum less smile reduced this inessential fear of death as the woman sauntered through halls.

Though tall, the woman's face was childlike, younger than Arcane- presumably, and as Arcane observed; she found no signs of magic. If she were a witch, would she not have been able to conjure magic to allow her to speak? Could she not have closed the door without moving, or moved Arcane without even the flick of a finger? Arcane knew how to figure out the minor details, and as she watched Sybil's face observe her turns, she knew she was a mere human.

Sybil's feet halted as an enlarged door appeared in their vision, by the end of the hall, double doors loomed over them. There was no door knocker, no way to show someone was there, not even any doorknobs.

Arcane's heart hammered in her chest, and she peered at Sybil in a hope for directions, however she had already begun her departure, her figure disintegrating the further she descended the hall. She was presumably a busy woman as she walked quick on her feet. Either that, or the woman was terrified of what was behind the door. Arcane couldn't blame her- especially because the doors were too eerie and looming to be welcoming, dark and silent.

The entrance leisurely peeled open as Arcane took a step forward, and she anxiously slipped through the slit of the door. As soon as she fitted herself in, the door creaked shut behind her, and she was struggling to adjust to the darkness of the room she was within. A thick silence overcame the room with the creak of the doors closing behind her, ceasing her escape.

A small light blew out with the current of the door closing, which left the only light being the dim setting of the outside world through the single window by the queen size bed. Arcane took a sharp breath of cold air, the temperatures had dropped, and rain began to patter against the glass window. It was comforting to not be outside during the rain, but the splatter of the rain unsettled her against the eeriness of a dark room.

Through the dim light, Arcane observed the silhouette of a figure standing leaned against the bed frame, and as she inched closer, a white light appeared within the fingertips of Mistress Mori, silently, she flicked the orb of light into the chandelier above, and rather than fire- it was a glowing blue and white mist of light that replaced the darkness. The white absorbed the room, neutralizing the emptying darkness into a delicate warmth that immediately released the anxious knots in Arcane's shoulders.

Arcane blurted her words out immediately at the sight of the woman shrouded in darkness.

"Do you like watching people?"

Arcane couldn't hold back, though she didn't intend to sound so harsh.

Her whole heart, her whole life was on her sleeve now, open to the world to see- or at least, for the one and only Mistress Mori to see. Her eyes blankly scanned Arcane as she appeared untroubled and satisfied for someone who had just intervened with death, and watched it flash before her eyes. Perhaps the death was something she was used to, but that idea only made Arcane more unsure of the woman standing before her.

They had spoken once, yet Mistress Mori knew so much.

Mistress Mori knew she feared fire, Mistress Mori had known she was leaving her room prior, had somehow- heard the conversation. She knew to give her a notebook as evidence that what she said was 'true.' She knew both Ito and her would jump from the balcony when they did. Mistress Mori saw what she wanted, saw what she needed to, *but how?*

She knew too much.

Arcane despised that, she wanted the Mistress to be conscious of such a fact.

THE TRIPLE MOON | 65

Mistress Mori barely faltered, she only peered away, hair framing her eyes- covering them from identifying any form of emotion in those pretty black orbs.

"I'm trying to protect you."

"Are you really?"

"It's my duty to protect you, there is no alternative to keeping you all safe."

"Sure, keep telling yourself that."

"I mean it. I was born to protect the people I love; it is my duty as the Mistress of this Coven, Arcane. Your life means as much as everything to me."

Arcane couldn't care less.

Arcane's eyebrows narrowed, and she sauntered closer. There was a rumbling, striking fear that wouldn't falter, and it was reminding her that she neither knew nor trusted the woman in front of her, despite her powers.

"How do you do it?" She sneered. "Watch everyone?"

"Magic."

"You know what I mean."

At this point, Arcane had sauntered-rather stomped to the point where Arcane's hot breath fanned the shorter woman's face. As Arcane peered down at her through the hazy white glow of the lights that only whitened her sickly texture, she found Mistress Mori's face almost looking...dead.

Though, dead people could not walk or talk- and this woman was doing exactly that.

The shorter woman leaned against the frame of the bed, taking a sharp breath that tripped Arcane out of her furious, almost entranced haze, she peered away from the woman's delicate pale lips- back to her naturally narrow eyes.

"It's an ability only few witches receive by chance. It's rare, almost extinct. It's called astral projection."

Arcane huffed excessively, clearly disrupted.

"How did you learn?"

"I know you don't want to know this."

"You don't know me."

"I know you more than you realize."

Arcane's blood began to pump, hot- thrumming in her ears, hot through her veins.

"Because you've been watching me?"

Mistress Mori barely faltered.

"If I had not been watching, had not been alerted of heart rate increase- you would have lost a life, as would Takanashi Ito."

Mistress Mori stood taller, now, swiftly moving around Arcane swift enough the taller woman's eyes could not keep up. She was as if a scent passed through as she rounded the desk within the middle of the room. It was ancient, carved wood and overcome with books, enchantments, and ornaments as if the woman restlessly studied till her fingers bled from papercuts. If someone told her so, Arcane would not be surprised, there were blood stains in the pages of the books.

Arcane didn't want to admit she was right, she only aggressively crossed her arms over her chest, peering away in a hope the shorter woman hadn't recognised the way she roamed both the room and the other woman with a lack of discretion.

"Listen, Arcane. I need you to trust me."

"As a stalker, or as my superior?"

Mistress Mori narrowed her eyes.

"I don't watch you nude, if that's what you're scared of," She rounded the table, resting herself against the desk across from where Arcane stood, the tip of her lips raising in keen interest. "Though if you like that sort of stuff, it can be arranged."

"You're my superior."

"You don't act like it."

"How must I trust you to answer my questions truthfully if I barely know who you are, or whether you'll even listen to me?"

Mori shook her head. "What do you want to know? Then, get on with it. I told you I don't have much time- we may have nine lives to live through, but I have spared enough."

Arcane rolled her eyes, standing closer- enough that the light of the mist above shone colour into Mori's eyes, and her scar upon her cheek was visibly radiating against her sunken skin. She looked as though she had not slept in weeks, though still basked in a delicate beauty.

"How old are you?"

"I'm nineteen."

Arcane narrowed her eyes, and it equalled Mistress Mori's disinterested gaze.

"Liar."

"Why would I lie about something as immature as age?"

"You talk like you're four thousand years old- you walk like it too."

Mori ignored the woman, not finding the insult hilarious as she watched Arcane's lip rise for a second before dissipating. Arcane didn't care if she found it hilarious or not, she was still upset- fuming. She still wanted and yearned for answers.

"How are you a Mistress at nineteen?"

It was peculiar, throughout Arcane's entire life, she had grown up knowing the older, more aged, and knowledgeable women, most powerful, became Mistresses of their Covens. Mistress Mori was only a year or two older than her, it was stunning- actually. Either she was effortlessly powerful, or all they had at the time. Arcane, despite disliking the women, did not believe the latter.

The shorter woman seemed less than willing to answer the question.

"I was created by a previous Mistress of this Coven. I was born to be a Mistress."

"You always lived here?"

The shorter haired girl nodded reluctantly.

"My sister was the Mistress before me, and whoever I will create, a child, will be the next Mistress- or whom I please, I suppose."

It was a given fact that witches did not need a man to create life. Women with magical properties could easily create life itself, whether that be plant based, or the real human life of a child. Arcane was created by her Coven, and seemingly, Mistress Mori was created by the Mistress prior to her sister's reign. It seemed the people of this Haven knew the dangers of the hunters, and to preserve life, ensured there were enough witches to continue the prideful existence of witches.

"What happened to the girl?"

She took a sharp breath, shaky-almost.

"You must be honest with me if you yearn my trust."

The Mistresses face illustrated no reaction to her words.

"The girl you saw was Vera Roe, she was nine years old. She was born here, her parents left her to me as a Guardian."

The pregnant pause made Arcane realised that although Mistress Mori was that of a Mistress, she was only still a teenager, a teenager vividly without parental guidance. She was quite frankly, alone. She was doing this on her own, protecting a Coven of witches by herself.

The information made Arcane question how the others had all died. Vividly, Mori's creators, nor her Sisters were alive to this day, nor the witches that had left to rebel, or Vera Roe's parents.

Arcane found herself sitting attentively into the seat closely across from Mistress Mori. She didn't protest as the taller witch sat into the ancient wooden chair. There was a thick silence as Arcane deliberated her words, faltering her stare from the Mistress when the latter caught the brunette studying her face.

"We assume it was hunters."

"Hunters? You're telling me they know of this island? That we live on here?"

"I'm afraid so."

There was a second of pregnant silence.

"Are you not scared I will tell everyone?"

"No, I don't."

Arcane swiftly silenced herself, the woman's tone oozed authority.

"I know you want to help; I can sense it. I placed a warding spell, that displaces people- makes hunter's leave the area, they usually don't find anything. They never have, till now."

Mori eyed Arcane, accusingly. A way in which made Arcane snap.

She thinks I led them here?!

"You truly think I led them here, that I'm the reason-"

"No, I don't. I think we have a traitor."

Arcane stilled herself at the robotic tone, unable to process the woman's words.

"Something has happened, has changed, and now the hunters are on the island, they can see where the children go, where we all go. Vera always knew the rules, to always stay in groups, to never stray too deep into the forest without me. She knew the risks; *she knew the rules.*"

Mori's voice was coated in a strain that she struggled to hide, clearly, she was well at covering up the negative emotions that stemmed from Vera Roe's body being found burnt to death, hanging from a tree. Arcane observed the way Mori teared her eyes away, finding interest in the floor as she silenced herself, lips folded into a thin line of discomfort. After a thick silence of deliberation, Arcane broke.

"You think someone gained her trust, took her out there?"

Mori nodded, stiffly.

"I don't take pleasure in putting my effort to my Sisters, but you have eyes that I do not have. I am but a loner, hidden in my room. It would be peculiar for me to attend outings, especially seeing as I never did so."

"I understand I have to help now, seeing what I saw, but what about Nipuna and Sybil? Why not them?"

"They will be working alongside us, privately."

"I truly did not expect you to follow me to find Vera's body. I… Apologise for exposing you to such a sight, truly."

Arcane shrugged.

"I've become accustomed to it."

"Nothing great comes from accustoming yourself to the dead," There was a long, belated silence as the two peered to each other, The Mistress cleared her throat- and Arcane peered away, fearful the older woman caught the redness of her cheeks. "Nonetheless, do you have any more questions? I must leave soon."

"I want to help, but in return you must consider my suggestions, on a rebellion- on fighting back. Revenge is all I want in return."

"It is not revenge you want, you want justice. It is too different; you are too good of a person to take revenge. Perhaps you have it in your mind, but you do not have it in your heart."

The way the Mistress peered to Arcane abruptly made her vulnerable, more human than witch.

"Will you think about it?"

Mori nodded; empty eyes unblinking. "Your ideas and your experiences made me question whether staying here is the safest option. It is the safest, but since Vera's death- we need change. That does not mean leaving and fighting a war we cannot win; it means weeding out the devils within our heaven."

Mori stood, dusting herself off.

"I need you to keep a watchful eye, log things you find peculiar, please."

"How do you know it wasn't me?"

Mori reluctantly gulped, peering to the rain that pelted against the window. A flash of unsureness clearly outlined she did not want to admit anything.

"I was keeping my eyes on you, and you were always where I assumed you to be."

"Why didn't you see when it was happening? Why didn't you get a wave of shock or adrenaline as she was being murdered?"

Questions littered her head, though Mori could not answer them. Even the Mistress Mori struggled to find the answers to such simple, knowledgeable questions.

"I couldn't figure out where she was, the connection I had connected to her numbed, I was completely blinded, I could not find her no matter how hard I tried to fight the spell on us. The spell restricted my tether to her, if it hadn't, she would be alive."

"Is Sybil, Nipuna and I all you've talked to about this?"

"Nipuna and Sybil are my closest associates; you can trust them with your life."

"Like I can trust you with mine?"

THE TRIPLE MOON | 71

There was a sarcastic bluntness to Arcane's words, she enjoyed bothering her and watching as Mori's face dropped- or stared with an emptiness that was hard to interpret. It was almost a hobby in her eyes, a way to bother the most powerful, it made her feel superior.

"I would die for you or any other sister in this Coven, I promise on my own life."

Arcane nodded distastefully, peeling away.

She struggled to trust those words as she stood to her full height, peering down at the Mistress.

"When will I see you next?"

"The ball, I expect."

"That's a week away."

"Five days, actually."

"What will I say to you?"

"You will say nothing unless you have to send me messages. If it's urgent enough, find me, or I will find you. You must not act as though you know me, it will create suspicion."

"But…. Why me?"

"You would've been a suspect if it were not for the fact, I have been monitoring you. I have suspects, but I need you to be my inside eyes. You are one of few who have seen what happened to Vera, so you must help me now."

Arcane began to turn away reluctantly, nodding. Upset by the fact she'd have to pretend as though she knew nothing of Mistress Mori, for her own good of course, but it still irked her to no end.

She struggled to walk away, finding Mori's eyes admirable to look at, her long fingers tapping at the desk were distracting, her narrow eyes always watching, her black hair framing her sunken face. She waited, walking sluggishly in a hope to hear her voice once more.

Her voice was hoarse, yet honeyed, nonetheless.

It was strange, her beauty, her voice were enchanting, despite her blunt and lack of emotions- Arcane urged for more of her time. She was infuriating, frustrating, yet comforting. Perhaps it was the strange fact the woman was watchful, overly observant and protecting from afar.

She wanted to scream to the world about how she finally met and discussed with Mistress Mori, the boasting was what she wanted most, looking at Ito and showing her, she was superior, she was more important, that she had in fact won.

"There's a rat, Arcane- and we need to exterminate it, fast."

6

Rigor Mortis

Barely a week had passed, barely a week. Not even three days had gone by since Vera Roe's death. She was merely a nine-year-old child- who drifted too far from the path, and fell into death's heartless, callous grasp.

They had hoped she would be the last.

But she wasn't.

Arcane knew, deep in her empty heart, that Vera would not be the last victim.

There was an emptiness to the halls of the haven, a disoriented lack of connection between the people trying to survive and reality. Arcane struggled to address and process what she had seen, who had died, how they had died, and who had possibly done such a thing to a child.

She didn't know who to trust, even Mistress Mori- and her overwhelming sense of comfort was questionable beneath the trailing fear of death around every corner. Her power was admirable and principled, the fact she could kill anyone she would like caused a chill to run through Arcane's spine as she twisted uncomfortably in her chair.

The notebook Mistress Mori had provided for her sat idly in her hands as she glossed words over with her feathered ink pen. The library was mostly empty aside from the few teenage girls sifting through the books cradled into the endless rows. The ticking of the clock hanging from the roof, and the quiet shuffling was the only sound within Arcane's mind as she struggled to go over where Takanashi Ito had been in the past few days. It was expected for her to be estranged- carless with time and whereabouts, but the strangeness could not be overlooked when girls were going missing. Not only so, but one of the twins wasn't present at dinner- which was an hour ago, though her sister only muttered that she was just busy with her dress.

Arcane still struggled trying to identify which sister was which, only being able to through mannerisms rather than physical features. Hino, Arcane remembered, was the moderately exclusive sister, while Miu was rather amiable, sweet spoken. That's the simplest way to tell the two apart.

She wrote the day down, and the lack of whom she remembered seeing. It was hard to watch the whole of the haven, though her specific group was easy enough to tally down.

She began to mindlessly scribble spells and incantations she wanted to pursue from the witches' learners' book into the free pages in her notebook, struggling to mouth the names correctly through her tongue and parting wrongly through her lips.

"This is so useless…"

"Reading is in face useless, my little dove-"

Ito crashed down onto the table, her legs enclosing Arcane in her seat as the abnormal woman peered down at her with mismatched eyes, glaring with her mischievous smile. She had not been at dinner, but she was here now, flouting all her strangeness.

"What do you want?" Arcane muttered, snapping the notebook shut and stuffing it into her bag as she sat stuck between Ito's legs on the chair, struggling to keep a steady stare anywhere but in the direction of the odd woman.

"Aw," Ito sniffed dramatically, eyes teary and faking melancholy as she leaned in close, her hot breath, the scent of mint on her tongue as her chest heaved for breath. "But I've missed you so very much, I only wanted to visit."

"Why didn't you make dinner?" Arcane furrowed her brows.

"Why are you so persistent today, so- stern, it's scary..." Her voice was layered with a sort of mockery as she slipped off the table, finding a seat on Arcane's lap and leaning into her face menacingly. "What's on your mind, little dove?"

Arcane fought to lean back into her chair enough to give her breathing space. There was no use as she inched her eyes away from the glaring woman on top of her, she was angry- furious even, but she controlled herself. Ignored the lingering attraction, buzzing through her body.

"Where were you? Takanashi Ito?"

Ito scoffed. "It's not important, I wasn't hungry. Now that I admit that I'll add in the fact I demise Sybil's food, her steak is never rare for me."

Arcane rolled her eyes, and as she began to push the girl from her, a blood curdling scream echoed throughout the halls, it shook the bookcases, and the two immediately ditched their spots without a second to lose, sprinting towards the screams.

Ito was agile, and swift on her feet as she overtook Arcane and her faltering ankles as they barged into one of the younger girls' bedrooms. Ito shoved the door in, it snapped on its hinges, and swung open abruptly with the force of her weight and her magic intertwined.

As Arcane followed close behind, the trail of blood dripping from the opening of the door made a shiver of dread reach through every inch of her body as her fingers urged to pull Ito back from the view of whatever was inside the room.

There was a burning, overwhelming stench, and memories of the past began to consume Arcane's mind, bodies, burning, fire, bodies, burning, fire, consuming her vision, blood, clouding her sight. Though as she blinked, she was seeing someone who was no longer her sister, but a girl unidentifiable to her.

There, in the middle of the bedroom was a charred figure of a young girl, her dress tattered-burnt to crisp like her complexion.

"Oh my god," Arcane muttered- astonished, a tight pain stabbing through her chest, muting her ears from the cries of the girl holding her friend's body. Through hazy eyes, hands grasped her shoving her away and against the wall.

"Wasn't expecting that much blood," Then Ito's careless giggle, one beneath her breath. Arcane shut her eyes tight, absorbing the feeling of hands on her to pretend as though the stench of blood and gore was still not breathing down her lungs.

Panic began to set in as the running of soft feet pelted down the hall. Children were coming to see- she struggled to breathe, begging, begging the girl was breathing, begging there was a pulse, begging Mori could do something before it was too late.

The abrupt panic shoved Arcane out of her trance, when she realized these feet, this movement- came from the young girls. The young girls were just as shocked by the screams and cries, confused-young girls who did not deserve to see death, to look it straight in the eyes.

"Wait!" Arcane pulled away, shoving herself in front of the door as the girls began to cascade in. She cried out, her hand shoving forward in hopes of halting them. They would not budge, and a flashing light cascading over the door as Arcane absentmindedly cast a blocking spell. A blocking spell Ohno had only just taught her, something she had only just recently grasped.

She stood- legs and arms stretched defensively, frozen as the girls argued, unable to see through the haze of her blocking spell through the door. They urged Arcane, aware of the dangers

"Girls," Nipuna's figure parts through the crowd, her towering form visible beyond the hoard of young girls. "Leave," and when they didn't, a poisonous snap echoed throughout the hall.

"Get out, now."

Her icy voice broke their trance upon the door and the sobs muffled behind it as they disrupted and dispersed, the chaste sound of sobs echoing through the halls. Nipuna peered away, her hands dug into her pockets- as though to hide the shake and fear.

THE TRIPLE MOON | 77

"I need you to leave as well," She then turned to Ito, "Both of you." she sneered.

"Will Mistress Mori be an acquaintance to this interesting meet-"

"Is that all you care about?" Nipuna sneered beneath her breath, inching close to the estranged woman. "There is a dead girl, and you rather discuss the concept of love and sex? When will you learn?"

"Learn what?" Ito narrowed her eyes, glaring up at the woman.

Nipuna's breath was furiously hot against the mismatched woman's face.

"That she has never loved you, do you not wonder why she does not allow you to visit anymore? You are a lost cause, Ito."

Her face twisted from an emotionless facade to a wide- large smile that emitted a rather fearful reaction from the other two women.

"Oh," Ito giggled. "You'll see..." She stepped away, unable to peer away. "I'll show you."

Ito did not pull her eyes away from Nipuna's form as she twisted from the corner and descended from the area, her feet gradually lacking in an echo as she departed further. Once the woman was completely absent, Nipuna peered to Arcane- expectantly.

"I advise you to leave, Arcane."

"I can help."

"This is a dirty business, death."

"I have looked death in the eyes once, I can do it again if it prevents others from having to."

Nipuna scrutinized at Arcane for a long second, hard- questionably. She was unsure, despite Mori's wise words to trust this woman. She knew deep down she could, with Mori's word. But did she want to trust her? With her life, with her word? If Mori had not told her to, she would never.

Nipuna observed as Arcane released the blocking spell of the door, hiding the horror inside the room.

"Fine," She muttered. "I hope you can stomach the deceased."

Arcane huffed, trailing behind and trying to reduce the pain that came from hearing the sobbing.

"Trust me," she muttered. "I can stomach it."

Observing, Arcane held back the watering tears at the girl who hugged her friend's dear body in her hands, curled up into her chest with the head lolling to the side. The girl's hand lay outstretched, almost as though reaching for some sort of salvage, some sort of way to scream *help me, please, someone, anyone.* Almost as though, they were looking to be saved by someone.

"Akuji?"

The name was barely heard over the sobs, the scratching of nails against charred skin. The girl holding her friend peered up shakily through blotches of tear-stained skin.

"Nipuna?"

"What happened?"

Her voice was soft, surprisingly, chaste- sensitive.

It was something Arcane had not seen before.

"She- she- I," she began to hiccup.

"Take your time to talk, we aren't rushing you." Arcane muttered, standing as far away as she could. Nestled close by the door frame, observing the blood- though aware of the fact her room was rather intact for someone who had been tortured before being burnt to death.

"She wasn't here earlier, I p- p - promise. I do, I t-truly promise," Sobs racked her little form, she was only a few years younger than the two women, only a teenager trying to survive in a murderous world, where she was wanted as prey amongst the predators.

A waft of easy amenity sunk through every inch of Arcane's form, she observed as both Nipuna and Akuji's shoulders slumped, clearly relaxed. It was as though a presence settled the girls, allowing the poor girl to find comfort among the unease and fear of doom. The girl holding her friend's body took a deep breath, a lack of a shakiness in her voice as she struggled to blink away her tears.

"She was gardening earlier,"

"With anyone?" Nipuna quipped.

"Uh...Honestly, only a few younger girls. She said she'd be back for dinner. I waited for her here, but she never turned up by dinner, so I left to eat and came back to this."

"Do you know the girl she was with?"

THE TRIPLE MOON | 79

"Uh…" Akuji blinked, her dark eyes streaming tears, though she had considerably relaxed since they had first found the girl's body. "They were young, they couldn't have done this."

"We need names to figure out when and where she went afterwards, please-"

"These girls won't be hurt, we promise." Arcane cut softly as Nipuna bashfully struggled with her words as she stood eerily above. Watching the tall woman, Arcane realized there would be little comfort that came from an emotionless, lanky woman standing over you and your dead best friend.

"Um…Their names were Moxi Legg, and… Frankie Rand, they're a few years younger than me- maybe twelve give or take, their room are downstairs."

Nipuna seemed to barely be able to recollect who the two girls were, as she side eyed Arcane. The lanky woman pulled a piece of paper from her pocket, her fingers ghosting over the parchment- the girls watched as the names sketched themselves onto the paper with literate handwriting close to what Nipuna's was, italic and slanted.

"Take this to her,"

Arcane already knew who she meant.

She left swiftly, although with lingering eyes on the girl holding her friends remains close to her chest. The dull eyes looking up to the ceiling ss she rested, cradling into the warmth of a human- suffering body. A pang of pain shook through every part of her body, numbing her fingers as the shaking- crying sobs began to echo through the room once again. Arcane fiddled with the red bow around her wrist, trying to erase the pale dead body, lying in blood as she trailed the path to Mistress Mori's private quarters.

As Arcane stepped to the large entrance of Mori's bedroom, a hand grabbed her shoulder urgently, spinning her around. Arcane furrowed her brows as a shock penetrated through her, she had not heard anyone coming, and she despised how distracted she had become.

Blinking, she peered down at Spring, who heard her shoulder with shaky fingers.

"What are you doing?! We have rules to stay in our room!"

"I- I was-erm-"

"You can't run off like that, please, it scares me."

"I was just running an errand."

Spring furrowed her brows, peering to the door. She scoffed a little beneath her breath, more surprised than questioning.

"For whom?"

"Sybil, being mute you know- she needs written messages delivered to people." Arcane numbly and instinctively waved the writing, before stiffly shoving the paper beneath Mori's door. Curious eyes watched her as Spring began to lead her away from the door.

"That's sweet of you, but seriously, you could've died!"

Arcane rolled her eyes, rather playfully at Spring's words.

'Totally."

"Take this seriously! There's a rumour someone died!"

"Yes, I did hear that."

Spring huffed. "Well come on, we have orders to be locked down. We have to stay in our rooms for a few days till Mori gives all clear."

Spring clung to Arcane, wrapping her hands around the brunette's biceps as they walked through the dimming halls of the Haven. It was eerily silent aside from the mile away sobs, the silence- was so present it was almost as though it made sound, ringing in the ears, the drips of invisible rain along the wooden floorboards. It began to create an imaginary sound among the hollowness of the night.

"Ohno's rooming with us, she doesn't like sleeping alone during this sort of stuff."

Arcane shrugged, she was less than bothered, rather relieved she felt as though she were making someone feel a little more at ease, a little more comfortable in this fearful period.

"Assumed she didn't like me,"

"Oh," Spring laughed grimly beneath her breath. "She doesn't like many people, or at least, she pretends she doesn't."

"Who is the one person she hates the most, then?"

Arcane muttered, struggling to pretend the dead body she had seen was still not in the corner of her vision or in front of her every time she moved or closed her eyes. She peeled the door open, observing Ohno as she made a makeshift bed on the floor where the incantations previously were made. The books were moved to the edge of Spring's bed, candles moved to the corner of the room.

"That's obvious,"

Ohno was walking out of the bathroom as she replied, cleaning her glasses with her pyjama shirt. Despite the sleeping attire, she wore a uniformed set that followed the dress code, a white buttoned shirt, black pants, and the soft red bow to tie her hair back.

"We all know who I hate the most,"

Spring shrugged as Arcane furrowed her brows, though as she observed the two slip into the designated beds, the memory of having dinner with the relentless arguing of Ito and Ohno across the table.

"Oh, yeah…"

"Takanashi Ito is a loose cannon," Ohno muttered, though as she began to mumble and curse, Arcane found herself tempted to the concept of a hot bath as she distractedly disappeared through the door. As she sat in the hot water, absentmindedly scrubbing her skin raw, her burn almost like dirt she urged to remove from her skin, their voices quietly carried.

Arcane, with little knowledge she had of magic, mumbled a few words, trying to push herself into hearing through the confined walls and into the next room. She concentrated, hard enough her nails began to dig holes into her palms.

She took a sharp breath, flinching enough the water lapsed over the bathtub as the sound of their voice echoed abruptly in her head. She truly did not think she had trained enough to be able to do this, she supposed Ohno was just a good teacher.

"How's she been?"

"Arcane?" Spring's voice was exaggeratedly hushed.

Silence, supposedly- Ohno did a physical gesture.

"She's been okay, I guess…"

"I guess?"

There was another long pause, enough Arcane furrowed her brows.

"She's not liked the others, she's sweet, and kind-hearted, but something happened to her before she came here, and it's clearly made her react differently to how most would."

"Elaborate."

"I'm usually a good sleeper, you know- only wake for the toilet. She always seems to be awake, though. Whenever I wake up, she's always wide awake- and she seems less inclined to come out with me if I have plans."

"She's introverted."

"Yeah…"

"Maybe the ball will change that."

"Oh, that reminded me. I'll be a little late to that- I have a date I'm going with; can you take her with you?"

"Does she have an outfit?"

"She has a basic one, a long black skirt and a fancy white blouse. She can match a white corset with it if she wants."

"If she even wants to go."

Silence, then Spring's voice again.

"Don't you think it's a little strange these things have started happening as soon as she comes?"

Silence, long, and hard. Enough for Arcane to impatiently drop underneath the water, holding her shaky fingers over her face as she listens to their shaky breathing on the other side of the door. The lack of breath made her want to gasp through the water consuming her, her throat burning as she feared the next words.

How dare she.

"Yes, but…One rumour of a dead girl, and Vera missing isn't much to worry about yet."

"I know, I just…This has never happened before."

Silence.

Arcane couldn't wait any longer for a reply, she burst from the water, gasping- having a gulp of air as her eyes blurred, her heart beating dangerously against the ribs encapsulating it.

THE TRIPLE MOON | 83

"Honestly, Ito has more drive to play around with rumours and people than any other person if we are deciding to point hands, though a witch doing this wouldn't make sense at all."

That's all Arcane had to hear as she tuned out, resting the back of her head against the edge of the tub, peering up dainty at the blank white roof, and observing the black mist the dropped from the top-like snowflakes in the snow before it twisted into a hand, within the fragile pale hand, was an envelope.

Through the dark, was lurking, observant eyes- staring back as she shakily grasped the envelope. Arcane could memorize those eyes effortlessly, the natural narrow, the darkness of those orbs through the little light on the other side of the mist. There was a sense of comfort that overcame Arcane despite the lack of familiarity that came with knowing the Mistress Mori.

As her hands grazed lanky fingers, the mist dissipated, as did the comforting figure within it, and once again- physically Arcane was alone, although he was unsure whether someone watched her, as they sat at their desk of blood-stained books.

She twisted herself so her stomach and chest laid against the edge of the bath, shakily, her exhaustedly drained fingers- wet and wrinkled like an old lady tried to peel the envelope from whatever was inside, presumably a letter addressed from Mori to herself.

Dear Miss, Arcane Amunet,

The solstice is almost upon us.
Which means the festivity of the ball is upon us.

You must promise to find me, once the least eyes are upon both of us.
We must discuss the matter of contention at hand.

Arcane took a deep breath, though as she scanned longer, a thud echoed throughout her insides as her heart plummeted, the emotions draining from her, enough it hurt to breathe. Arcane took a sharp, strangled breath- her breath catching.

We found another child.

This is the third.

I am not addressing this to any of the students, this abrupt demise may as well cause an uproar, nor will they know we speculate this is a person of our own, and not the hunters doing. Our Sisters do not deserve to be lied to, but it is safer this way.

If you need any comfort for the hardships that comes with the commitment you are doing for me,

You know where to find me. I have anything you shall need in my vicinity; I will make sure to accommodate.

Sincerely-

Crow Mori,
Mistress of Venfic Island's haven.

7

Solstitium

Arcane had always presumed everyone felt the irrelevant sense of death leaning over themselves in every second of every day, though the more she absorbed Ohno's tendency to ignore these signs made her realize she was a loner when it came to such. It seemed she herself was the sole person fearing what tonight would bring. No one else seemed to perceive tonight as being a catalyst to the ending of their existence, only her.

"Stop struggling," Ohno muttered from behind, her short figure struggling with little strength to tighten the corset around Arcane's outfit, her heeled boot digging into the taller woman's back, forcing the two to struggle balancing with the weight. She groaned beneath her breath at the little change Ohno's pulling made, and after a pregnant silence. Listened as Ohno conjured a spell that automatically tightening the corset- jolting Arcane back as it tied it up before the strings dropped without command.

"I won't look stupid, will I?" Arcane muttered, referring to the elegance of Ohno's dress. It sat tightly amongst every inch of Ohno's body, illuminating a figure that was often unidentifiable due to the layers of uniform she most commonly wore. It was a soft pastel blue-satin, it almost looked as though Ohno was a different person altogether.

Arcane peered down to her own outfit- to the basicness of her skirt and blouse, and the corset that only added a sense of fashion. Without the white corset paired with her white blouse. She'd look like a house maid of sorts, not what was expected from a person invited to a celebration of the solstice.

"It suits you."

"Are you calling me basic?"

Arcane eyed the shorter woman as she scoffed beneath her breath, edging her glasses up her little button nose. Her narrow eyes rolled, vividly unimpressed.

"I'm just being honest, I think you need to do something with your hair," Ohno sat herself onto Arcane's bed, patting beside her. "You haven't even brushed it," She scowled begrudgingly, whipping the brush from the drawer, and bashing it through her hair with little answer from Arcane.

The unkempt girl peered to Ohno, observing the red bow in her hair.

"Why don't you use a different colour?"

"Why?"

"It doesn't match your dress."

Ohno ignored Arcane scoffing. "Who cares."

"I don't," Arcane muttered, rolling her eyes as the girl took another relentless blow to her unkempt hair, before she irritably wrapped it into a loose bun. "I was just curious."

"There."

"Thank you," Arcane muttered, peeling away and walking to the door.

"Hey... where's your red bow?"

Arcane observed as Ohno placed it around her wrist, furrowing her brows and watching as Ohno rolled her eyes, again. It seemed the girl's entire personality was being frustrated at people and making it blatantly evident.

"Spring gets upset if you don't wear it, it's a sort of- sentiment thing to her," Ohno only proceeded after the silence. "The day Nipuna stopped wearing hers Spring cried into her pillow for three days. Nipuna claimed it was itchy, but that only made her cry an extra day."

"Oh..." Arcane muttered, reluctantly leaving it wrapped as they began their way towards the ball, taking turns, stairs, and more corners before finding the hallway towards the entrance of the ball room overloaded with young girls in prissy dresses and suits, some-dressed rudimentary enough that Arcane found herself sighing in relief.

At least she wasn't a loner.

As the two girls slipped inside of the ballroom, overcome with elegant candle lights and a grand piano- as black as night with keys moving unprovoked, floating music consumed the room, instruments that lacked artists, their keys moving alone with the sense of magic erupting within the vibrant air. Arcane peered down, searching for Ohno close beside her.

"Hey, who was Spring's partner any-"

Ohno had already left her side.

She huffed degradedly beneath her breath, aware she was now disorientated' standing in the middle of a bustling ballroom, observing the cluster of synchronised dancers. Despite the overwhelming sense of fear- the loneliness despite being in a crowded room, the girl's synchronized, elegant dancing lulled Arcane into a delicate interest as she stood observing. The woman, despite the past couple of harrowing months, seemed content in one another's arms and presence, this perceived harmony shot a sense of jealousy through every nerve in Arcane's body. She hoped that one day she could have that sense of comfort and harmony with these girls, but it felt as though it would take her hundreds of years before she could truly warm up to their love.

The dresses mingled with a raw beauty, the palettes vastly congruent to the winter and the solstice- the dresses flowed with soft colours of greys and blues, many finding comfort in the colour of black, with their hands grasped in one another's as they danced to the harmony of the magically playing instruments. The reddened moon peered down on the witches through the little window on the top of the sphere roof. The little window towering above was entangled with ancient artwork, it was spick and span- brand new, despite the fact the art was clearly created hundreds of years ago, the creators Arcane expected- were to have passed, though their art remains to acknowledge their once existence as the living.

Arcane found a sense of familiarity as she peered up into the depictions of forest creatures mingled with dancing girls amongst the roof above. She craned her neck to peer at the painted Triple Moons further towards the window upon the roof, the slated crescent moons depicted mischievous simpers that peered down on Arcane as the laughter and music began to distantly dissipate within Arcane's ears. The artwork above pulled her into a state where the outside world did not falter her mind's reeling ideas. It was almost as though her mind floated amongst the stars and the moon within the night sky, the sound of people long distant in her ears.

A breath tickled the back of Arcane's craned neck, and through a breathy laughter- Arcane snapped away, swinging back to find Takanashi Ito peering at her with those mismatched eyeballs, narrowed flirtatiously as she stood idly by, tempting herself to come closer.

She wore a tight pair of suit pants and a coat, with a lace corset beneath. She looked rather attractive for someone who was likely to kill her- a wolf dressed in sheep's clothing, it seemed. Her grin was almost threatening if not for the obsessively loving pair of eyes. She had slicked her uneven hair back, but did not bother with makeup, it seemed she liked to fashion her scars, rather than hide them. Her scars were almost inspiring to her, that or- they were a statement.

"You look ravishing," She purred, her black nails dragging down Arcane's chest, catching in the lace of her white corset as she edged close, her breath was velvet soft against her lips. She had a wafting fragrance of honey dew as she edged closer- Arcane was sure that metallic smell of blood was still on her clothes, more than on her clothes, stuck to her very skin. It immediately reminded her of whom they had found only a few days prior, dead in a puddle of their own blood.

Arcane eyed the woman, curious.

"What do you want, Ito?"

Ito blinked, her lips rising into a manic, shaky smile.

"I just want a dance."

Her hand delicately reached from Arcane, fingers desperate.

"I've never danced before."

Ito narrowed her eyes despite the smile.

"Pretty please, little dove?"

"There's always something you want out of my presence."

Ito hummed, "I suppose my offer still stands in regard to those *'thrill rides'* as you called them, Dove."

Arcane memories resurfaced, and although Mori had told her to keep information and communication of one another on the downlow, it seemed Arcane could not hold back the yearning to edge Takanashi Ito on about what she desired and what Arcane had.

"Oh, there's no offer anymore, I already found her."

She knew she wasn't supposed to say so.

She told herself she wouldn't.

Yet? She still did.

Ito, for a second, blanched in complete shock.

"What?"

"You were right when you said she smelt divine," Arcane muttered, standing shoulder to shoulder with Ito, observing as her face broke, eyes narrowing and her teeth clenching. "Like soft parchment paper, have you touched her skin recently? It's as soft as silk, like she bathed in citrus-"

"Arcane," Ito sneered. "Let's not lie."

"You can tell I'm not lying," Arcane scoffed, the air heated, waft of magic erupting. "You're using an incantation to tell whether I'm lying, what is it telling you?"

Silence.

Then, she sneered.

"No, you aren't," she edged close, long nails dragging down Arcane's chest, looking for a sort of- chilled reaction, like the tingling of the spine and the jolt in Arcane's eyes, but there was vividly nothing. "So, how did you do it? Did you bargain? Throw your life away for her attention, beg at her feet? Please, you begged, didn't you?"

Her voice was pleading now, begging beneath the sound of chaste music.

"Oh," Arcane scoffed. There was a rage of adrenaline, a sense of- I'm finally winning this game, Ito. You will not have a hold of me for much longer in such a weak state of grovelling. It seemed with such a simple fact, Ito was on her knees, and that only pumped more power into Arcane's veins. "I didn't need to do anything."

"Sure," Ito sneered, breath hotly fanning the witch's small- almost invisible smirk. "Sure, you didn't, I'll ask her myself. You may have not begged, but you never have been affected by her like I have, I promise you that, Arcane Amunet."

Ito only began to manically giggle as Arcane did not budge from her stand- her eyes furrowing as she replayed what Ito had said, though it seemed she was saved from her abrupt enemy as Spring came bounding forwards, completely ignoring Ito.

Arcane began to realize she enjoyed watching Ito act so erratically, but it seemed the woman enjoyed the same thing, received and given.

"Arcane!"

Ito sneered; words spat beneath her breath- something Arcane was unable to grasp before she disappeared throughout the crowd. She departed without a glimmer of a goodbye as Spring clutched onto Arcane's shoulder, pulling her down to make equal eye contact, a gleeful smile erupting upon her rosy lips.

"Ohno did well with you! I was worried you wouldn't even turn up."

Arcane anxiously peeled away as Spring let go, she wiped the dust from her outfit- the remnants of Ito once holding her, her scent still present in the air. She wasn't sure whether she was relieved or bothered that Spring had interjected. Being close to Ito meant answers could come from what she had been doing, her presence often quenched that loneliness, though with what consequences what Ito was a suspect?

"Who was your partner?"

Spring's smile dropped. "My partner? She shared a room just down the hall from us, I don't know where she went."

Arcane nodded, observing the upset downturn of the little blonde's lips, though despite this- her dress was beautifully crafted. Though not to the standard of the twins, the dress had its perks, it was tight before it grew from the waist, a cute pink dress that matched her red bow that was tied to the strap of her dress.

It wasn't the pigments expected to be worn at a winter solstice hosted by Witches, cherry pink wasn't a conventional colour. Though Arcane assumed she had done so to illuminate the room, flourish amongst the gloomy hues and tones of the ballroom. It was true, Arcane was obscured in her dark clothes compared to Spring Lee's lively dress.

"You look nice, I like the corset. Is it Ohno's?"

"Yes, she found it lying around. I couldn't imagine her wearing it though, it's quite- revealing if it weren't for the blouse underneath."

Spring shrugged, eyes roaming the ballroom, catching on the dancers across the floor, spinning and twisting in each other's arms. "Still, you look wonderful."

"I look like I did the bare minimum."

Spring scoffed. "You do not! Even if you did the bare minimum, your bare minimum is beautiful."

Arcane shrugged her shoulders, struggling to feel any sense of beauty with the mediocre outfit, she crossed her arms over her chest, resting her weight on her hip as she listened to Spring start to gush about her partner for the dance- presumably, her name was Beatrix, a girl that usually sat at the table with them but never seemed to attend anymore, finding them exclusive and uninteresting for her time. She ate on her own and didn't attend anything, Spring clarified. Which was why Arcane hadn't heard of her till now.

Spring rambled on, searching for her through the crowd.

"She's quiet, nice- but quiet!"

"How long have you talked to her like this for?"

"Like this?" Spring quipped, unsure what Arcane meant as she peered up through blonde lashes.

"Romantically, I mean." As Arcane struggled to get the words out, pink clouding her cheeks at the awkwardness, Spring's face seemed to mirror this as she slipped closer.

"A week, maybe. I've been visiting her for a while."

Arcane, although quite content with Spring's actions, still sensed that greedy pang of jealousy through her chest, a shrivelling sort that made it hard to breathe. She was beyond jealous even, being alone trying to find salvation in a world that wanted you dead, left out of touch, starved, she was alone for almost a year looking for the haven, why was she so surprised she yearned for some sort of love as compensation?

Although Spring similarly had a life lacking the current contact of family support and love, Arcane was getting no support or comfort, while Spring was able to bounce back and find a sort of replacement, from the love of a family- Arcane would not, and could not recover, her nightmares progressive, her mourning common in the mornings, horrible in the night ss she held her pillow as though it were a person holding her back. Spring was falling in love, it was obvious to the scrunch of her nose when she said Beatrix's name, and the way her eyes glowed.

Arcane knew love would never come easy for her, she was an outcast- someone unable to overcome the obstacles life had thrown at her. If she could not fix herself, no one else could do it for her, that's just, not how she worked. She didn't believe in other people's support in life, either she did it herself, or she died trying. Her fight was internal, and no one could fight that out of her but herself.

She applauded people like Spring, people who could fall in love, people who realized comfort and support helped the pain and the recovery and made life worth living- but she could not imagine such a thing ever happening to her, not at all.

A figure appeared behind Spring as she continued to ramble, Arcane barely able to process her words.

"Hey," Beatrix, presumably smiled lopsided, their long black hair framing their round face, they were pretty- tall, merely taller than

Arcane, dressed in a fancy blue suit with one of Spring's signature bow wrapped on their pinkie.

"Arcane right?"

She nodded, awkwardly peering, searching across the ballroom for any sign of distress, or Mistress Mori and Takanashi Ito.

"I've heard a lot about you from Spring, but-" They halted, as if unsure on what to say next. Although Arcane wasn't fazed, barely looking at the two and rather searching the room for the person she needed to find before the end of the night.

"Could I take Spring from you for a few minutes?"

Arcane broke from her search, blinking.

"Uh, of course. You don't have to ask me."

Spring spared her friend a sympathetic stare, she was alone- and Arcane was too awkward to stay like that any longer. Spring assumed she'd leave back for their room sooner or later.

Though that was not Arcane's plan, she observed as Spring disappeared through the crowd, hand in hand- before she began to search for the small feminine figure of Mistress Mori. She knew it would be one of the hardest things to ever do. The woman was heard, but never seen, a gust of dust amongst a sparkling sky of stars, Arcane assumed it would take her hours before she'd get a glimpse of her, if she decided to turn up that is.

Though she was aware of the direction Takanashi Ito had gone through the crowd- her figure had disappeared around one of the pillars, and towards a corner concealed by silk, almost like a curtain that disclosed a small hall that led to a balcony.

Despite how much Arcane hated having to argue and be within the general vicinity of Ito, she followed. The unhinged woman was brilliant at stalking a specific someone, and this someone was whom she needed to find tonight. If she found Ito, she would find Mistress Mori not too far behind.

Furthering from the loudness of the ball, and closer to the chaste softness of voices behind the red curtain, the tranquil waft of cold air shifted through her face, allowing her cheeks to soften their redness, and a relieved sigh to part from her lips.

Her heeled feet halted at the broken sound of laughter- the cackling, Ito style of laughter that was condescending. It echoed throughout the small space, and barely past the curtains shielding the party. Arcane took a sharp-quiet breath, allowing herself to sync their voices and despite the distance- be able to hear their hushed voices flawlessly in her ear.

"Your presence is a paradox, have you realised that yet?" Her cackle of a voice whistled in distaste.

It didn't take long for Arcane to realize whom exactly she was talking to.

Her low voice chuckled, and for once- there was a string of emotion that emitted from the Mistress' throat, something more uncommon then most liked to admit for their superior.

"How so, Ito?"

There seemed to be a gruff sound that came as a reply, almost as though Ito was frustrated.

"Preaching protection and affection, and then throwing us in the dirt like trash-" her voice was gravelled, angry, and spitting. "-We haven't seen you in months, all you do is hide away. Ever since we were children you did it. You are a paradox."

"Do not bring that up again, Ito. You know how hard I'm working-"

"Not hard enough."

Arcane fisted her hands by her sides, never would she have expected For Ito to disrespect Mori like that so blatantly and with such bitterness. A surge of fury seeped through her, she couldn't truly pinpoint why, but Ito's comment rubbed her completely in the wrong direction.

"Where have you been then, Ito? I suppose you assume I do not keep watch of this place?"

There was a thick silence, and Arcane began to understand what exactly Mori was implying. She proceeded, this time- with vigour pulsing through her, echoing in her voice. "What have you been doing, Ito?"

Sound of rustling clothes followed, a grunt, a sound of skin on skin- and the silence.

THE TRIPLE MOON | 95

Arcane edged forward, aware of the soft creak her feet made against the old wooden floorboards, it had started getting trickier to hear- even with the spell, particularly when the ballroom only illuminated, the melody heightening.

"You already know-" her voice came out strangled.

"Say it."

"No."

The silence was thickening, choking down their throats, Arcane could hear the faint breathing they emitted, though Ito's was shaky, as though she knew she was overstepping the boundaries.

"Say. It. Now." With every word was a harsh silence, Mori's voice gradually ascending into a colder tone of distrust. A grunt followed.

"*Death*, don't you dare play stupid with me just so you can hear me admit it."

The air shot straight out of Arcane's body, the life draining from her face.

Arcane began to leap through the curtain in a fit of rage, but a force halted her, her legs bound. She peered through a furious shimmering sight to find the black fog wrapping dreadfully up her legs, like tentacles along her skin- cold and caressing up past her skirt's materials.

Arcane furrowed her brows, confused beyond comprehension- unsure what Mori's plan was. She wanted to rip the woman on the other side to pieces, to drown her- burn her, so why was Mistress Mori holding her back?

"Death? *Ito*, who is dying?" There was a strange gentleness in Mori's voice. Arcane could not process why there was such an unexpected softness aimed at the traitor, the rat of the bunch, caught in a trap.

"You already know what."

Ito's voice began to gravel, begging.

There was no prickling of Arcane's skin, not a single indication Ito was lying.

"Say it, Ito."

"I've been trying to kill myself; you know why, you're always watching me."

Silence, the sound measuring from Arcane's ears for a split second, her mind too overwhelmed to process the words. She no longer resented the woman, no lies spewed from her mouth. She was being vulnerable and open, and now Arcane felt horrible for having heard such a private conversation. Although, Ito did not seem disappointed, rather mediocre than anything else.

Arcane wasn't sure what was better, but now everything began to make sense. The bandaged arms, the lack of sight in her left eye, the scar along her face, the strangely cut hair and long, nails with scabbing red blood underneath.

"I enjoy the thrill. I live off it," She whispered, sensually. "You used to give me that thrill- Crow. Now...Now you just threw me away, demanded me to recuperate on my own. What am I supposed to do other than chase for the excitement?"

"You compare my attention to the thrill of dying?"

"Of course, I do."

She made it sound as though it were obvious, plain sighted.

A sharp breath, one that was hot in Arcane ear, almost as though Mori stood close by her side, but that was not true- she stood on the other side of the curtain, though it seemed Mori was very much aware she was there, listening.

"You are-"

"*Crazy?* I know, you've told me. But if I'm honest, I love it when you call me that."

"This conversation is migrating, I am not here to talk to you about your romantic emotions, nor your thrill rides. You cannot do this anymore, Ito. What will make you stop?"

"You."

"You know I cannot give you that."

"Then, Arcane Amunet."

WHAT???

A long, pregnant silence, one that Arcane did not love.

"What of her?"

Arcane's face began to redden, the cold air could not compensate for the abrupt amount of embarrassment. Arcane begged for the plan not to backfire, and Mori would not be furious at her for egging Ito on about having her attention. Though that was the overthinking talking, Mori wasn't an aggressive person- well, she assumed she wasn't.

"Ah," a cackle, quietened behind the curtains. "So, you have met her."

Silence.

"She and I, what do you say... get along well." Ito continued. "Imagine, have you tried calling her your little dove? She goes all flustered and hot, it's exhilarating. Now I know how it feels, Mori- when you do it to me."

Mistress Mori scoffed beneath her breath.

"I don't need to imagine."

There was a distant prickling behind Arcane's neck. The lie was detected instantly after the words rolled off her tongue, a lie that hardly distinguished the truth. Mori could imagine, she did imagine, it seemed. Arcane's face reddened, stomach starting to do somersaults.

"And you presume her romance will be equivalent to mine?"

Arcane observed the black magic shifting away, almost like a beacon as Mori proceeded.

"No, it will not be, but it's nice to try."

Ito cackled, and it only loudened as Arcane shoved past the curtains, her figure walking straight into Mori's smaller figure on the other side. Arcane observed with narrow eyes as Ito's hands hazardously gripped the collar of Mistress Mori's formal burgundy blouse, hands pale.

"Aw- Look what the cat dragged in."

Mori did not seem fazed by Ito's proximity, seemingly used to the intimacy her character brought to most conversations. The room was exceedingly modest, barely enough room for the three girls to stay put. In the low light on the small hall before the doors that led them to a small balcony, Arcane observed the dimness of Mori's face, the way her eyes continuously appeared in and out of focus.

"Mistress Mori, are you okay?"

Silence as Ito giggled, eying Arcane.

"Ah, so thoughtful, Arcane."

Arcane ignored the woman entirely, observing the Mistress with keen interest, waiting for her to come back from whatever engrossed her as the said woman peered away absentmindedly, concentrated on an idea or vision that was far off.

"Yes," Mori blinked, "Thank you."

"So, you both planned this, then?" Ito quizzed. "You know, you could have just asked, I would have been more than delighted to join."

The two other women visibly furrowed their brows, peering to one another and hoping Ito would provide an explanation, though Arcane did not need one, she already realized what Ito was applying as the half blind woman shoved Mori into the other wall, causing Arcane too, to be shoved back by the magic shove of her hands.

A dry chuckle left Mori's lips, mocking- it was something Arcane had never truly seen, though it was gone before Arcane could even preserve the memory.

"You're quite feverish."

"I know you like it like that-"

A surge of irritation hit Arcane- no, not just irritation...envy.

"We aren't here to play around Ito," Arcane sneered, urged to shove her away, though kept her hands grudgingly to her sides. "You saw the dead girl when you were with me in the library, witches are dying day by day. We need answers."

It finally clicked in her head.

Her face distorted into a twisted, unfair smile- mocking, more mocking than Mori's previous laugh aimed at her.

"You thought I was the culprit?" She pulled, reluctantly away from Mori, vividly struggling to part as she eyed Arcane's scowl, finding joy in the way her eyes narrowed in irritation. She shrugged bashfully, and as she did, her suit jacket rode down, her chest more visible.

"I don't enjoy killing others, only oneself. Though I do have exemptions to that testament."

Mori shook her head, and her lanky fingers grazed the small part of Arcane's back, beginning to rigorously lead her out of the small hidden area. Though as she spoke, she slowed to look Ito straight in her eye.

"I knew it wouldn't be you, Ito. But I cannot take chances, not now."

"Not ever it seems," Ito narrowed her eyes, though it dissipated with her fanged smile. "Well, I have no promises, it would be so easy just for you to come back to me- one knife too close to my skin and you're in front of me, how delightful.'"

"I can stop you from anything without lifting a finger, Takanashi, do not try me. My affection is not needed."

All three women were aware of the lengths Ito would take to get Mori's attention.

It was dangerous.

"We don't need another dead witch, Ito- despite how much you infuriate me." Arcane muttered.

With those words, the two left Ito inside the room, her groans evident as Mori pulled Arcane to the corner of the room, hidden from the crowds. It seemed despite her popularity, she feared attention. Her face displayed this, although mostly concealed and lacking emotion, her eyebrows pinched together, her shoulders tense and her fingers pressed hard into Arcane's back, causing the girl to struggle to keep her composure with the woman's closeness.

Mori pulled Arcane close, aware of the soft smell of candle wax on her skin, unaware that Arcane could smell the smoke and lemon scent of Mori's clothes. Her breath was hot on her neck, lips a\second away from caressing the skin. Arcane struggled to keep her composure, moving in front of Mori to keep their prying eyes away from her short physique.

"Have you perhaps seen Nipuna?"

Arcane pursed her lips, bending down an inch to meet Mori's narrowed eyes.

"No, I haven't."

"The twins?"

"Sora yes, but Miu? No…But, you know Miu wasn't at dinner last night?"

Mori nodded. "I do."

"Sora said she was getting her dress prepared, but I haven't seen her at all today- she's a sucker for praise, I'd assume she'd be here by now."

Mori nodded, faintly.

"Follow me, will you? We must search for them."

"Do you know where they might be?"

"I can sense Miu isn't in the building."

"And Nipuna?"

Mori was silent, ignorant to the question for a minute too long.

"That, I do not know."

8

Silva

"Follow me."

Arcane furrowed her brows in question, though was more than willing to trail the Mistress as she gripped her arm in a death like grip- pulling her through a small door that led to the kitchens down the hall from the bustling ballroom party. They wanted through the doors to the kitchens without a hassle, the wafting smell of divine foods, honey, chicken, cake, and pies overwhelming Arcane's senses.

There, Sybil stood awkwardly, waiting patiently. She wore a long pale dress, matching her pale skin. She seemed quite dressed up, very refined, though too reluctant to join the party as she stood busying herself making what seemed to be a human size cake, half-finished on an antique counter. There was flour =all along her face and dress as she lacked an apron.

"Sybil," At the voice, she perked up, expectant and waiting for command. Her eyebrows rose more as she peered at Arcane who despite the jolting chills of Mori's hands through her blouse, smiled the only way she could: awkwardly.

"Please, monitor the ball. I must find Nipuna."

At this, her mood vividly deteriorated. Silently, she clapped her hands across her dress to rid of the flour, nodding and leaving through the door they came through.

They trailed through the huge kitchen covered in utensils that hung from the roof. Arcane followed as Mori slipped through one of the kitchen doors, sauntering down a spiralling set of stairs before slipping through a creaking door that took them out to the back of the haven. This was where the back gardens were, behind this- a large, looming forest, shrouded in darkness.

Arcane's voice shattered the silence like broken glass.

"Your tone makes me worry."

Mori halted, peering to Arcane through the wisps of dark hair.

"Oh, I apologize," She began, beginning to walk again, her grip unfaltering. "You see, I have always struggled masking my emotions."

Arcane furrowed her brows. "I find it more unsettling the fact you have no emotions. There's not even a flicker of emotion in those black eyes."

Mori did not falter, though Arcane sensed a pang of pain, unless it were her own regret as the words burst out from between her lips. "I didn't mean it like that."

Silence as they broke through the garden, making it to the entrance of the tree line. Mori's fingers sprouted a blue light through her fingertips, a lightness within the dark of night.

"No offense taken; emotions are everyone's weakness in the end. It is better to have none than too many."

"You know," Arcane muttered. "I think I disagree."

Mori seemed to ponder the words as they sauntered through the forest, though the conversation was broken by the sound of a large crack that echoed through the darkness. Arcane stilled, breath short in her throat.

"Why do you think Nipuna will be down here?" Arcane began to double guess her position. Was Mori truly to be trusted? She was leading her through the dark forest, alone. What if Mori was the one killing these girls, she was, in fact the strongest out of all- gifted by the magic of the Coven leader, having trained for some many years, studied for so long. She could potentially kill them all if she pleased.

But she wouldn't, Arcane told herself.

But you barely know her.

You've put your trust into a woman you have only just met.

On What?

The fact she makes your heart race.

Witches have spells, Arcane, she could've bewitched you to like her.

Shut up.

SHUT.

UP.

She may just be using you.

Taking you to your death.

Mori's hands moved to Arcane's shaky palm, squeezing before parting from holding her any longer as they trekked through the darkness of the night. It seemed that one glimmer of comfort was a mistake or Mori's, she gave space immediately after, almost as though she had pricked her finger on barbed wire.

It seemed Mori was more of an Empath Arcane took her for.

What comes of killing innocent girls?

Coven leaders have immeasurable power, only the weaker of people who yearn for power would bother to side with hunters and kill their own to gain power and more lives. IF it were anyone, it would be the weakest, or at least, a professional actor.

"Nipuna was scouting in the afternoon; I saw her last by the lines of the trees. She must have lost the time, or decided not to come to the ball..."

"That doesn't seem common to her."

"It isn't." Mistress Mori muttered.

"And Miu? Why would she be here?"

Mori was silent, unable to look at anything, she was specifically negligent to Arcane's curious eyes.

"You're on edge." Arcane eyed the way Mori's fingers shook that held the ball of white, blue fire.

"I know," she muttered. "I felt the tether of string that I have of her. You see, I can see everyone one of you through an internal tether of string I place in my mind between every one of my students. I can feel when these snap, they can happen often, small- implications. Sometimes they snap by accident, but sometimes they snap on purpose."

"But this?"

"Every girl that has died, Arcane- their tether has not just been snapped from me, but I can feel it shrivel and die while still connected, almost as though the person is taunting me as they kill them. They use an incantation to blind my sight, unable to use the tether or find where they may be, I have to feel them die."

"Have you felt it yet?"

"This one snapped, I have no sense of where Nipuna is right now, Miu's has not- I sense her through the forest, but something is-." She cocked her head to her heeled boots, blinking, trying to diminish the haze in her sight and mind "-something is clouding my vision."

"Someone, not something." Arcane muttered.

A hollowed-out sense of dread echoed throughout every nerve of Arcane's body, almost as though Mori's hand had broken through her skin and ribs to rip her heart from her body. Perhaps Arcane was being dramatic, but deep down, she knew they may be too late.

Though Nipuna was experienced and highly intelligent, would they be able to fight off hunters, or one of their own?

"Come," and with the single chaste word, Mori pulled Arcane close- breath caught in their throats for a synchronized second, Mori swiftly twisted them away through her blackened mist, the sight dissipating from Arcane's eyes. A second occurred, and Arcane shakily pulled away as their feet landed on the softened ground of the forest. They were deeper in the forest than before, the rough sound of crickets and the distant splatter of water against the earth's surface louder in their ears.

The rain, to their relief, had halted a few hours ago. Though it seemed neither girl realized at all it had been raining while inside.

Arcane's voice began to echo as she called for Nipuna, voice beginning to hoarse the deeper they trekked, though Mori's presence only soothed that fear for only a short amount of time.

A crack echoed once again, silencing the two women. This time, it was close, too close- like a hot breath in their ears, climbing down their necks. Mori inched closer to the sound. She placed herself against the tree, and with delicate movement indicated with her fingers for Arcane to stand closer to her, shielded by the tree.

Arcane furrowed her brows, her lips parting- but Mori's lanky pale fingers, icy cold to the touch, caressed silence to her lips. She shook her head, 'be quiet.' before her finger pulled away as she twisted to look past the tree.

Arcane numbly placed her shaky fingers to where Mori's once was, the touch vanishing like the smoke of incense. She observed, back pressed to the bark of the tree as Mori observed through the folds, watching the movement.

As another crack came, Mori's figure dissipated- and Arcane was left alone.

Alone.

I AM ALONE.

NO.

No.

Where is she?

Where did she go?

Arcane snapped away from the tree, turning to find a hunter's form nose diving into the hardness of the ground, through the moon's bright, guiding light, Arcane observed the blood that coated the grassy terrain- as snowflakes began to descend from the sky.

Arcane observed Mori's black mist transcended to the next hunter- who was deemed too slow as his head twisted strangely, a crack echoing as his neck snapped. It seemed that was the last of the hunters, and Arcane sensed no mercy from Mori nor herself as she left her spot hidden behind the overgrown tree.

She assumed there were no more hunters.

She had checked every corner, every step- every sound amongst them, though some hunters were too skilled in their trade, and Arcane could not hear them approaching. The abrupt sound of feet kicking rocks alerted Arcane enough she twisted on the spot, face to face with a Hunter- a boy, only her age, pulling the trigger on his crossbow.

The arrow, aimed directly at her heart.

Arcane narrowly dodged the arrow, the fletching grazing her cheek as a surge of electricity shook through her body, urging her to move.

There was a second where time stopped, and Arcane held her breath- swiftly enough she chanted within her brain, begged herself as she shoved her hands forward. Magic surged through her body, humming- thrumming, tickling every inch of her.

She had cast a barrier, one that ejected the hunter across the forest, knocking his head with a crack against one of the towering trees of the forest. A surge of fury overtook her, hunters in their land, in their home. *How dare they.*

"How dare you even think of touching me."

The boy was barely conscious, shakily trying to stand despite the blood pouring from his face.

"Vermin," He hissed. "All of you."

"No one said you have any right to speak to me." Arcane sneered. Her mind flashed to her burning Sisters, screaming, crying- begging for another life. Her hands outstretched, magic dislodging a sharp piece of branch from the tree beside her.

"They'll kill you, al-"

The branch pierced his figure without second thought, Arcane's hands going numb as they dropped to her sides, staring at the dead hunter with the sharp branch impaled through his, leaking blood on their land. The fury did not simmer down, it only increased as her sister's faces shimmered in her vision reminding her of what she was intending to do to not just one hunter, but to all of them.

She relaxed her tensed shoulder, taking in the cold breath of mother earth as she turned to find Mori standing, knees bent inwards,

THE TRIPLE MOON | 107

hands grasping her heart as though she had been pierced by the branch Arcane had ejected.

Though, she wasn't.

Arcane lurched, flushed- overwhelmed. For a second, she thought she had harmed her, as though her resentment had truly, and finally overcome her, and she had killed the one person who provided her with a sense of comfort.

"Mori!"

The sound of her name on Arcane's tongue ruptured her pained haziness.

Mori stretched from her hunched form as Arcane's fingers encountered the skin of her wrists. She peered up through wisps of hair, observing as Arcane searched relentlessly for the injury, aware of the hunter's blood on the Mistress' clothes, splattered on her cheek.

"We're too late." She sneered through a throaty whisper. "I felt it, they killed her."

The words made Arcane freeze, fury overwhelming her.

"Where?!"

Mori did not need to reply, morphing the two into a black mist- casting them upon the two hunters' observing the hanged and burnt figure hanging upon an overgrown tree. Arcane froze, hoping, begging the dead body was not who she thought it was, that it was not Nipuna, or Miu, or some poor girl who had gone missing, or taken in the night.

Please.

No more.

No more death.

No more dead girls.

Arcane couldn't mouth words, couldn't move- couldn't think as she watched Mori stop the arrows that whizzed through the air, aimed at them. They stopped mid-air, the wind stilling for a second as the two Hunters observed in shock, before falling- limp to the floor as the arrows flew back, straight into their eyes, out the other sides of their heads.

Mori withered in fury, unable to tear her eyes away from the dangling dead body- though, nor could Arcane. Her eyes unblinking, a hot tear slipping from her eyes, dripping down her cheek. The pain was unbearable, despite the fact the person was unrecognizable.

Though as Arcane peered closer, she realized the figure wore a dress, little colour still engrossed, but still- the same colour of Miu's ball gown.

"Miu," Arcane swallowed her agony, her throat itching- croaking, aching as she held back her tears.

A loud sigh of relief erupted through the trees, and Arcane snapped her head towards the figure tied up against the base of one of the trees. Her dark, lanky form could not go unnoticed, nor the natural glare directed at her.

"Nipuna!" Arcane cried out, racing- but being overrun by Mistress Mori as her black mist sunk like fog through the air. She cut the chains with a heated gaze, fire sizzling away the metals holding the dishevelled Nipuna.

"I worried the worst," Mistress Mori's solemn voice was almost unrecognizable.

"At least you are here now."

"Not in time," Arcane muttered. "If we were a little earlier-"

Nipuna was helped up by the two, a limp evident in her leg, dried blood covering her attire.

"None of us could've known Miu would be next." Nipuna choked through cracked lips and a dry, aching throat, there was a pain more than physical in her voice. "I'm so sorry, Crow…. I thought I could stop them. I…. She shouldn't be dead; she doesn't deserve that. What will Sora say, they- they can't live without each other."

Tears dripped down Nipuna's cheeks as she blinked hard, hoping the vulnerability would disappear.

"It should've been me, Crow. They had so much more potential, they had more time."

"Please, Nipuna," Mistress Mori whispered. "Do not overcome yourself with grief. Miu's gone, we cannot lose you either."

THE TRIPLE MOON | 109

There was a solemn silence as they stood, helping Nipuna to walk again on her two feet, testing the waters and the level of injury. Her head lulled, she evidently had a concussion through her mannerisms, which only made it harder for her future recovery.

The Mistress pulled away.

"You two must go, there will be more coming as the moon passes. Help dress Nipuna's wounds; I will come to you both once I'm done."

"We aren't leaving you to do this alone, I can help you-"

"Arcane."

"You act like you're the only one around."

Mori narrowed her eyes.

Arcane would not back down, it would be stupid, futile to leave Mori to have to bury her friend, to have to fight off remaining hunters if found on her own when she had an abled person beside her, willing to do anything to assist.

"That's an order, Arcane." Mori muttered, inky black eyes empty, without life amongst them.

"See, there you go- being all heartless and obscene. I'm not leaving, you can't clean this up all on your own."

There was a distant sound of noise, feet beating against the ground. Voices. Hunters.

"I can fight, you saw."

"Saw what?" Mori snapped. "That wasn't a fight, Arcane."

Arcane went to bite back- fury, eating her from the inside, but Mori beat her to it. Her dark eyes narrowed, face devoid of emotion.

"I was a fool," Mori sneered. "Thinking someone like you could listen, I gave an order. Do you want us all to die because you would not follow your superiors' orders?"

A pang of agony shifted through Arcane's heart, her face twisting into something Mori could not place, though she could effortlessly sense the pain like it was her own. She had truly thought she had done well. A prickling sensation itched down Arcane's neck, through her spine.

"Leave, now."

Arcane only glared, filled with rage before the two were consumed by black mist, leaving Mori behind.

The black mist led the two back into the haven, though it seemed the two stood awkwardly in the middle of Nipuna's personal room. It was a little smaller than Mistress Mori's, without the desk, but a seating area by a fire.

Arcane numbly sat Nipuna down on the long couch. She observed as she irritably rested her head against the arm rest, dangling her injured leg from the couch. Arcane rapidly went to work, sifting through the draws by the wall Nipuna had exhaustedly pointed to, finding the equipment she needed.

The work would silence her mind, remove the Mistress' words from her head, and her friend's body- dangling from a rope.

She pulled up the sleeve of her pants, observed the long cut down her calf, seemingly a knife of sorts- perhaps a throwing knife. Silently, she dabbed alcohol, careful and surprised at the lack of reaction as she pressed gently to the wound.

"I was worried you were dead." Arcane broke the benumbed, grieving silence.

Nipuna lulled her head to peer down at Arcane as she worked.

"I don't die that easily."

Arcane huffed, beginning to stitch after a peering to Nipuna for consent to begin.

"What happened out there?"

Arcane was aware that traumatic experiences were hard to retell, especially so soon. She was expecting silence, an excuse to be quiet, a snap- but no.

"Sora told me Miu had not attended dinner because she was finishing off her gown for the ball. Sora had said she would just eat in their room, which was true. I visited to check after dinner."

Nipuna took a sharp breath, compressing the pain with controlled breathing as she proceeded.

"She was there, working on her dress. She had just finished as I came in, though she was short of material for her headpiece. She was exhausted, and impolite, as always. She was complaining about the lack of time she had to make the dress, I was tired of her complaining so I ignored her and left."

Nipuna's eyes distantly peered to the wall, her mind in another place.

"But now I wish I had stayed, even just for a few extra minutes."

"I'm sorry," Arcane whispered, hot beneath her breath.

She knew beyond words how it felt.

"I'm sure you know what I mean when I say I'd take her place, one hundred times over, even if we were never close."

Arcane nodded, shaky hands trying to concentrate on the stitching.

"Anyway," Nipuna whispered, staring up to the roof of her bedroom. The room was warm, fire illuminating the room, casting shadows on the roof. Nipuna observed how often Arcane eyed the fire, a flicker of concern in those chocolate-brown eyes. "I checked everywhere; she was nowhere in the palace."

"You assumed she was in the forest?"

Nipuna nodded grimly.

"I found her shoes first, hanging on a tree- like a warning, a sign."

"You think the hunter's put them there?"

"To provoke us, yes. It worked. I stormed in as soon as I found her, she was alive at the time."

A pang of grief overcame Arcane.

Nipuna watched her die.

"I thought I had trained enough, but their weapons were laced with fire- I was too busy warding them off when they began throwing poisonous knives and slashing me with swords, there were at least twenty of them, one of me. I was knocked out not long after killing only one of them."

"Wait...You're telling me that's how many there were?"

Nipuna furrowed her brows.

"What?" Nipuna was beyond confused, the pain along her leg clearly getting to her as she drowsily rested into the couch, unable to process certain words thrown at her.

"We only killed five before finding you."

Nipuna stilled.

"There's still fourteen." Arcane urged, "we have to go warn Mistress Mori."

"No," Nipuna muttered, "Not all of them would've come back. Most Hunters are cowards, they fear us more than we do them. They're like snakes, they hiss and attack on sight, although if you stomp your feet against the ground, they slither away frightened."

"I don't believe that." Arcane sneered, holding the needle like a death grip in her hands.

"Do you trust Mistress Mori?"

The name made that same pang of fury overcome her, she was so hurt, so disappointed in herself. Mori was not pleased with her, it seemed, disappointed, she did not care for her, not like she had hoped. The woman put her power and her standing before anyone else. Arcane tried not to make it personal, but the woman's lack of emotion made it difficult to not feel as though her resentment was aimed at her.

"That depends."

"Liar," Nipuna hissed beneath her breath.

"How would you know?" Arcane muttered, placing the utensils down, finished as she grabbed the gauze to cover the stitching. Her hands shook as she tried not to ruin the placement against the wound.

"I may be concussed but I'm not foolish. You blindly followed her through that forest, you trail her like a hound, hunting for her. I see the way you glance at her, more than any ordinary individual would look at their superior."

Arcane was silent.

"She may act apathetic, but she appreciates you more than you know."

"No, she doesn't."

"I've known her for fifteen years."

"You don't know me, though."

Nipuna scoffed. "If she inquired you to come with her, she knows you would be valuable by her side. I can sense you took her words personally," She gave Arcane an expectant look. "That's the awful thing about Crow, her emotions and her words never work well simultaneously."

"Of course, I took it personally." Arcane sneered, standing and wiping her hands against her long-bloodied skirt as she walked her way to Nipuna's bed- sinking into it. She didn't want Nipuna to see the way her cheeks turned pink in humiliation.

"I thought I did well."

"I'm not dead so, you did to me."

"Not to her though!"

"Whatever, talk to her about it if you're so hurt."

"No." Arcane petulantly muttered, curling herself into a ball on top of Nipuna's neatly made bed. Silence sluggishly ensued, but the girl, cursed by fire, blood, tears and death could not sleep, did not dare sleep. She waited until the sun rose, then, when Mori still did not come, her eyes stayed open, body unable to sleep till the sun hit past noon, and snow began to stick to the glass windows, coating the ground.

The coldest part of winter was coming.

Arcane always enjoyed winter the most, it meant her Coven 'hibernated,' as her Sisters liked to say. They collected their food for the season, did not leave their homestead and remained safe away from the winter.

Her mind wandered to her family, unable to drift into sleep. Unable to sleep without knowing Crow Mori was still absent, out struggling against the winter, and the hunter's who had consumed the forest.

She did not move from Nipuna's bed, not even when Nipuna stood, limping to the door where an anxious Sybil stood. They disappeared together, leaving Arcane to shrivel away, worry, fret, cry- agony consuming the hollowness of her heart. Miu was gone, Mori disliked her, all these witches were dying, there was a traitor amongst them, weeding them out from the vulnerable to the powerful.

Sooner or later, Arcane realised the students would have to know what was happening by now.

114 | JESSE PIPER

They came back an hour later, though finally it seemed- Arcane's tears had exhausted her, she was asleep as Sybil lifted her sleeping, benumbed body, moving her to a more secluded room. Arcane could sense the faintness of a cold touch on her, hair tickling her face before she nodded off again, the scent of sugar and apple pie in the air.

Arcane awoke as the sun was setting, a whole day she lied down- anguish overcame her, hurt more than grief consuming her guiltily. She realized the silkiness of the bedsheets in her grip, the citrus- parchment smell in the air.

They had moved her to Mistress Mori's room.

A note sat by the pillow beside her, sloppy handwriting and blotches of ink covered the note, forcing Arcane through teary, bloodshot eyes, to read the words more carefully.

> *I decided not to put you back in your room with Ohno and Spring, like Nipuna had told me to.*
>
> *Nipuna claims to sense hurt in you, so I say we fix that.*
>
> *Do not tell Nipuna.*
>
> *-Sybil.*

And then, an awkward smiley face underneath her signature.

A tear slipped her eye when she genuinely thought she had none left to shed. This tear was wholehearted, sweetened as it dropped to the writing, blotching the paper. The girl placed the note in her pocket. She didn't want to lose her kindness, it was beginning to become rarer in this monstrous, woman eating world.

She rested herself back against the pillows, allowing her body to sink into the softness of the bed. Her mind half-heartedly envisioning hands around her body, holding her tight. She drifted off, eyes staring at the setting sun through the dark room.

Her resting mind turned to self-consciously criticizing how dirty she must be, and the fact it'll stain the bedsheets, although she realised it was a modest retaliation for what Mori had said to her.

The same words she repeated in her head, all night.

9

Ignosce Me

Warmth overcame Arcane as she curled deeper into herself. It had taken her a long time to get comfortable after Miu, after Mori- after all those spiteful words, but as soon as she smelt the waft of citrus and parchment, dug her hands into the silk sheets- she was out, flashes of fire in her sleep, though nothing compared to the monstrous nightmares of every other night, something soothed her as she slept, a comfort overcame her enough for her body to truly rest, body untensing, unravelling upon the bed.

Fingers caressed her hair, trickling down her cheek, lining her jaw; it tingled and stimulated every inch of her body. She blinked through the darkness, the sole light of the hanging white, blue lights of the chandelier.

As Arcane rose, abruptly aware of long fingers caressing through her knotted hair, she found no one beside her. There was no weight beside the bed, nor warmth. She observed the black mist across the aged, wooden planks, following the haze of black to a figure leaning over her work. Her head dipped down to the pages as her back arched down exhaustedly.

A spike of pain echoed throughout her body, Arcane wiped the wetness from her eyes- realizing Mori seemed less then interested in

Arcane, and ultimately- what she felt was merely a lingering dream, a way to escape her nightmares, because Mori was not near her, she was hunched over her intricately drawn maps and transcripts.

Mori didn't dare turn as Arcane's body ruffled the bed as she sat up, crawling to the edge of the bed, and observing- unsure, as Mori scanned her eyes over the writing. It seemed Arcane had slept until nightfall, the blue light of the moon cast through the window, glinting the paleness of Mori's side profile as she turned to peer over her shoulder.

Her face lacked emotion as she pulled away from her work, straightening her figure, cracks were subtle as her bones popped.

"Did I wake you?"

Her voice was hoarse- like Arcane's, the sort of voice that becomes throaty after choked tears.

"No." Yes.

Arcane tried to speak with the lack of emotion Mori held, wanting it to come across as how disinterested and disheartened she was. She peered away, unable to look Mori in the eyes as she wiped her ink-stained hands on her dirtied long skirt.

It was then Arcane realized she limped as she walked, and that there was a small cut along her cheek, the blood dried along her cheek, down her jaw. There was dirt mattered in her hair, covering her destroyed formal attire.

Arcane feigned not caring, but the small sound of concern that bubbled in her throat told both women otherwise.

"I left things wrong," Mistress Mori muttered, still- she waited patiently for signs of a reaction from Arcane.

"You did."

"I-"

Silence.

Arcane couldn't cry anymore, but her hands fisted by her sides, she edged forwards, leaning from the bed to look closer at Mori- see the regret in those inky black eyes. She saw them. It only made her more furious.

"I don't want to talk to you. I don't want to look at you. What use am I to you, anyway? It seems as though I provide no use to you." Fury oozed from her voice, detachment aching throughout her body like wildfire.

Silence.

"I am beyond disappointed in myself, Arcane."

"You should be because your words harm. I chose to help, that's all I've ever wanted to do for you. All you do is drive people away, and you don't care if you have to harm people to make sure they leave you alone."

Arcane had no clue as to why a burst of self-confidence hit her so hard, talking to her superior like that provided her with a sense of independence, a sense of power. Though, this hatred aimed to Mori was better than melancholy. Arcane furrowed her brows, slowly admiring the way Mistress Mori bent her head down, hair framing her face.

Slowly, she dipped to the floor, hands outstretched.

She was bowing down to Arcane.

"What are you doing?" She whispered, stunned beneath her breath. Her voice came out hoarse as a white mist parted from her lips. The room had a haunting coldness, and as Arcane dubiously slipped her hands into Mistress Mori's outstretched ones, she realized her hands were even colder, like death held her in an embrace.

"I did not mean what I said. I apologise but do not expect forgiveness, and I will do anything you ask to rectify what I said. I did not process how severe my words were till I sensed your heart ache."

Arcane's hands were clammy within hers. There was an abrupt self-consciousness within Arcane as she pushed herself to the edge of the bed, her bare feet touching the wooden floorboards in front of the Mistress. Arcane observed the way the woman's head dipped a breath away from her knees, face unrecognizable underneath the tangle of hair.

"Why did you say those things to me, Mistress?"

"Call me Mori, or Crow. Please."

"Do you deserve that?"

"No," She whispered, almost unrecognizable. "No, I do not."

After a cold, stiffening silence, she proceeded- answering the question provided to her.

"You were stubborn, I cannot- I've never been able to overcome a person's stubbornness. I turned to cruelty, cruelty which was untrue, like venom in my mouth. You always made me proud, you know. I-don't know how I had the stomach to say those hateful words to you, I am forever indebted to you."

Arcane's breath became short in her mouth, her pains, slowly-gradually unravelling inside her stomach. An internal weight lifted, though there was still that haunting fear of disappointment inside, beckoning her to leave, to never look back, to hate Mori's guts, and claim her words were lies.

Mori peered up through wisps of black hair, cheeks flushed.

"I have never met anyone like you before."

Arcane furrowed her brows, disbelieving.

"Yes, you have," There wasn't rudeness in her words, but a chaste-painful denial. "You've met countless people with better power than me and people just as ordinary as me. Ito, Nipuna, Sybil, the twins-" Her voice faltered, realisation dawning her. She went to pull away to wipe the brimming tear, though Mori held tight, pulling her hands close to her face, her breath hot on her bruising knuckles.

"You are more than just your magic and your power, Arcane."

"That's not true, you know that" Arcane muttered. "You were born to be powerful; you've been told your entire life that your magic and power makes you who you are. Without magic, you wouldn't be a Mistress, I assume that's what your Guardian's told you."

"What someone is told is not exactly always correct, is it? I told you something untruthful earlier, perhaps my Guardians merely did the same thing," Crow Mori pressed on, urgently. "What you did yesterday was beyond my expectations, you held yourself well, I am beyond proud of you and your efforts. What would I do without you? Arcane?"

Arcane peered away, silent- in denial.

"I- you scared me, when you made us leave you alone there."

THE TRIPLE MOON | 121

Soft lips pressed a chaste kiss against Arcane's bruised knuckles. A shaky breath caught in her throat, shock- slowing her down. Her heart began to hammer against her ribs as she watched Mori stay in the same position, lips a breath away.

"I wanted to protect you."

"And endanger yourself? How many more were there?"

"It doesn't matter, they're all gone now, I'm alive, am I not?"

"I know there was too many, fourteen I assume?"

Mori shook her head, not refusing it but rather ignorant to responding as Arcane pressed on.

"I'm not that important for you to risk your life for, I could've stayed to help. Risking my life beside you is better than leaving you to fend off hunters by yourself. You may be a Mistress, but you were just a teenager a year ago."

Silence.

"You are important to me."

"Don't lie to me."

"I would risk my own life for anyone here," Mori muttered, Arcane listened- trying not to deflate, aware Mori could sense such intense emotions. "Arcane; do not think so lowly of yourself, I priories my loved ones over all else."

The brunette took a sharp breath.

"Also, please, stop teasing Ito- you're driving her insane. She's been banging on my door for weeks now, she'll be trying to get through the window sooner than later."

A small smile tipped on Arcane's lips, relief seizing both women's lungs as the fear of hatred and fury wafted out of the air. A subtle softness remained between them as Mori sat bowed beneath Arcane.

"But it's so exhilarating."

"I know it is."

Arcane enjoyed the way her heart hammered, bursts of adrenaline overcoming her as she peered down at Mistress Mori- she was unsure where these emotions stemmed from, but she liked the way it made her feel. Like she could move a mountain, slay an army of hunters.

They sat in a long silence, till Mori removed her hands from Arcane's, allowing the comfort to dissipate as she disappeared through mist, a small door creaking open as the mist pressed through it, candles lighting within the next room.

Arcane hadn't even realized there was another door, unless-it was a secret, private room. Arcane observed the bookshelf that appeared askew, moved to the side. Presumably, the case covered the door. Arcane waited, listening intensely to the sound of heeled boots hitting tiles before the sound of steaming water hitting what seemed to be a bathtub.

Arcane perked up, numbly, and achingly trailing the black mist till she found herself halting, resting her exhausted body against the door frame. The dull touch of Mori's lips still lingered on her knuckles.

"What are you doing?" Arcane whispered, though she was more than aware Mori was capable of hearing.

She observed the woman as she filled the bathtub with abrupt speed, boiling water edging from a floating vase, water endlessly pouring despite the lack of space it provided.

"You need a bath."

"I smell?"

She was abruptly self-conscious as Mori flicked her hooded eyes upwards to peer at her.

"No, you're tense."

"Oh," Arcane nervously muttered, edging herself into the room, her bare feet shuffling against the chilled tiles. "What about you?"

"I shall go wash your dirty clothes."

Arcane furrowed her brows.

"You are dirtier than me, no offense."

There was no offense in her face as the corner of her lips raised.

"None taken. Nonetheless, I never leave this room- you do. More people see you then they see me."

"You aren't wrong." Arcane shrugged. She muttered beneath her breath that 'it still seemed wrong,' but Mori purposely ignored it as she sauntered out the room.

THE TRIPLE MOON | 123

"Just drop your clothes, I'll be back to grab them- if you don't mind."

"You've seen me naked before." There was a sense of teasing in Arcane's words.

Mori peered over her shoulder, tensed, and baffled. That was the most emotion Arcane had ever seen on her face.

"Pardon?"

"When I was bathing, you sent an envelope. I could see you watching me through the black mist."

Mori's cheeks flushed, and she instantly retreated into a black mist, leaving Arcane to ponder and undress on her own. She admitted the sweet nature of Mori despite her lack of outward, straightforward affection by the way the candles were consumed by a white, blue light, rather than the red and gold shimmering of a normal fire that consumed her nightmares and made her relive the same night over and over every time she saw it in her vision.

She skimmed her shaky, aching hands over the scar littering her shoulder, down her back. She was aware Mori had seen it, seen the vulnerable side. Though as she pondered it within the large bath, consumed in warmth, she realized Mori was the only person who she believed wouldn't judge whom she was over her body.

Not only so, but deep down, Arcane's sole comfort came from her. Despite her inner demons, her presence was soothing, like a sleeping forest that nestled you in the leaves when cold. She lulled her head against the edge of the tub, sinking deeper into the bath and stretching out her legs. She couldn't do this in her own bathtub, this one was luxury compared to her small one.

Self-consciously- as she usually did, she scrubbed extra hard at her scar, subconsciously expecting for the scars from fire would come off like dead skin. Her limbs aching and crying out as she uncurled herself, stretching her legs out- something she could never previously do.

The door creaked as a black smoke reappeared, Mori blindly peering away from Arcane, observing everything else in the room other than the naked woman in her bathtub.

"Uh-" She muttered, turning away bashfully, unable to meet Arcane's gaze as the bare woman wrapped her long hands over the scars of her shoulder, along her back like a snake's trail amongst sand. Arcane observed the citrus fruits held within Mistress Mori's palms. Her fingers looked dainty as she rolled them along the texture of the citrus.

"You can look."

A small sound emitted from deep in Mori's throat as she blinked, the pinkness of her cheeks lightening as she edged beside the bath, losing the colour in her face again- she was direct to peer at the face rather than anything else. She was aware of the self-consciousness, perhaps, she sensed it- like a stench.

"I bought you something to assist with your wounds."

Arcane furrowed her brows, slipping to the edge of the bath and resting her head on her hands, allowing her to see Mori's face with more detail up close. The waft of citrus overcame the air, and Arcane peered curiously.

The water lapped off her skin as she moved, steam arising from her skin. Arcane eyed the way Mori's eyes faltered, unable to steadily look at her and instead peered away entirely. She outstretched her hands over the inflated bathtub, eyes clamped shut.

"What are you doing?"

"A healing spell."

Her voice roughed, eyebrows jittering as the two citruses enclosed in her hands, the juices of the citrus slipping down her wrists, dripping into the bathtub. She stood still for a second, mumbling quietly- incoherent words even with Arcane's gift enhancing her voice in her ears. The citruses disappeared in a black mist as Mori threw what seemed to be ginger from her pocket, the stench wafting in her nose as it mingled into the water.

Mori removed a knife from her side, slicing a thin cut along her palm.

Arcane jolted.

"Hey! Mori, Please, what are you doing?" Arcane lurched in desperation- a chill of shock penetrating through her spine. She

THE TRIPLE MOON | 125

grabbed Mistress Mori's hand in an iron grip, observing the way Mori had no sway for her strength, squeezing her palms and transfixed as the blood dripped gently down her palm and into the bathtubs water.

"You must sacrifice for the better good, Arcane." Mori muttered, opening her palm, observing as blood began to mingle in the citrus. Arcane was beginning to worry, but that worry immediately relaxed into gratitude as her aching limbs began to soften and become reposed within the water. She observed in fascination as the blood and citrus twisted the water, into a sparkling white liquid- overcome with the scent of citrus, and metal.

"It will heal you, I should- get going."

Arcane held tight to Mori's wrist.

"Stay, for me?"

She hated being alone.

Mori should've known that.

Her face contorted into something that defined being unsure, eyebrows furrowed, and head cocked as she peered down to the women relaxing within the tempting bath water, Mori struggled to hide the raise of a smile at the corner of her lips as Arcane vividly relaxed into the bath, no longer self-conscious of the scar along her figure.

"What do you need from me, Arcane?"

You.

Your time.

Your attention.

Everything.

All of you.

"I just don't like being alone. Would you talk to me about magic while I bathe?"

Mori gradually nodded.

"Of course, I can do that."

She moved to grab the small stool by the corner of the room, though a surge of confidence hit Arcane, her hands tight around her wrist. Mori furrowed her brows, turning to watch Arcane as she smiled mischievously. Arcane had never imagined feeling normal again, never imagined channelling her old self again- but it exhilarated her, the way Mori watched her, like a wolf stalking her prey.

"You're just as dirty as me, come in."

Mori froze, though Arcane did not falter her advance- she observed intensely the way Mori's knees knocked one another, the way Mori's eyes darted anywhere other than Arcane's naked, exposed figure.

"I don't think that's a good idea, Arcane-"

"What if I say please?"

Arcane pulled Mori close, drawing herself out of the white water, skin glistening in the low light of the white candles decorating the bathroom. Mori's breath halted at the closeness. She reposed herself as professionally as she could- though unable to say no to the abrupt skittishly thoughtful smile on Arcane's tired face.

"Fine."

Arcane immediately pulled away, reclining into the water as she observed as Mori disrobed- a lack of timidity on her facade as she stripped off her skirt, though left the red blouse she wore from the ball, it swept long enough over her thighs as she stood to her full height.

"This isn't professional."

Arcane rolled her eyes.

"You say that every time I'm around."

"Your hair needs to be washed anyway," she muttered as she slipped her bare foot in, followed by the slinking of her body beside Arcane. She was much shorter in the bath, now- the space beginning to cramp, Arcane having to look down.

"Is that supposed to be an insult?"

Mori's lips edged up into an exhausted second of a simper.

"Perhaps, what of it?"

"You're a real good comedian," Arcane muttered, twisting to sit against Mori's figure, sliding down so Mori could reach her hair easier. Arcane found herself resting sleepily into Mori's figure as her fingers began to lather in Alma- a liquid most witches used to cleanse themselves. She struggled to ignore the speed her heart hammered against her ribs, or the way she snapped her thighs together beneath

THE TRIPLE MOON | 127

the white water, observing as the bruises on her knees unhurriedly healed. Mori's chest vibrated she spoke, her heart quiet- dull against Arcane's head.

"You did well today."

Her hands massaged through her hair and into her scalp, lanky fingers emitting a chill against her hot skin.

"You said that."

"I feel as though I haven't said it enough. You're- you're special, Arcane."

Arcane twisted to look up at Mori, a tired smile upon her face. This abrupt closeness was not as overwhelming as she was expecting, it seemed Mori was always interested in her, to some degree, and vice versa. The close comfort was mutual as they peered to each other, breath fanning their faces, analysing every inch of one another's details.

Arcane began to realise how much ease she had, so abruptly.

"Wait a second," She sat up. "What did you do?"

Mori rolled her eyes. "Would you like to elaborate?"

"This healing spell, it only heals the physical?"

"It's a small spell, heals the emotional and small physical characteristics of a body."

"Oh," Arcane relaxed. "That's why…"

"That's why what?"

"I don't feel so anxious."

The words came out wrong, confusing- not right. They didn't work like Arcane had planned them to.

Mori's face lacked a reaction except for the purse of her thinned lips. Any normal person would have been offended, argued even. However, Mori was different, she was patient.

"I make you anxious?"

"I- a good anxious. I promise. I wouldn't have invited you to share a bathtub with me if I didn't like you."

Mori relaxed her tensed shoulders, shrugging.

"I don't think this is as intimate as you may believe."

Arcane raised an eyebrow.

"Take that shirt off then."

Mori ignored her, peering away as her hair covered the brightness of her pale skin. She did an entire one eighty, completely pretended she heard nothing of the sort.

"You wanted to know about spells?"

Arcane huffed, crossing her arms over her naked chest and reclining back into Mori's massaging fingers across her scalp, before she started lifting the white water to clean through her hair.

"This spell is making me quite confident."

"You always had confidence, Arcane. Your experiences only shadowed it."

"You know me too well, now and then it feels as though you're in my body."

"I was born Empath, so…"

"Wow," Arcane scoffed exhaustedly. "Really caking it on aren't you."

Mori rolled her eyes. "Empathy as a magical ability can be learnt too, but to what extent- born bearers may be able to yield it more efficiently. I don't mean to boast, but I can sense how you feel every second of every day."

"I…Don't know why my parents never taught me. I wish I knew how to conjure spells and incantations."

Arcane twisted in the water, her arms resting beside Mori, leaning close to her heart, hoping to hear the distant beats against her ears. As she rested into her chest, she struggled not to yawn as she listened to Mori's muttering, her chest rumbling faintly.

Mori silenced herself, beginning to ponder in the silence as she analysed Arcane's facial features, from the pointed nose to those wide brown eyes, long lashes covered in the wetness of the water, her tan skin glistening.

"Where was your home?" Arcane halted at the question, the healing bath could not overcome every obstacle, unfortunately. "If you do not mind me asking."

Arcane trekked her memoires back to before she began her wretched travel to finding a saviour. It would almost be a year since what happened, she realised. The weeks at the haven began to allow her to recover despite the horrors still dwelling within the halls.

"My family was in INDUSTCOR, a small little state called Mika."

Mori listened, silent and intensely.

"Mika, I thought it was an abandoned state for hundreds of years after the Necromancy War."

"The...What?"

"Apologies, I should explain." Mori shrugged. "It is one of the reasons we are still hunted today, the King ordered necromancy witches to be seized and hanged for the threat they caused...We never truly caused carnage, it was always the misconceptions of the Hunters, praying for our downfall." Mori seemed deep in thought, "but enough of that, that is the past. So, your family hid in Mika? That is where the necromancy witches resided, specifically."

To be exact, Arcane never truly learnt of what her families magic was. She knew Guardians passed down Coven capabilities and powers through blood, but she only knew so little. All she knew was that Spring's was chlorokinesis, Ohno's was super intelligence, Nipuna's was rumoured to be advanced empath. Other then that, either some girls did not receive any, or they did not know.

"We were the biggest Coven in Mika, the only one actually. There were seven of us."

"Seven..." Mori muttered.

Seven was so little.

Now, there was only one left of the Amunet family.

"Truthfully, the Amunet family have always been renowned for their necromancy, but this was hundreds of years ago. Perhaps the magic of necromancy died off in the bloodline, or perhaps your family did not teach you to protect you."

Arcane furrowed her brows, her breath fanning Mori's pale face. Despite the seriousness of the conversation, Arcane couldn't seem to take her eyes off Mori's form- to the way her blouse began to mould across her chest, to the way her breathing came out shallow and hoarse.

"You're telling me my bloodline can harness Necromancy?"

"Anyone can, but as a Amunet Witch, your blood is strongly inclined to power it. My blood could not sustain a resurrection like you could. If you wanted to learn, I can assist as much as I can."

Arcane couldn't believe it, her family had truly not told her the bloodline passed down such a magic ability? If Arcane could harness it, she could bring back whomever she wanted.

Arcane gawked at Mori.

"I could kiss you right now."

Mori's eyebrows rose abruptly.

"Uh- Why, exactly?"

"You're just so perfect, so kind-hearted." Arcane scoffed, before clearing her throat. "Thank you, I would really love to learn."

"It is scheduled, then. I shall drop off some novels for you. I cannot do much, but I do know of some books that will assist you and figuring out if you do have the ability to harness Necromancy."

Arcane, overcome with the sense of movement from the abrupt information, pulled Mori into a tight hug. She sensed the way the air was thrown from Mori's lungs, the way her hands ghosted the bareness of her back as their chests pressed together, skin sticking to clothes.

Mori held tight, her hands ghosting scars- her breath short as she arched her back into her touch.

The two's bodies moulded together, the temptation of intimate closeness and lips touching hot in the air, but neither took that step, despite the yearning for it.

They lay in the hot water for a while longer- the citrus seeping into their scents as Arcane stayed lying against Mori, her head resting against her shoulder- and despite the nakedness, lacking discretion from both parties as they bathed in the soothing presence of one another.

"It is my pleasure to help you Arcane, but we cannot lay here forever expecting the horrors to dissipate."

"Must we leave so soon… Please, I want to know more of you. You're a shadow, all the time- a figment of imagination, you always disappear, and I can never find the right time to give you all my attention."

"You act like this is the last time you will talk to me; I hardly think talking naked in a bathtub is better."

"It is, "Arcane whispered, close to Mori's ear. "I have confidence here."

"You should always have confidence."

"I always seem to lose it when you're around."

Mori's cheeks went flush.

"Shall I give it back to you, then?"

Arcane smiled, cunningly- like a cat.

Their lips close, too close- yet too far. The yearning, thrumming through every inch of them, though neither of them pressed close enough for their lips to mould into an ecstasy. Mori's eyes peered from Arcane's lips to her wide brown eyes, an emotion of glee within them that Mori worried she'd never truly get to see.

After a second the smile on Mori's lips was short lived as her eyes glazed over, they emptied and blackened as her body stilled, a sick paleness overcoming her face.

A sense of fear rocked across Arcane's body, something must have changed, a tether snapping, a pain- something was wrong, gravely wrong. Mori was still in her faze, her hands dropping from Arcane's waist.

"Mori?" Arcane shook the woman by the shoulder's, panic beginning.

She disappeared into a black mist, a little piece of paper falling from above her place. Arcane groaned dramatically- a way to distract herself from the doom and fear consuming her thoughts. Tension imploded in her body as she caught the paper, aware writing would meet her on the other side.

Mori was gone.

But not without a note.

You must attend, tonight- as the clock strikes midnight.
At the dining hall.

Please.

Arcane peered through the wisps of wet hair over her eyes, her hands forming an enchantment that warped a clock into a room, the stench of magic overcame the citrus of her skin as she glanced at the ticking clock.

10 o clock.

10

Conventus

Arcane stood with the rest of the women within her ranking, standing stoically behind the backs of their chairs. It depended on what sort of a person the witch was- but most of the girls held their hands behind their backs, patiently withering away with unease. Others, like Spring Lee- bit at their fingernails, beyond anxious, waiting- hoping to be provided with answers.

Ito surged through the doors; bandaged hands outstretched dramatically, the sound of the ancient doors opening rumbled through the unspoken dining room. She observed the categorized seating arrangement, aware her seat had not moved- but that was not what she cared so much about.

Because Arcane's seat had been moved.

The girls observed as Ito sneered. Her eyes narrow, a smirk tugging on her face as she idly sauntered behind her chair- body weight pushed to one side, hand on waist. Her eyes did not falter from Arcane, Arcane whose chair had been moved, moved to be seated beside the head of the table.

Arcane sat beside Mistress Mori's chair, and Ito's visage only oozed with animosity.

Arcane observed from the side of her eye, the way Ito stalked her from the other side of the dining table. She did not dare look away, watching the way Ito evaluated their distance. Though Arcane could not watch forever, not when four members of the typical table arrangement, not including the deceased, were absent.

It stirred un unsure, fear in Arcane. One she despised, the longer they waited for their counterparts, the sooner they worried they were not coming at all.

Nipuna, Sybil, and Sora were missing.

Oh, and Mistress Mori.

Though that was expected of The Mistress.

Although the witches were summoned to an imperative mandatory convention, majority of women expected Mistress Mori to not attend, she never attended meetings. She relayed messages onto Nipuna as an alternative, who would represent her in a more formal manner then which Mori could present herself in.

Ohno nudged Spring from beside her, knocking her out of her musing. Arcane blinked, peering down to Spring's anxiousness, providing a pointed look at the way the girl destroyed her nails. She hid them behind her back, shamed by her self-sabotaging.

"I'm sorry, I'm just panicking."

Arcane's heart plummeted as Spring resumed, her face was faintly pale in concern, an absence of shade in her frequently bright cheeks, she wasn't cheerful, but rather grimacing.

"You heard what happened right? Miu's gone," She croaked, hard to hold her tone as discomfort spread on her appearance. "What are we going to do without her?"

Miu.

What are we going to do without Miu?

Arcane's heart happened against her chest, boisterous in her ears. She feared everyone could hear it. Somehow, the word had spread, and now the girls knew of what had happened. She knew Mistress Mori didn't want this, but it was better than lying to them. Lying, Arcane realised, was like betraying her own Sisters.

To pretend Miu wasn't dead, was a crime.

"We strive, we continue. We protect." Ohno muttered beneath her breath, overhearing from beside Spring. She too held back her tears; hands clasped tightly by her sides.

"I don't think I can do it," Spring's eyes welled, and Arcane's hands rested on her shoulder rubbing small circles before delicately pulling away, watching Spring's face soften as the entrance automatically opened with a draining creak. Nipuna sauntered through, Sybil trailing close behind.

Arcane observed the way Nipuna struggled with the wound on her leg, her leg dragged, sluggish. She covered it well, the witches that knew nothing of what happened those nights ago, would not see it as anything.

"You may sit."

Ohno furrowed her brows as everyone began to rest into their designated seats.

"Is this all of us?"

"No," Nipuna muttered. "We wait on one more."

The group would speculate for the next minute, who was it? Sora, or The Mistress? Could Sora really face reality right now? After her best friend, her soul sister, her everything was dead, and all that was left alive was her other half?

Ito did not rest her legs on the table this time, she sat lent forwards, eying Arcane- with a steak knife in her hands. Arcane tried to ignore the heat of thew woman's eyes as she spoke up through the shuffling of the older witches sitting.

"Where did you get that knife, Takanashi?" Arcane started, shocked to see it. They may be in a dining room, but there was no food or utensils being presented before them. Arcane peered at Nipuna, who had a dispassionate scowl as she looked through the corner of her eyes.

Ito narrowed her eyes to Arcane, threateningly.

"Where did you get your confidence?" Ito quipped.

Arcane furrowed her brows.

"Excuse me?"

"You're excused."

JESSE PIPER

Arcane narrowed her eyes, she did in fact find the reply laughable. Though right now, she could not stomach laughter, her mind was overcome with the vision of Miu's dead body, the unease of this meeting eating her alive.

Spring cut in before Arcane could snap and crack.

"What's your problem, Ito? If I'm honest, you've been quite strange as of late. We all know Miu's death wasn't some coincidence, nor the other girls."

Ohno blinked, realizing what Spring was implying. Her voice aroused over the callous, unsure silence and spectacle of the dining table.

"You have…Haven't you. You've missed dinner, I barely saw you at the ball."

Ito rolled her eyes, groaning.

"I think you need a new prescription for those shitty glasses, four eyes. I was at the bloody ball you blind roach-"

"Oh, how dare! -"

"You're the only one to talk Ohno, you haven't been to your own room in weeks!"

"So, you're watching us now? That's quite suspicious." Ohno sneered, she leaned forwards in her chair, hands smacking to the table, rattling the girls into a rise of conflict. Ito stabbed her knife into the table with a power aggression that overshadowed hers, standing as the other girls began to argue, rising- some beginning to point fingers.

Mori was right, the deaths would leave to shambling.

They were realising someone inside had to have done something.

Nipuna rolled her eyes, her face falling into her hands.

Arcane peered at the two empty seats down the table, the seats Sora and Miu would've been sitting in, they would've whispered in one another's ears before they began to rant, pointing fingers as Miu sneered and Sora would try to calm the situation down. Arcane was uneased the longer it took for Sora and Mori to finally attend.

Something was wrong.

THE TRIPLE MOON | 137

She tried to ignore the accusations and the screaming and threatening, imagined the twins grinning, gushing, and snickering before that vision dissipated, and her nails were digging cuts into her palms.

"I'm so sick of this," Arcane breathed beneath her breath. She was sick of the fighting, sick of the unsisterly treatment of one another, the accusations, the things humans did to them, yet they were doing it to one another.

She stood, her chair tipping down to the floor with a *knock* from the speed. "I'm so sick and tired of accusations and hatred and yelling." She cried out; voice hoarse. The girls halted, still, waiting as Arcane eyed the members of the table, ire in those brown eyes.

"We are family, we are *Sisters*- not enemies. We cannot keep accusing one another like we are in a war, like we are challenging one another," Arcane held herself well, chin raised. "If we keep doing this, we will not find a way to stop the death and carnage, it will be too late- we will kill each other before our enemy kills us."

Ito leaned into the table, arms flexing to hold herself upright.

"You're talking like someone I know." Ito sneered.

"Don't start, this is not the time-"

"You know, I find it quite strange ever since you got here, everything has started happening. Vera was the first, from what I heard, she died only a day after you arrived. Is that not a coincidence? *Dove?*"

Ito had never had such malice when talking to Arcane. She knew deep down, Ito was not doing this to create disruption, she was doing this to make her confess her relationship with Mori. The relationship most would protest, the favouritism, the privacy of it was something no girl would appreciate in such a time, especially when all of Mori's undivided attention was on Arcane, and not them.

Arcane narrowed her eyes, she peered at Spring, urging her to protest, but she sat with her head down, staring at her scabbing fingers and edges of her school skirt. An aching sense of disappointment surged through Arcane's core, no one would support her but herself, it seemed.

"There's no coincidence, I promise."

"Do you, perhaps- have anyone to protest my statement?" She sang, fanged teeth slipping from their confinements behind her pursed lips.

"You're making this personal, Ito."

She scoffed. "Where have you been lately? Spring, do you know?"

Spring ignored the women, peering away anxiously.

"I'm not a part of this, Ito. Leave me alone."

"You know, hogging The Mistress to yourself won't solve our issues, Arcane. Perhaps the reason you cling to her is because you're trying to kill her too, take her life and replace her as Mistress. I think everyone deserves to know you've been in her bedroom."

Nipuna grumbled out of the folds of her fingers against her face as Ito began to sneer.

"This is unprofessional."

"And you're a sorry excuse for a professional," Ito sneered, she edged over the table- wanting, yearning to be closer to Arcane, who stood across from her- unable to tear her eyes away from Ito's menacing glare, there was a glimmer of sarcastic melancholy in those mismatched eyes.

"She doesn't like you, not like you like her, Arcane."

Fury overcame Arcane, like a match to the fuel. She narrowed her eyes, pain shooting through her palms as her nails dug deeper inside of her. Ito's words were getting to her, it was evident, and Ito admired it.

Arcane scoffed.

"You're jealous, I get it- but why do you have to ruin my life for it? I would never hurt any of you, you're my family, my Sisters. I've been with the Mistress helping her, you all assume she does everything on her own?"

"Jealous?!"

It seemed that was the only word Ito picked up.

"Evidently."

"You stole her from me, Arcane- I am not *jealous*, I am *furious*."

Arcane rolled her eyes.

"I didn't steal anyone from you, she just never liked you- she was exhausted by you, you and your manipulative games to make her all yours, you make her responsible for everything you do, so she comes back to you."

"Please!" Ohno barked, although the group was blinded by the argument at hand. It cut her off mercilessly.

"How dare you, I was here before you- long before you. If anyone, you're the one killing us for our magic. I wouldn't be surprised if you were working beside Mori."

Nipuna lurched up at the words.

"This is preposterous-"

Ito began to crawl on top of the table, inching closer and observing as Arcane held her ground from her advances.

"Or maybe she's just using you. You smell just like that citrus scent, the love potion she puts on herself so everyone that smells it loves and admires her," Ito sniffed the air, smiling cunningly. "You smell just like spell, citrus and her blood? Right, I thought I was right."

Arcane stilled, breath caught in her throat, a tickling at the back of her neck.

"She's going to fuck you then leave you in the dirt."

"You're lying."

"She did the same thing to me."

"Ito," Nipuna sneered "This is an important meeting, not a roast night," though her voice was silenced as Arcane held herself tall, seething her words like she was talking to the very people who murdered her Coven, her family.

"I lasted longer than you, though- didn't I? I don't believe a word you say about love potions, because frankly- you know nothing about love. You wouldn't even know what it feels like, let alone what it smells like."

Arcane leaned closer, hot breath fanning the pretty woman's pale, irritated face.

"You're a dirty liar, she left you to the dust because she deserves better than a nagging, accusing bitch like Takanashi Ito."

As soon as her name was purred out through her pursed lips, Ito lurched through the air, tackling the girl onto the floor. The air was punched from her stomach, she couldn't breathe as her body collided with the wooden floorboards, weight overpowering above her.

The knife was in Ito's hands in a second, raised above her head as she laid on top of Arcane upon the floor, legs tangled within one another, pelvic and hips bumping and grinding as they fought over one another., desperate to survive.

The girls lurched up in shock as Arcane caught the knife before it pierced her face. Arcane pushed against her power for dear life, death flashing within those pretty eyes. She watched as fury consumed Ito's face, before a smile tipped on her lips.

The entrance door creaked open menacingly. Arcane watched as Ito's body was thrown off her by an overpowering black shadow, colliding full force into the dining table. Arcane scrambled up, girls crying out.

Ito lay limp on the dining table as Mori appeared behind her through a black mist and observing as blood trickled from where Mori had smacked her nose into the table.

Ito's breath knocked from her lungs as she eyed Mori from over her shoulder, her heart hammered in her chest- Mistress Mori's eyes alight with fury, though her face was slackened, empty of a reaction.

"Ah- Mistress, you're quite-" Ito gulped, a strange groan edging from her lips. "-Late."

Mori glared down at Ito with an expressionless appearance; none of the girls were able to crack the cypher of her devoid face.

"You're pitiful, Takanashi Ito."

Ito giggled, finding a strange adrenaline rush that did not follow with an ouch of pain from her words.

"Only for you, Crow Mori."

Mori pulled Ito up from the dining table by her hair, fingers digging into her scalp. It seemed that rather than pain striking her face, ecstasy clouded the girl's eyes.

"Your insanity is beginning to deter others, Ito. Do not keep it that way, or I will deter you."

Mori did not smile, did not alter the way her eyes glared with emptiness as she pulled away, her hands retracting as though she had grazed fire.

Ito straightened, stretching her back like a cat as she yawned. Every single member of the group's eyes were upon the Mistress, watching- observed and beyond stunned as she took her standing in front of her chair, at the end of the table.

She did not look at Arcane, did not watch as she awkwardly stood, dusting herself off and finding Ito standing close by her seat. Arcane elbowed the girl purposely as she sat and peered to find Ito gleefully looking down at her, negligent to leave her place- like a cat attached to their owner, tail wrapped around the ankle.

Her emotional changes were giving Arcane whiplash, one moment they hate each other, the next Ito is beaming at her. Perhaps Ito had gotten what she wanted after all.

"I apologize for my lateness," Mistress Mori muttered, empty eyes surveying down the table, sight catching- tongue lapsing across her top lip as her vision crossed Arcane's. Though to anyone else, it was invisible. Arcane couldn't forget Mori's eyes, even as she peered away- listening to the anxious breathing of Spring beside her.

She didn't hate Spring, not really.

She understood to an extent why she didn't want to say anything.

Fear changes people, makes them weak and constrained- ignorant and blind to the truth.

"My lateness speaks louder than words itself," she began. "There's been another body."

It seemed the whole room tipped upside, flipped, rolled. Arcane held back the disappointment and found the touch of a hand as Spring held hers beneath the table. Her hands were sweaty, shaking beyond control.

Beatrice had tears in her eyes, crossed arms, gnashing, angry teeth. Spring's eyes brimmed with tears; head hung low. Everywhere Arcane looked, people were hardly able to hold back their anguish.

"Sora committed suicide an hour ago."

Arcane's whole body fumbled, unable to grasp her words as Spring's fingers held dangerously tight to her, pleading in a hope to fix what had been undone.

"She's...Dead?"

Ohno's voice was a hot whisper over the heavy hoarse breathing of girls trying to hold back tears. Ito even seemed damaged, head watching her fingers dwindle, the blood of her nose having dried into her fingernails.

"Not forever, no; She's dead, but she fortunately had a life to spare."

There was still no celebration.

Only signs of apprehensive relief.

"She has been moved into intensive care. Her soul needs time to revive her body."

"How many lives does she have left?" tears sprung from Spring's eyes; voice hoarse.

"She has less than you, more than some."

"That's not the point, Spring-" Nipuna muttered. "She killed herself because she could not think of a way to restore what had already been undone. We are not here to mourn; we are here to deliberate."

Spring faltered, unable to look Nipuna in the eyes as Mori's voice boomed.

"I called you all here in a bid to alter what disparity we have fallen into. Too many witches are dead- you are all aware. The hunters are upon us already. Miu's death was our clear indication of their closeness."

Ohno edged her circular glasses up her nose.

"Mistress, I am glad you realized this is a team effort."

The sentence was not backhanded nor cruel, it was a soft chaste response. Ohno observed the way Mori's shoulders stayed in the same incline of tenseness, her eyes droopy- her figure walked with a fatigue that was almost unrecognizable if Ohno did not observe so well.

"I presume you have a plan?"

Ohno shook her head.

"I would, but I have not seen the hunter's, not seen how they fight- their strategies I cannot counter."

THE TRIPLE MOON | 143

Mori nodded, dissatisfied. She leaned into the table, resting her palms to assist in holding her upwards. As she peered up, her black hair shielded the bags beneath her eyes. Arcane's breath left her lungs, how could she be so unravelled yet so magnificent all at once?

"We just need a way to protect ourselves."

"We cannot just protect anymore," Arcane muttered, she couldn't seem to look at Mori- fearful of the reaction she would get due to her unexpected arise in conversation. "For all we know, there are hunters within this very room. At this point, with the amount of death on our doorstep; all we can do is fight."

Nipuna nodded.

"I despise the fact I'm agreeing with you, but you're correct."

Arcane would've been offended by Nipuna's reply if it weren't such a serious discussion.

Mistress Mori's hand outstretched lazily to indicate to both Nipuna and Arcane.

"I must say I agree, despite how much I do not want to admit it. We were sworn into privacy, into secrecy. Now, we are threatened and dying each day. Protection will not save us, Arcane taught me that."

"We should add a ward, a way to turn them away." Ohno added input, to which the group nodded.

"It won't do." Mori muttered, crossing her arms over her chest. The group was silent for a second, observing as Mori thought, she sighed before she began.

"'I wasn't planning to leave so soon, but it must be done."

Spring jolted from her chair, likewise to the other girls in the room. They're outcries of protest overcome with their fear of death and the lack of protection no Mistress would mean. The sound was overbearing as girls argued.

"Silence." Mori muttered, and like a hypnotized crowd, silence became of them all.

"It came to my attention- It is situated within the forest, close to the edge of the Venfic Island. I have no clue how many there are- only of the amount we have already encountered. The more they appear, the more there will be. I must go, do you understand?"

Her authoritative voice was beckoning, soothing and overwhelming at once.

"I could do it, search the area of hunters."

Ohno scoffed at Ito's words.

"Why could we even trust you to do that?"

"You trust me enough, I'm not the rat- Ohno. Use your magic on me, I'm not playing tricks on you."

Ohno shook her head, aggressively crossing her arms.

"And what of the rat, Mistress? We all speculate it, someone had to have been inside to kill all those girls. Hunters cannot come inside, someone has to be working for them, one of *us*."

"There is no rat."

Lies. Mori, they could effortlessly tell you were lying- if they just tried.

Though there was no prickling in Arcane's neck, she furrowed her brows, the way Mori's eyes, for a split second- peered at her. *What...was she trying to tell me?*

"Whoever is killing us, one by one- was never one of us. Even if they were one of our witches, they will never be a part of this Coven. So, there are no rats; I realize now- they are not betraying us, for they were never once one of us."

Ohno nodded. "Rats are deserters, but if you never truly belonged- you cannot desert us."

Her voice was thick in the air.

"Again," Mori muttered. "Don't overthink it. You girls are more than capable of protecting yourselves, as well as the younger girls. Nipuna will stay in charge whilst I am away," Mori removed herself from her position, walking across the dining room, past the chairs as she addressed others.

"Mistresses of the Coven Mori have not made any official orders of attack in hundreds of years since our exclusion from the world. This is something none of us have experience on, we have never fought in our ancestors' wars. Now, you must follow me and my words. Is this understood?"

Her words played around amongst their heads as they nodded.

"Sybil and Nipuna will look after Sora as her carer till her soul is within her confined body once again. None of you may tamper or visit her body. We all know this may take a few weeks, let alone months. Ohno," her name leaving her lips caused the girl to jolt for a second before recovering.

"I entrust you to place an additional ward whilst I am gone. Spring, you will assist. Beatrice-" Mori's voice distantly rang out in Arcane's ears, her chaste voice like a soothing melody to accompany sleep as Arcane observed Nipuna's perplexed face, and the way Sybil rolled on the balls of her feet, behind her.

Arcane leaned forwards, breath quiet.

"Where is Mori going?"

"Mistress Mori," Nipuna corrected with a hiss.

"Yes, where is she going?"

Nipuna rolled her eyes, the usual acrimony consuming her face; from her scowl to her narrowed eyes.

"She's scouting the island."

"Yes, in the forest- but where exactly in the forest?"

"You aren't going."

Arcane scoffed. "You aren't the Mistress."

"She entrusted me to make sure you don't try to follow her."

Arcane narrowed her eyes.

"I wouldn't even do that," Arcane hissed, leaning closer across the table.

"Yes," Nipuna sneered. "Yes, you would."

Arcane groaned.

"She shouldn't be going alone."

"She's the Mistress of a Coven of one hundred girls, I think she's pretty qualified."

Arcane had a gut instinct, she couldn't agree. Mori was only one, against a soldering army of men, of Hunters who wanted to kill them.

Could she really keep herself safe? Nipuna couldn't, hell- Arcane couldn't.

"This doesn't feel right."

Nipuna huffed. Eyeing as Mistress Mori discussed the ward with Ohno, deep in conversation as the rest of the witches discussed, and or listened along.

Nipuna inched closer over the table; their voices chaste against the planning of war.

"It doesn't, I know. But it's the only way we'll know where they are exactly, how many they are- and, who knows; Mori could find out who the enemy truly is."

"You know she can figure out which one of the witches is working against us?"

Nipuna went to speak, but Ito's voice rang out over all others.

"I mean not to- interfere with the discussion, but Mori?" She called.

The woman who was called bristled, yet nonetheless listened as she straightened herself, moving back to her chair by Arcane. Her hands skimmed the top of her chair, her scent of citrus wafting through Arcane's nose, her presence lighting Arcane's anxious mood as she sat down in her chair.

"It's Mistress, how many times do you need to be told?" Ohno hissed beneath her breath, glaring.

"What is it, Ito?"

There was a genuine look in Ito's eye, it took Arcane back a few seconds, unsure how to process it.

"Why would someone want to kill their own family?"

There was a thick silence as Mori observed Ito, a look of memory glistening in those dark eyes.

"Power," She whispered, though despite the whisper, the whole world could hear the complexity of her words, they weighed down on everyone. "While the Hunter's kill us mercilessly, the witches begin to kill each other for power, for lives. Our world has crumbled, rather than loving one another- living in harmony, witches realize the power that comes with killing others like themselves,"

Mori proceeded.

"Whatever Witch is killing us; they are gaining our lives and our magic as they do so. They're selfish, killing their own for power. A Witch that kills their own becomes a monster, something that cannot be reckoned with."

"So," Ohno muttered. "If someone were to kill both my soul and my body-"

"They will receive all the power you once had, all the lives they took from you, would be theirs. Therefore, some of the cruellest of witches live for thousands of years. They steal their own, feast on their own, thrive off their own."

"It sounds..."

"Merciless." Spring muttered with tear-stained cheeks- she had not taken the news or Sora lightly, gulping. The vision of her dead, recovering body wild and scathing within everyone's mind. "How could a person do it so mercilessly? Without regret?"

"How could anyone do it at all?" Ohno muttered.

Mori disregarded the two's more private conversation as she proceeded, clearing her throat, and crossing her legs at the head of the chair. Arcane struggled not to observe her with hawk eyes, an ogling, obsessed observation - like a predator scouting for her prey. She looked away as Mori caught her eyes.

"In this world, Witches are beginning to turn upon one another, we are no longer selfless and enlightened like we once were in the name of history. Our genocide and the War has made us become narcissistic, ignorant to one another, we no longer perceive each other as Sisters, but as enemies."

Mori gave Takanashi Ito a scathing look, to which the girl only smiled menacingly.

"Which you evidently illustrated- Ito, but we shall not perceive it personally."

"I have one more question," Ohno raised her hand before immediately dropping it, realizing she was not a child that would be called upon. She was a member of the highest level ranked girls in the Coven, she was more than just a child.

Mistress Mori nodded, urging her to proceed.

"In the worst scenario, what happens if you don't come back? When do we start worrying?"

The question made Arcane shrivel up, made her body feel as though it were a ticking time bomb- about to explode. She did not want to think about that scenario. Not at all. If Mori disappeared for too long; the ward would dissipate, panic would turn to disarray, and Mori herself would be gone.

Arcane could not fathom what she would do without her presence always lingering, her voice always chaste and informative, her touch faint yet yearning.

"I'll be only a day, if everything turns out how I would like it to," Mori muttered. "Later than a week, then you start to worry, but that is unlikely. Understood?"

Ohno nodded promptly, a tight-lipped smile on her face. As though she could not hold back the glee of having a face-to-face conversation with the Mistress herself. It had been years since Ohno had a normal conversation with Mori, she could barely remember their last meeting.

Mori stood, dusting off her clothes.

"Thank you all for attending."

Then, she was gone.

The black fog was left behind in her wake, the group started, slowly falling from a trance as the girl's stayed seated, waiting for Nipuna to speak; who sat glaring away in no general direction.

"You heard her-" Nipuna sneered, snapping, and standing, dusting her clothes, and swerving from the table in a way that covered the evident limp in her side. Sybil followed close behind her, a gum-less smile directed at Arcane that made her heart increasingly lighten.

"Do as you are ordered," Nipuna sneered. "This is a serious matter, who knows what our Mistress will come back with."

As Arcane stood, Ito gave her a menacing smile, licking her cut lips.

She only narrowed her eyes as a reply.

11

Exitium

Three days had passed.

"I cannot fathom the fact she has left us," Ohno muttered, eyes absorbed into the writing of the book she was reading; a short novella of mystery as the girls curled into the comfort of their beds. Arcane wasn't fond of it, to put it lightly, not when Ohno was too invested to even look back at her as she talked.

Spring seemed more apprehensive, as she paced the room.

"I can't keep still, I really cannot."

"Relax," Arcane muttered, although she may have needed to take her own advice, because she was not relaxed. Her shoulders were tense, eyes sore from her lack of sleep, her eyes scanned over the messages of her notebook. "She'll be fine."

Ohno and Spring halted, staring questionably- but said nothing.

"Was Ito being serious, about the Mistress?" Spring asked.

Arcane's cheeks went red, "Do we not have more important matters to discuss?"

Spring playfully shook her head as she climbed onto Arcane's bed, resting beside her. "Hmmm.... Nope. There's nothing else to talk about."

"Why do you care so much?"

150 | JESSE PIPER

Spring shrugged, to which Ohno replied- suspiciously.

"She looked at you like..."

"Like she looked at everyone else?" Arcane scoffed. Internally panicking.

"No," Ohno could not put her finger on it, as she traced the words of the novel. "She gave a personal look to you once or twice, and- Takanashi Ito has an animosity for you, which she did not always have."

"Ito is deranged," Arcane quoted Ohno, to which she only huffed.

"Anyway," Spring cut, lying her back into the bed and staring at the ceiling longingly, tiredness drooping in her eyes. "I can't believe there's a rat."

"There isn't a rat, there's an enemy. There's a difference."

"Yes," Spring solemnly muttered. "Yeah, you're right."

Ohno nodded distractedly.

"If it's anyone, it's Ito."

Arcane struggled to hold in her bottled fury, these girls were really starting to get on her nerves, she'd barely spent time with them, and she wanted to smack them both repeatedly over the head. They should be doing more important things than accusing people.

She knew they had good reason; Ito did almost stab her to death.

But she knew it wasn't Ito.

Ito wanted to kill herself, not kill everyone else. It wouldn't make sense, there was no reason for Ito to kill others for power, especially because she wanted to kill herself so desperately.

"But-" Arcane took a sharp breath, beyond confusion. "-You used your magic did you not? There were no lies."

"People have spells and incantations that hide lies, Arcane."

She said it as though it were obvious, but it didn't seem obvious- because Arcane had no idea how to do such a spell. As though Ohno sensed it, she pointed to a singular book by a burnt-out candle on the floor. "That book has lying spells, ways to cover and tell. Easy stuff, especially if you know how to detect a lie already."

"Thank you," Arcane muttered. "But think about it, most of us have no reason to kill one another. What will power give us if it means killing the ones we hold dearest? Who would want that?"

THE TRIPLE MOON | 151

"An insane person," Ohno muttered. "Like Ito."

"It's not her, honestly at this point I think you guys have a hate love relationship."

Ohno startled.

"Very funny."

"I try to think of anyone that would honestly help the hunters, and my mind goes blank." Arcane whispered. She did not get an answer.

Arcane flicked through one of the spell books on the floor. She skimmed the pages, reading through the spells until Spring's snores were evident in the room, till Ohno curled into herself, book closing against her hands wishes upon the bed sheets as her glasses twisted strangely on her face as she slept.

The brunette wasn't initially waiting for them to sleep, but she realized this was the best opportunity to leave, when no one was watching. Not even Crow Mori.

There was nothing better for Arcane, it was either; succumb to the devils of the night, consumed by a sleepless sleep of nightmarish dreams, or stay awake in a hope she'll figure out who the enemy of this Coven truly is.

I mean, who else is going to make sure Beatrice is patrolling the haven?

The night obscures the vision, the eyes begin to see faces, moulds of people- shadows that move like the humans, sound like the humans. The snap of a twig as it falls from the branch is now a figure's foot snapping a stick in too. The mind creates illusions within the darkness, no person can overcome what the mind makes them believe.

Crow Mori had known this from a young age.

Her hidden figure, folding into the shadows, was an illusion to the eyes. There was a sense of superiority, the fact that as she stood in plain sight yet completely clandestine- these hunters assumed it was their mind playing tricks on them, and that they would have to get used to it as they consume Witch Land.

Her Mothers had always told Crow that illusions were key.

"You are weak, Crow- but your illusion makes you powerful. While you look in the mirror and see a weak girl; the witches you protect see a liberator."

As she grew to the current age, the voices never left her head.

You are weak.

But your illusion will make you appear powerful.

They were right, though Crow would never admit it. She would spit on their grave before she admitted they were right.

Her fragile figure was well hidden in the darkness of the forest; nevertheless, if she had no magic, she would be dead. She had no capability to fight without her magic, neither did she have beauty beyond her strange, intimidating glare. Magic made her beautiful, her power made her invincible, without it she was nothing.

Mori twisted into the tree as footsteps sauntered past, her black eyes following the trail of three hunters- boisterous and playfully drunken as they scurried back to the campfire.

She knew how dangerous this was.

The Coven's Mistress, standing in plain sight of a Hunter's camping grounds. She was only shy away from the campfire, the light illuminating around her, aside from the shadows she hid within- of course. She took a sharp breath, her mind begging her body to lose that human tendency to acknowledge the fear strumming inside of her.

"You are not allowed to fear things, Crow."

Her mother's voice was always in her ear.

She took a sharp breath, observing the figure that ducked into the largest tent within the scattered campsite across the clearing. Two hunters stood guard, crossbows at their sides, lazily held in their hands- almost like instruments that were hardly cared for. They wore dark uniforms, but careless faces.

She observed the way a younger pair of boys played a sort of game by the fire, cards dispersed in their hands. Her eyes softened at the innocence, at the sense of shame drumming through her, before her sister's hoarse voice echoed within her head.

"There is no remorse, if you don't learn that sooner or later-You'll be dead before you're eighteen."

Her words were always ironic.

The sound of voices snapped Crow from her deep deliberating.

"Oi!" A bellowed voice echoed. "Where's the Captain?"

"The only place he ever is, you dimwit. In his tent!"

Mori shifted away from the tree and into a fog of black, finding herself now sidled into the darkness behind the tent, on her stomach as she flicked a gust of magic to hold the bottom flap enough to see with one eye. She observed inside the tent, shrouded in darkness and as silent as a mouse.

A young man sat cross legged upon a wooden chair, long hands caressing the work along the desk. He was tall and lean, tan skin glistening against the lantern by his side. He was scanning over what seemed to be maps, Crow realized.

She narrowed her eyes, and listened in as the other man came in.

"You ear' anyfin?"

His accent was unrecognizable, though Mori had never travelled outside of the island, and most of the witches did not have such a unique drawl. She tried to get comfortable, however was more than aware she was lying down on the hard ground of the forest, there would be no comfort.

"Yes, I did." His voice was throaty, lacking emotion.

His wild black hair framed his face, Mori could not tell his age nor perfectly see how he looked beneath it. Though his voice prevailed a rudeness from it, it radiated onto the man who had come into his tent.

"What's ya' plan? *Fian*?"

Fian. Crow pondered.

What a strange name.

Though she couldn't particularly talk, her mother had named her after an animal. One that was more perceived as a rodent than any other descriptor.

"The ships come in tomorrow night; we have enough time to prepare before we begin our assault."

The younger man, smaller- thicker in places where one would carry a heavy load, was evidently hesitant- his long fingers raking through his ginger hair.

Crow's heart hammered against the wet ground, loud in her ears. She wasn't sure whether it was the beating of their heart in her ears, or her own as she listened closely. She fisted her hands against the wet ground, feeling where snow had melted. She began to digest the dilemma at hand, finding herself becoming more and more furious as the seconds occurred, which only led to her being unable to bottle it up.

"How many do we have?"

"Enough."

His voice twisted; Mori could sense his abrupt discomfort as he cleared his throat. He straightened.

"Now, Prepare the weapons. Douse in oil and Ricin. We begin our war as soon as our fellow soldiers make it to base."

"Why don't we plan a day to rest? *You* need to rest, Fian. Many of the soldiers wouldn't have slept for days on that boat. Even then, we haven't even got a full scout of the haven yet. Why don't we wait till the Witch gets back to us?"

There was a sincerity in the ginger's voice, one that made Mori question their relationship.

"We aren't deliberating what my plan is, I'm ordering you."

"Understood," The man slightly faltered, though his wide human eyes showed an anger that needed to be quenched. "I await your orders for war."

"Leave me." Fian flicked his ring covered fingers gently towards the door, and he watched callously as his partner left the room to himself. There was a ringing, in Mori's ears- hot, her cheeks burned, her hands shook.

She couldn't understand, couldn't process how she was feeling at this very moment.

There was an Army of Hunters coming to kill them all.

Crow Mori was left to observe the way Fian sauntered around the room, pacing up and down. His eyes trained across the map upon his desk, red string attached to knives that delved into formation, into strategy and plans of death and decay. It was so close, yet so far.

Fian's body was a shield against such advances. He had a towering height, and despite the sheer speed of Mistress Mori- she knew better than to expect herself to survive standing with a leader of an Army of Hunters.

They train from birth, live in treacherous conditions- they live to kill, they are born to kill.

Mori always told herself the Hunters and the Witches could never truly live in harmony, for their birth was intentions that crossed one another's paths dangerously. Witches lived with a power the hunters lived to destroy. She had grown up seeing what it did to people, she knew it would never end.

The Hunters after the Necromancy War grew stronger through the years as the Witches decayed. They used their own magic against them, their own weaknesses to a breaking point. Witches were no match for fire, poison killed their lives individually and too efficiently.

Even if Mori would steal the map, the potions on the wall could very much kill her- though she was aware of her talents, she was also more than aware of theirs. She took a sharp breath, observing the array of weapons across the floor, hanging from chains in the tent. They shined against the light in all their iron glory. They were sharp, edged in poison and oil- they intended to take more than just a body, but a Witch's soul.

Crow did not want to admit it.

She was petrified of the decisions she had made.

Truthfully, Crow did not know what she was going to do. As the days passed, her suffering was more obvious, her pains clearer to the eye; she was still only a child, in her own eyes, perhaps even to everyone else's. Protecting her Witches took a toll on her body, her magic exhausting to limits where she could not perform simple incantations.

How could a child keep her Coven safe?

Now, she wished her blood sister was still alive, and begged in another life that she would never have to be the Mistress.

She never wanted this.

Crow was never a leader, her mother used to remind her of it every day.

Mori was her illusion, her fake self; a way to make her Coven consider in a improved life.

Even Crow Mori couldn't believe in an improved life.

Not now.

The impending doom was always, and will forever be upon them, ever since the beginning of the war between humans and witches, and the rise in power of hunters. She should've given up long ago.

Mori pulled away, unrolling from the ground. She found herself taking a deep- controlled breath before shifting into a black mist. The dizziness in her head only became apparent for a second before she stood in front of a figure.

"So, you kept your word."

Fian halted his pacing, peering to Crow.

He had wild, blue eyes- like the ocean.

"I do not break my promises, Fian. Do you think of me so lowly?"

"Any Witch in my presence is deemed lowly, even the helpful ones."

12

Ferox

Her feet were silent as she trekked through the halls, her breath chaste against the numbed quietness of girls in their rooms, giggling and discussing to lighten the load of being isolated in fear of death. In some sense, Arcane was privileged enough to not be aggrieved over the fact she was disobeying orders from her superior.

She hadn't found Beatrice, she even knocked on her door to no avail. As the moon began to descend into the sky, illuminated the shadows of her body as long and slender against the floorboards beneath her feet. She aimlessly inspected the palace, before finding herself stumbling to Mistress Mori's door.

It ominously towered, cascaded with intricate details along the door. There was no doorknob, Arcane reminded herself- it was locked from the inside. Of course, it would be. Arcane huffed. Deep down, she had no reason to be in Mori's room, but she at least wanted to be there when she came back.

She wanted to be with her, so bad- her whole body ached without her presence.

As though Mori was a cure to a deathly illness that plagued her body.

Arcane sealed her eyes shut, hands pressed into the door. She listed the spells within her little head, reminding herself of the minor spells and incantations she found that allowed her to move through shields. The pulsing of the door told her enough, Mori had been intelligent enough to ward her room off from anyone but herself and the people who knew how to break a ward.

A hard gruff sound emitted from Arcane's mouth as she pressed into the shield, imagining herself falling straight through- magic resonating through her shaking fingers, coming from her heart, through her nerves.

Her body tipped as the door slipped open, and as soon as she tumbled into the room, the door slammed behind her. It was rough, an echoing resonating through the empty room- wind had knocked books over from the desk, and Arcane stumbled up-cursing and cleaning it all again.

"She'll know I've been in here now." Arcane swore under her breath, struggling to remember what book went where. Her fingers skimmed an opened envelope by a few books piled up. While the books titles upon the spine were things like '*NECROMANCY*' '*DEVILRY*' and '*THE TRIPLE MOON.*' Arcane found herself more transfixed with the envelope.

It was ripped carelessly, the stamp non-existent and missing with a patch showing where it once was.

Stop prying.

No.

She'll be furious.

She won't care.

Arcane slipped into the chair on her desk, resting into the scent of Mori's parchment paper- the distant stench of blood still tinged in the air, like the taste of pennies. She pulled the envelope into her hands but found no letter.

"What the fuck?" Arcane groaned. "That's not fair at all."

She flipped it, finding no address to a person on the letter.

"Perhaps this isn't hers…"

A voice emitted from across the room, a throaty, giggled voice that jolted Arcane from the chair. She stood on the tip of her toes, expecting to have to run for her life as the voice echoed throughout the dark room. She analysed the doors, the walls, and windows- but relaxed as she found no malice to Takanashi Ito's hidden figure.

She stood resting against the door to Mori's private bathroom, outfit dishevelled, her hair wet and tangled. The stench of blood was prominent in the air now. Arcane could not see why though, Ito's lips were sealed, eyes hooded as her body sat lazily shadowed in the dim light.

A twist of unsureness overcome Arcane, especially seeing her in a locked room that she even struggled to get through. There was a shimmer of envy- consuming her from the inside out, but she told herself Mori did not want to have anything to do with Ito.

"How did you get inside?"

Ito pointed to the window, as if it was obvious.

Oh.

"What are you doing here?"

Arcane did not have a friendly tone.

"I just wanted to enjoy the silence," She lied. "Mori always hated it when I did it, it only makes it more exhilarating- you know? Fearing being caught by her."

Her cackle was muffled through the darkness as she skipped out from her resting position, the letter in her hands as she sidled on top of the study, shoving the books back onto the floor aggressively to make room. Her body twisted to look down on Arcane, her pale face glistening with the white light of the moon through the window Her empty, pale eyes slow compared to her other- glaring one.

Arcane lost her breath, she had never truly been able to admire her face, the way the bones of her face jutted from her skin in a strange and delicate way. Her brows were often furrowed, lips always pursed into a scowl, her mouth always tainted red with blood as she whined.

Though that admiration was overcome with Arcane's fury as she reminded herself of what had only happened a few hours prior to now.

"I cannot believe you." Arcane snapped, straightening herself in Mori's chair, her eyes screaming daggers at the woman idly resting on the top of the desk, her skirt riding up her thighs, white blouse unbuttoned inappropriately as her hands waved the letter Arcane had wanted to see in the air.

"Can you never hold all that anger in? Can you not spare me some respect?"

She only giggled.

"Oh, little dove, I was only playing."

Her fingers caressed the wood of the desk as she reclined back onto her elbows.

"You attempted to kill me- stab me to death in front of all those girls, including the Mistress herself. *Are you crazy?*"

Ito raised an eyebrow, seemingly unimpressed.

"Why yes, I am."

Arcane rolled her eyes as her mumbling continued.

"You're scared of what they think?"

The questions caught the brunette off guard.

She took a sharp breath.

"Give me the letter, Ito. You know I want it." She sneered as she reached for it. Ito jolted away, her breasts jutting out as some sort of barrier between Arcane and the letter raised in her hand.

"Do you? Do you really want it?" She teased, a strange glimmer in her eye.

"Yes!" Arcane snapped. "I do! I want to see it."

"Admit you're scared of the girls, about how they perceive you- admit you're scared of Mori leaving you, just like she left me. Then I might consider it."

Ito's face inched closer as her hand holding the letter furthered away. Her breath was hot on Arcane's skin, her fanged teeth a bite away from her neck. Ito's eye scanned the bareness of her neck, the lack of a blazer on Arcane's shoulder's, the way her thick eyebrows always narrowed furiously in her direction but diminished when she thought she was not watching.

"I shouldn't need to admit anything to you, lying is a fool's gamble."

"You're scared of what they think."

"Of course, I am," Arcane snapped, breaking the facade of carelessness. Ito savoured the way her face broke, admiring the desperation in those wide brown eyes. "We are both suspicious in their eyes- we look like killers. Not only are you a maniac, but as soon as I came here people started to die. It would've been fine too if only you kept your bloody mouth shut. It isn't fair on either of us, I know- but stop accusing me, you'll get me killed!"

Ito rolled her eyes menacingly.

"You're so scared of what they think," She scoffed, not able to understand the severity.

"Because I am not powerful enough to fight off a Coven of Witches who think I'm the one killing them!"

Ito scoffed, again.

"Do you really doubt yourself that much?"

"Nipuna is a six-foot giant, Ohno has the intelligence of a century old Witch-"

"But Spring cannot even grow her plants, Sora is nothing without Miu. I want to kill myself; If I was in a fight, I would want you to kill me. Nipuna is injured, and Sybil is only a mute human girl. You could effortlessly beat them, one versus the rest."

"And Mori? You believe I could kill her?"

Ito chuckled beneath her breath.

"Perhaps if you're outraged enough."

Arcane furrowed her brows.

"What do you mean?"

Ito shrugged dramatically, clearly reluctant to confess the truth, going on a tirade about something else. "Your emotions fuel your magic. I can see that, most Witches just absorb their energy, but your body absorbs emotions. It's quite intelligent, actually."

"All those girls know more spells than I have ever learnt in my life. I only knew recently that there are spells that make lies be perceived as truths. I'm almost eighteen and I did not know that it's humiliating."

Ito scoffed. "Yet you broke into this room quite easily."

"It was a minor warding spell. Easy things- now stop distracting me." Arcane reached for the letter, but Ito was too fast as she analysed every muscle spasm and movement of Arcane's body, the way her biceps flexed through her blouse and her wrists unintentionally cracking before she were to move around in the chair.

"Anyway...They speculate we are the enemies, little dove- we have an enemy amongst us. While they try to combine loose ties and make some sort of sense to the disparity, we don't need to. Because I know, and you shall know."

Arcane furrowed her brows as Ito continued.

"You're telling me we know who the witch is that's working with the Hunters?"

Ito narrowed her eyes. "Yes," she handed Arcane the letter. "We do, and it's obvious."

"Beatrice, right?" Arcane whispered, to which Ito cackled with wide eyes clearly with confusion.

"No? Not her, she's weird, she can't even attend dinner without crying, the bitch is useless."

Arcane couldn't find any sense of sanity in the woman's strange words. Before she pulled the letter into the diminishing moon's light as it began to disappear over the trees, the morning sun began to rise over Venfic Island.

Mistress of Venfic,

This is a formal invitation.
I hear of your talents, aware of your tracking, observant skills.
Find and meet me.
We must discuss plans.

Candidly Captain Fian Venator.

Arcane could not process the words pressed harshly into the paper. She reread them, over and over and over until her eyes hurt and her breath came out short and panicked. She narrowed her eyes, reading it again, standing, pacing, before her breathing began to choke her.

How could she?

"What is this?"

Ito smiled, cunningly.

"A letter from the Hunter's to Mori."

"What...Does this mean?"

"It means Mori is with him now, working with him- talking to him. When she told us she was scouting the forest, she was truthfully meeting with the *'King of Hunters,'* *slimy Fian.*" Ito sneered, she jumped from the table, hands twisted into fists by her sides. Arcane could barely hold back her tears as she stared into Ito's fuming eyes.

"You're wrong."

"I'm not," Ito bellowed. "She's the sharpest of us all, it makes sense- did you not think of it once? Did you never question where she always vanishes to, why she's never around?"

"No, it doesn't," Arcane snapped back. "Mori...Mori promised."

"She's working with the enemy," Ito sneered. "No, she is the enemy. Enemies, do not promise things, Arcane."

Arcane's body stilled, the letter dropping numbly from her hands as the tears began to crumble from her eyes. She cried out, shoving Ito away. The fury overcame her, like a bomb about to diffuse, about to kill them all. She didn't know what she was going to kill, but she couldn't hold back- her whole body ached in pain, throbbed in a sense of betrayal.

"She was the killer, this whole time?"

Ito spit her bloodied saliva into the ground.

"She watches us all; she was never able to help anyone- it makes sense. It was always Mori, she was the one giving them intel, she was the one killing those girls for their power, for all those lives," Ito seemed to have an abrupt epiphany.

"A Witch must sacrifice all but one of her lives for the power of a Coven leader. All Coven leaders have one life- When Mori lost those lives, she realised she could not bear the risk, so she kills. It makes sense! Her entire family is dead." Ito whispered. "Right? It makes sense."

"Who cares now," Arcane sneered. "She has more. She won; she will have dozens at this point."

Arcane couldn't truly wrap her head around it.

It's just…

"It doesn't make sense."

Ito's entire body transcended, a burst of fire in her eyes, white magic exploding from her body as she erupted. Wind emitted from her as she yelled and cried and screamed.

"IT DOES!" she screamed. "ALL OF IT MAKES SENSE. I AM SO SICK OF YOU'RE BLIND TRUST FOR HER. Can you not see what she has done to you?! You trust her, over evidence!"

Arcane straightened, narrowing her eyes threateningly through tears.

"Is this the only evidence you have?"

She couldn't make herself believe what she was seeing.

The gust of wind gradually deteriorated, the window having smashed from the power of Ito's fury, glass covering Mori's bedroom floor. The chair had flipped, the books of the bookshelf thrown across the room. Ito analysed Arcane, relaxing her shoulder's back into their idleness.

"Yes," she sneered. "Who else could it be? Nipuna wouldn't hurt a fly, nor would any other girl," Ito rested herself against the desk. Arms crossed feverishly as a speck of a tear fell down her cheek. "-and despite how much I fucking hate Sybil, it isn't her either."

"Your hatred is suspicious."

"I just find it suspicious the bitch doesn't talk."

Arcane started, finding herself breaking inside.

"She's mute, Ito."

"How are you not furious?" Ito sneered, ignoring the retort.

THE TRIPLE MOON | 165

"I am! I'm trying not to cry." Arcane howled, tears freely flowing, fury- the aching want to strangle the woman tingling in her fingers, just so she would shut up, so she could stop lying.

"Imagine Ito, you love a girl enough to be vulnerable with her- and you find out she wants to fucking murder you!" Her cry was harrowing, it shook the floor, and Arcane couldn't hold it in, her fist collided with the desk- a sickening crack echoing as it snapped in half with the magic surging through her fists.

Ito faltered, stumbling away, and observing the damage as Arcane screamed into her hands, throwing the chair into the wall, and watching it splinter into hundreds of little pieces. Her entire body shook, and Ito questioned whether showing her the letter was a wonderful idea.

"I fucking hate her, I'm going to fucking kill her-"

Ito smiled.

"That's my girl."

Arcane only glared from over her shoulder.

"I am *not* your girl."

Ito only giggled, covering up the shock she still processed from the letter.

"I won't forgive you for trying to stab me, you know."

Ito barely deflated, only chuckled before tumbling onto Mori's bed.

Now, the smell of her was haunting, her room- ominous.

It was no longer welcoming or comforting- and all that was left in Arcane's heart was the hollowed-out place where Mori's presence once belonged. Now, she feared being here for too long, what if Mori appeared? The two at this point were vulnerable, she would snap their necks before they would even see her arrive.

"So, how are you going to murder her?"

"Not with fire- I'll do it slowly." Arcane sneered. Her eyes distantly watching the morning rise through the window, light overcoming the room, shining on her tear-stained face- showing the dust that was collecting within the room.

She was beyond furious, but also- fearful.

The one woman she trusted, was the thing she feared most.

"I'll strangle her, every time her soul comes back to her body, then the last time-"

"Stab her in the heart?"

"No, the stomach."

"Why?" Ito furrowed her brows from her position of lying down upon Mori's bed, spread out.

"I don't want it to be romantic."

Ito only scoffed before speaking up once again.

"You worry she'll make you feel bad?"

Arcane didn't want to admit it.

Yes.

Yes, I do.

I'm scared I won't be able to kill her.

"How much longer will this bitch take, I mean- I have no plans, but I wouldn't mind getting frisky if you know what I-"

The black mist began to appear through the darkness- more sluggish than routine as her body began to appear through the shadows of the room. Her ominous presence completely silenced the two girls, Ito left with the words spewing from her mouth.

Arcane froze at the sight of Mori shifting out of the black fog. She didn't think she could do it- Arcane realized, she couldn't believe it- deep down, her heart hammered, and she was unsure whether it was the want to kiss her or kill her, or both.

The disgust overcame her though, and she only saw a murderer.

Crow Mori's body was shaky, knees caving in with the step outwards from the smoke before it fizzled away. Her eyes were void, glazed over as though exhausted. Her pale skin glistened against the rising light of day through the window, and Arcane could see the cuts and bruises along her body, the blood that covered her blouse, the way dried blood covered the inside of her lips, as though she had bitten her tongue too hard.

The fury overcame her as she spied blood that covered the girl's lanky fingers- dried beneath her nails. She lurched, hands outstretched, grabbing onto Mori's collar with a brutal force, a power surging through her fingers.

THE TRIPLE MOON | 167

Mori did not protest her harsh touch as Arcane's abrupt strength sent her crashing into the bed, merely missing Ito. The deranged girl rolled off in time as Mori's figure snapped the headboard in half, and as her body fell into the bed, the powerful surge of her body caused it to tremble perilously before the legs gave out beneath it.

A gust of dust flew across the bedroom as the bed snapped completely at the impact, an echo raiding across the room as Ito merely missed a piece of wood that flew from the impact.

Mori lay stunned for a second, before her shaky, bloody hands ripped the headboard off her and propelled it through the room and into the wall, meters away from the two Witches- prepared and ready to kill.

Arcane's tear stained cheeks flustered as Mori stood onto the bed, her hair wisps in front of her furiously narrowed black eyes. Blood dripped from her lips, a long cut searing down her lip from the hit.

"What is this?"

Her voice was unnaturally husky, deep within her throat. There was an inhumanness to it as her inky black eyes glared at the women.

Arcane's breath left her lungs. Mori observed Arcane with more betrayal in those inky, black eyes than fury. It made Arcane falter for a second before the image of those dead bodies resurfaced. She was trying to play victim, assuming love would overcome the horrors.

"I trusted you- We trusted you." Arcane sneered, inching closer, observing the lack of movement from Mori. The way her body stood eerily still, waiting- calculating. It was ominous, the way she did not move a single inch, aside from the blood drooling down her face. It was almost as though she were possessed by evil.

There was a pregnant silence before Mori spoke up through the echoing silence.

"What are you talking about?"

Her eyes did not falter from Arcane.

"We saw the letter." Ito snapped, stepping beside Arcane. Her teeth bared, pen sharp in her hand. "I'm going to make sure you bleed out slow and hard, Crow."

Silence.

"I hate you. Why won't you say anything god damn it!" Arcane sneered, her hatred overcame her as Mori did not react- could not react. Perhaps those emotions were always. "You made us trust you- and I thought I loved *you*?" Arcane's voice cracked and deterred- overcome with emotion she could not place, and the words finally evoked shock in those monstrous black eyes.

Mori blinked, her mind clicking as she sauntered closer to them. "What?"

"You went to see him, don't act dumb. *You* are the enemy! *You* are the rat; *you* are the monster!" Arcane lurched forwards, tackling the girl into the ground so hard the room shook. She cried out, tears pelting, streaming from her cheeks as her hands wrapped around Mori's throat. She tightened, hard- hard enough to kill, she watched through tear-stained eyes as Mori did nothing but hold the hands that choked her, and her hands only choked harder, finding a strange shattering sense of her heart breaking into a million pieces as she watched Mori's cheeks flush red and her inky black eyes welling.

There was a long second where their eyes collided in a shift of conflict- her hands released for a split second, observing the way Mori's eyes stared back at her as though she could see through every inch of her being. This second of faltering allowed Mori's physical body to dissipate from beneath her.

Arcane stared at her hands in shock, listening to the echoed crack that came from behind her.

She turned, overcome with dread.

Ito was limp in Mori's arms, she slowly dropped her to the ground, the pens falling from her hands.

She placed the woman down delicately- not how a monster should have done it. She kicked the calligraphy pens across the floorboards and away from both women before she edged towards Arcane's trembling body.

Arcane sobbed.

"You killed her."

"No," Mori replied rather shocked- hurt in those empty black eyes. "I- can't believe you think of me so lowly."

"You killed them!" Arcane screamed. "Of course, I see you so lowly."

Arcane stumbled up from the floor, her ankles almost buckling.

"I'm going to make you pay!"

Arcane hurled a punch at her face, but Mori silently dissipated into smoke before appearing behind her once again, her feet silent, her breathing a wisp away in her ears.

Arcane twisted, hand outstretched to stab the girl straight in the eye with the calligraphy pen- although her hands were caught in the air. Mori held her hands back by the wrists, her grip was iron as the pen dangled seconds away from stabbing straight into the woman's eye.

Just a little closer.

Mori silently observed the way the tears streamed down Arcane's cheeks- the closeness of their faces wreaking more havoc as Arcane's body began to tremble, hating yet loving her deathly touch. The longer Mori gazed into those furious eyes, they more tears streamed down Arcane's cheeks, the more her hands tried to fight off her grip.

Arcane waiting for Mori's killing blow.

She flinched as Mori inched closer, eyes clamped tight- ready for the fatal blow. Expecting to wake in another few weeks to only die again.

She could not imagine she trusted the woman before her.

She truly thought Mori cared for her.

She would die, just like Miu- *trusting and weak, thinking Mori would be there to save you.*

"You.... Flinched?"

Arcane furrowed her brows, opening her swollen eyes to watch Mori let the girl go as though she were poison, or fire that killed at the touch. Mori stepped back, peering to her shaking, blood-stained hands, as though she was seeing someone else in her own eyes, perceiving something else, hallucinating something else.

Arcane numbly watched as Mori pulled away.

There was not much strength left in Arcane, so she watched, unmoving, struggling to stay upright.

Mori was too agile to beat.

"I didn't kill anyone, Arcane."

"You're a filthy liar." She seethed. "I knew, deep down you are the only person who is powerful enough to kill us if you wanted to. It would be so easy for you. So, fucking easy. I ignored my intuition because I thought you cared."

Mori's face broke- as though someone had just told a child their puppy had died.

Though, would Mori truly care if a puppy were to die?

Did murderers care for who they killed?

For who died?

"Arcane," Mori seethed. "I promise, I promise I didn't kill anyone."

Arcane stood numb. She knew she could not kill Mori, but she wished she had the power to.

"You expect me to believe you? The letter, Mori-" Her voice cracked, a betrayal evident in her voice. "You met with the enemy. How did he even get this letter to you if you were not-"

"It's a misunderstanding, I can explain."

"Can you?" Arcane seethed. "Because right now, all I see is a monster. You better start explaining, or I will kill you."

"You may see a monster- even I see one in myself, but not for what you think. *Let me show you.*"

Mori lurched forwards pleading, bloodied hands outstretching to Arcane's face, but she flinched away in disgust.

"Don't touch me."

Mori's heart broke, as did Arcane's.

"I will *prove* it."

"Prove what?" Arcane screamed. "That you aren't a heartless monster?"

"Yes," Mori seethed. "I will, I am a monster, but I am not heartless. Arcane, I promise over my own life, I would never hurt anyone. You know this, you know me."

Her voice was a quiet beg.

"I don't know you."

Mori's finger flicked, and Arcane's whole body went numb, she could not control an inch of her body, and she observed- panicked, tears straining down her cheeks as Mori's hands held caressingly against her temples, pressed like kisses- wet and covered in blood.

Disgusting.

Arcane's sight went black as a strange old dialect echoed throughout the air, Mori's voice haunting in the pitch-black darkness, her hands menacingly cold to the touch.

As she opened her eyes, she was no longer in the murderer's room, no longer confined and prepared for death on a silver platter.

She stood alone in utter darkness.

The stench of dark magic consumed the emptiness of nothing.

There, in the distance of darkness, a memory- as bright as a candlelight shimmered amongst the dusk.

"I'm in... your consciousness."

Her voice echoed, and she was met with silence.

Arcane willed herself to walk, her steps unfaltering without an existence around her. Her eyes set on the destination of a memory, far off in the distance. Though as she trailed colour, she realized there was more than just a single memory pocketed towards her destination.

Her hand outstretched to the bright light, and her fingers thrummed with power as she touched the light, a delicate memory clasped within her shaking hands before a flash of light overcame her, and she stood within a small, confined room. It was murky, the only light illuminating from the light that emitted from the bottom of the door.

The only other thing in the room was a bed, and a dresser- empty and desolate of any personal belonging but a frame of two girls, hard to see in the dark room.

The more Arcane took a second to breath, and for her body to relax into the state of the memory- she realized the room was akin to the size that would only fit a small child. The bed was well kept, the dresser dusted and barely touched, akin to the photo frame.

Arcane exited the room- finding that her body completely shifted through the door, and her touch was non-existent in this state of Mori's mind. She blinked, struggling not to panic as she fell through, finding herself observing the desolate halls of a large palace, or boarding school.

Presumably- The haven, only this was a memory, it was what the haven once looked like.

Arcane observed as a group of girls her current age, giggling as they walked through the entrance from the courtyard. They wore longer skirts, tights- ear muffs, their hair blown into their flushed faces, flowers, and fruits in their baskets.

One of the girls wore a flower crown, a chaste smile on her face as Arcane watched them leave. She then caught the sight of a smaller figure stumbled through the same entrance- unintentionally catching their feet on the steps of the door as they hazardously tried to catch up.

Arcane's heart lightened, at the way her knobbly knees buckled, and her basket flew from her hands. She collided with the wooden floorboards with an echoing smack, leaving the girl a crumbled mess on the floor as the girls further away left her behind.

Arcane winced, and despite her hatred for Mori- realised this childlike figure had no malice in her body as she panicked, trying to collect them as the clicking of heels on the floorboards were aroused from down the hall.

Mori looked no different- aside from the smaller figure, childlike face. Her cheeks were naturally flushed, rounder, more filled, she did not have her signature eyebags, nor that scowl. Though despite such a difference in physicality, Arcane could sense exclusion in those inky black eyes, the same shaggy hair framing her face, only it longer as a child.

"Crow," A stern voice called. Arcane halted from admiring the child, to observing as a towering woman with the same hooded eyes sauntered to her child. She stilled, peering down, and watching as the child picked up the last of the assortment of herbs, mushrooms, and peaches.

THE TRIPLE MOON | 173

"Mother," Her voice was merely the whisper of a baby bird. "Look."

"Where is your tutor?"

There was no reaction from her mother. Crow's mother's fingers distastefully outstretched, fanning the black hair from her daughter's face. She grabbed her cheeks with a motherless grip, leaning down as she searched her daughter's face.

Mori flinched as though her nails were hurting her skin, but her mother did not pull away.

They almost looked identical if not for her mother's sweeping blonde hair that ran down her back, and the way her mother was gifted with a towering height and sauntered with a sophistication Mori never exhibited.

They had the same, crescent eyes, pale white skin and the thin lips that was always pulled into a disinterested line.

"You're dirty, Crow."

"Elpis took me out to-"

Elpis, Arcane thought. *Who is Elpis?*

It seemed all the girls she had just seen were no longer present at the haven in current times, she had never seen them nor their intricate beauty before, their skin glistening and their lips bright with colour. If they were still present, they would be in their mid-twenties, and Arcane was aware mori was the oldest member of the Coven, everyone Arcane would see in this memory, was gone.

"Do you ever listen? Where is your tutor?"

Her mother let her go, as though the grime on her face was contagious and sickening to the touch, she stood to her full height, peering down on her youngest daughter as though she were barely recognisable.

"She- I don't know."

"How old are you, Crow?"

"I'm nine."

"Then you know better than to skip your classes." Her mother clicked her fingers and the memory warped as Mori's body forcefully dissipated into a black smoke. "Don't blame your incompetence and your laziness on your sister."

174 | JESSE PIPER

As she warped through the darkness, Arcane was unsure whether she was supposed to find these memories, or whether she was delving too deep in Mori's mind, sifting through the parts of her life she wanted nobody to know of.

Arcane found herself no longer in the halls of the haven. She stood within the forest, the moonlight basking her in brilliance. She could see the landscape around her, the way the moonlight shed its beauty amongst the trees, and how Crow stood older- beside her mother.

Her head was tipped to the ground, staring at her boots- unable to look away as her mother's towering figure leaned over her.

"This is the last time, Crow."

Arcane furrowed her brows, inching closer. It seemed all these distorted, crestfallen memories stemmed from the motherly figure in her life. Arcane inched closer- aware of the lack of sound her feet made.

"I just needed some time away."

"From what?"

Crow peered up, and Arcane could see the breaking of her face, the way her lips downturned into an upset grimace. Her voice came out exhausted, young- light despite the pain in it.

"From everything. I'm either stuck in my room studying, or I'm at the dinner table or the ballroom where everyone's watching. I've read every single book in that library; I have deprived myself of sanity." As her face was clear in the low-lit moon, Arcane could see the age of her face, this memory was at least three years after the last.

"That is your job," Her mother began to fume. "And what have I said? I am a Mistress, not your mother."

A small sound came from her mouth.

"Why did you even create me, then?"

"It was promised you would be good use to this Coven, that is why. It seems the prophecy was incorrect though. All you are is a nuisance; you're lucky Elpis is likeable, because I cannot have two dislikeable children."

Mori shook her head, her hands crossing over her chest. She acted older than her age, the way she watched people, the way she observed her scenery, and her mother's furious stance over her.

"You expect so much from me."

"Of course, I do," She scowled. "You are an heir to this Coven."

"Elpis is, not me. I won't need to ever lead this Coven, not when Elpis is around."

"Your dainty sister isn't going to be able to do it on her own," Her mother snapped. "Why aren't you like the other girls? You aren't hard-headed, you aren't independent, you're clumpy, and little. You cannot even control your own magic for goodness' sake- and you think going for a stroll in the woods when we have Hunters on this island is a good idea?"

A tear fell down Mori's cheek, and she did not wipe it away.

"I'm trying to be better."

"At this point, that is an impossible request."

Her mother pulled away, dusting off her long black dress, fixing her long-gloved hands as she gave her youngest a scathing look of disappointment that shattered Arcane's heart.

"All hope is lost if Elpis dies, and you are the one to take her spot once I am dead."

Then she was gone through black mist.

Arcane stood shocked, the harshness of her words shattering, overwhelming her. She observed as Crow's young body collapsed to the floor, tears streaming down her cheeks, hands shaking and the dirt piling on her knees, the stones scabbing her legs as she sobbed on the forest floor, careless to her surroundings.

Arcane was frozen as a taller body appeared through the trees, about to scream, lurch out to protest the dark figure, but found a young Nipuna sauntering out from their hiding spot. She was unidentifiable as she wore a long skirt, hair pulled back awkwardly into a bun, brown fringe framing her dark skin and long nose. She slipped beside Crow Mori on the floor, hands rubbing small circles on her back, letting the tears compile onto the forest floor, creating a little- almost invisible puddle of pain and rejection.

"I don't believe it."

Nipuna's voice was inelegant from the past memory. She was shorter, thinner with less muscle, and girlish. She looked nothing of what she was currently, boyish, and lean- towering in height. Mori was silent, trying to breathe as the girl proceeded.

"You aren't what she says, Crow."

"I'll never be good enough for her, no matter how hard I try."

Arcane stumbled as her body warped again, the image of the young girls sitting in the pale moon light disintegrating before Arcane found herself standing by a towering oak tree- the stench of magic consumed her as she observed the mythical size of it.

The morning sun began to rise over the hill she stood upon, her heeled feet a pile of mush in the wet grass. Despite her inability to touch, she found the gust of wind allowed her to breathe through the harsh emotions the memories within Mori's head provided her with. She was unsure whether she was supposed to see such memories, but it seemed these memories were more memorable than any other in her mind.

Shuffling broke her from her trance, she peered away from the sun gradually rising, the golden pink hue overwhelming the sky as she turned to the figure staring up at the tree beside her.

Mori looked only a year older than the last memory, she had grown into her current height, as well as the bags beneath her eyes, her hair had grown out, it was longer, combed and more feminine- but there was no lightness in her eyes, no sense of content as she stared off into the towering trees. Arcane furrowed her brows as she observed closely, the way a stray tear slipped down her pale face.

There was a swell of dread that pulsed through Arcane.

The memory wasn't as bright as she may have thought.

Beneath the tree was her mother's grave.

Mistress Tanith Mori.
From her birth in 260
to her demise in 749.

'One shall prevail and succeed within the clutches of death.'

THE TRIPLE MOON | 177

Arcane had never heard such words uttered. They were daunting-eerie to the eyes, to the mouth, to the ears, but it seemed they were the Mori Coven's dignified and very final words. Arcane was aware the Amunet Coven had their own, she cherished it, but as the months passed and her blood was merely within one living Witch, the words began to muddle in her head.

"Pray for the God of Death to accept the gifts of life to our lovers."

Arcane knew it wasn't the exact words she had just mumbled, but it was all she could remember. It was all she remembered as she buried her Sisters and mothers in their graves and engraved those words numbly into the tombstones. She was too drunk on pain to even be aware there were spelling errors, places where the carving fell through- though she would be the only person who knew she was the one who wrote it, so she found no shame.

Her Sisters would've laughed, after all.

Arcane huffed, tearing her eyes away from Mori's mother's ominous grave, she turned to observe the younger Mori, but found the real one peering back at her. She jolted back, squealing, expecting death- expecting to be grabbed and held down, silenced, and murdered within the mind.

But it did not happen.

"You have been standing here for quite a while." She muttered, searching Arcane's face.

She blinked, not having realized.

"I just…. Why are you showing me this?"

"You walked into this memory."

"Oh…"

"Somehow," Mori muttered. "Somehow you walked in. I always closed them off, placed them in the back of my mind. Your worst memories can be your disadvantage if you encounter Witches experienced in mental manipulation. If they are smart enough to get into your head," Mori pursed her lips. "So how did you find this?"

"It just took me here."

Mori was silent.

"Then I'm entirely vulnerable to you." she whispered.

Arcane was silent, her hatred still livid- but her inquisitiveness became the better of her, it ate her alive, she was aware curiosity killed the cat, but she was more than just a cat.

"How did your mother die?"

Silence, as Mori's eyes swept the tree. It was far from the Haven, away in an empty field overlooking the forest. There was an emptiness in those inky eyes, different to her fourteen-year-old self.

"She left Venfic to fight with other Witches against the crown of INDUSTCOR. Her body never came back, only a letter with one of her rings sealed inside, and the stench of burnt skin."

"There's no remains of her?"

"No. But I like it that way, it makes me wonder where her charred body was put."

Arcane nodded- struggling not to visualize where the body may have been left before she cautiously opened her mouth again. Her sister, she wanted to know.

"And Elpis?"

Mori sighed, dejected and dolefully.

"She replaced our mother not long after, she died when I was sixteen."

"Was she in any of your memories I saw?"

Mori shrugged, and their vision morphed till they were observing Mori back at the age of nine, her little figure curled into her older sister's form as she read from a sorcery book in her dainty, delicate hands. She was pale, with black hair just like Mori's, a flower crown ghosting her forehead, she was tall and slim- and had a smile that was worth a million pearls. It was glossy, glittering, twisted her eyes into warm crescents as she whispered to Crow as she nodded off on her lap.

"She was only twenty-one when she died," Mori turned to Arcane as her vision blurred again- but this time, the vision was bloodcurdling, a howling pain throbbing through Arcane's body as she stared at the charred body of Mori's sister, hanging from a similar tree Vera, the little girl had died on the first night they had truly met one another.

Arcane stumbled back, but Mori held her.

Arcane began to flinch back, expecting blood covered hands to hold her- but this wasn't reality.

"Look at her, Arcane."

Arcane held back her sobs, her sister's dress was shredded, the one intricate lace detail burnt to a crisp, she was almost unrecognizable, just like her own Sisters. She held strong, there was a reason Mori was showing her this.

"Why would I kill anyone, when she died just how they did?"

Arcane's breath choked her, eyes welled as she turned to Mori- observing the way her own eyes welled as she pointed up at her sister's mangled body. There was emotion that oozed from her, agony- and deprecating and rejection, all in one- this was her memory, her mind, and the air hurt to breath, it was as though Arcane was feeling what Mori felt when she found her sister's body the very night.

"I never admitted it, not even to Nipuna," Mori whispered, voice close despite the wind that whipped into Arcane's ringing ears. Above all else, Crow Mori's voice was a soothing comfort, a chasteness against the ringing, against the agony her heart seized in. "But the enemy was always at this Haven. Their first victim was my sister, Arcane. They killed Elpis just like they did everyone else, and I still have not had my justice."

Arcane could barely breathe, barely process it.

Could she truly believe this?

"You don't believe me." Mori's voice cracked- hope vanishing from her aching eyes, and her hold dissipated as she disappeared into a black smoke. Arcane heaved at the loss of contact as she shifted and disappeared until her figure landed into the soft grass of the forest, though now- the air was still, quiet- there were no dead bodies, but Mori's consciousness had left her entirely, and the brunette was alone.

She stood on wobbling knees, dusting the dirt from her skirt, and following the distant sound of chatter within the air. Her eyes peered at the large campfire, the horde of hunter's and their endless number of tents throughout the clearings.

Arcane did not dare count the amount, if she couldn't on her fingers, they were all doomed. Arcane couldn't help but think it was all Mori's fault, but the visions the memories, this memory. Mori was proving to her that it was never her, and Arcane was beginning to believe it- though, who could she trust but her own instinct?

Arcane followed the little trail of black fog that began to dissipate and found a tent larger than the bunch- lathered in lantern and chain, a flag of the INDUSTCOR royalty hanging in the air. Arcane had never known the hunters worked alongside the Kingdom, but perhaps it was not always like that.

She shifted through the tent flaps, her hands pressing through the material as though she were a ghost. She listened to the firm voice, and the chaste- emotionless reply.

She found herself staring at Mori and a man- tall, refined. He was lean, shaggy black hair and wide blue eyes- a human, a hunter. He had his black sleeves rolled up, scars littering his hands and arms, some looked like bite marks, others like scratch marks of nails and claws.

Presumably, Witches had not gone without a fight.

"Surprised you accepted my invitation."

Mori scowled.

"I came because I wanted to, not because you invited me."

"This conversation was needed, Mistress."

"This is barely a conversation, this is an argument, you invited me to your territory- the territory you stole from us, to threaten *my* Coven."

He scoffed, raking his lanky fingers through his black hair. He disbelieved her words. Arcane moved around the room, finding comfort standing close enough she could see both figures in the bright lantern light, though it seemed Mori's fog purposely created a shroud around her body- her dark eyes were hard to see through the blackness.

"We have...Quarrelled for long enough, so I'll be honest," He sauntered to his wall, dispatching one of his crossbows. The hairs rose on Arcane's skin, she peered, pale faced to Mori- expectant for her to do something as he loaded it, before aiming at her, it glinted in the lantern light, a liquid coating the tip of the arrow. "Surrendering will be your best choice."

"Surrender? Witches don't surrender, Fian- they fight."

"No, Witches do not surrender because they die before they can even beg for mercy. *I* have mercy," He sneered. "It is our job to kill you, but arrangements can be made for the more risqué of witches. I'm giving you a chance at life, over death."

Mori scoffed.

"What life is being chained up and drained of magic. We are not your slaves; we are not workers. You expect so much from us."

Silence.

"I suppose there was no point trying to get you to surrender, then."

Then, a cackle, a distasteful- unhinged, eerie laugh that came deep within her chest, it emitted from Mori's thin lined lips. She cocked her head to the side, her hair framing her irritated face. Her eyes narrowed threateningly.

"You think you can kill me? *Us?* My witches are more than capable of killing Hunters, we have done killed your kind for years."

He raised the crossbow up, the point of the arrow directing at her bare neck.

"No fire?"

"Ricin."

She only scoffed, triggering the hunter in Fian.

"Ricin is the second killer of witches. Fire is too messy; we don't want to burn my camp down."

"Who is we?" Mori mocked, as swiftly as she spat the words, her hands outstretched, her coat flying behind her as magic thrummed the air, uplifting the air. The arrow pierced the wind, shooting- aiming lower than the neck and straight for Mori's heart.

Arcane screamed, meaning to lurch forward, wanting to, but finding herself lost for words as the arrow twisted- shooting back in the other direction with the flick of her fingers. The arrow almost pierced the hunter in the head, but he dodged only a second before.

Mori visibly grunted, as he shot another arrow, its tip merely skimming her coat, shooting through the tent wall, and thudding as it hit a hunter on the other side. The man faltered, and Arcane watched a wicked, sinister smile tip Mori's lips as she grabbed onto the lantern, throwing it into the air, before creating a sword out of black mist, and piercing the lantern enough it exploded, the fire catching onto the tent, exploding into Fian's face as he dodged.

Arcane's vision blurred in a spark of a red explosion. She flinched, memories consumed with blood, fire, and disgust- her sister's faces drawn upon her vision at the sight of the fire.

Arcane breathed, reminded herself of the lack of pain that came when a spark flew her direction, passing straight through her body. Arcane kept her sights on Mori, making sure not to break her attention, urging herself not to shatter as the fire caught onto the tent's material, alight and burning everything that came in its territory.

Mori extended her hand, and an explosion followed outside the tent, shaking the earth as harrowing screams followed.

Arcane stumbled to the sound, leaving the confinements of the burning tent to find the bomb fire having exploding and ejecting everyone around it into the air, their bodies completely charred before the fire went out. Arcane started, shocked- heart hammering in her chest as Hunters had their weapons prepared as the Mistress sauntered out of the tent.

In slow motion, Arcane watched in shock as every arrow that came her way, was deflected, piercing the hunter on impact, cutting straight through their necks with a crack before they fell to the ground with a small 'woosh.' Mori did not flinch as her eyes caught the sight of an arrow before it was ejected back where it came- ending the hunter's life that tried to end hers.

There was a lack of remorse in those black eyes.

They had hurt her Sisters.

She deserved to give bloodshed.

She deserved the pinch of vengeance that came with every snapping neck, every halting heartbeat, every lack of breath. The Hunters had taken so much, killed their race till they were extinct- forced them

THE TRIPLE MOON | 183

into exclusion, into rejection- forced the world to perceive them as itches and not as humble creatures of chaste love.

Arcane found herself admiring Mori's swiftness, the way her fingers moved at the speed of light, her eyes always watching. Her mist trailed her like it were muse, and Mori was merely dancing amongst the slaughter.

The memory was fresh, the stench of blood as it splattered onto Mori was fresh in her nose, the smell of firewood overcoming her senses, Mori's pained face evident as a sword collided with her side- slicing clean through, before she caught his second advance, disintegrating the sword before the attacker's neck snapped, and he fell silently to the ground.

Arcane could not move as the hunter's body piled upon one another, every single arrow meeting its mark as it tried to pierce her. The screaming of the Captain urged them to stop shooting, to stop dying-and once his orders rang in their ears, and their attacks stilled hands shaking- breathes heaving from their dodges and swings.

Mori sneered.

"Count this as a warning," Her eyes pierced the Captain as he stomped out, eyes ablaze.

"I will kill every last one of you."

He chuckled, eyeing the dozens of his soldier's dead bodies, sinking into their own blood.

"This is a dozen soldiers. We have thousands, and we have a Witch."

"Who is it," Mori's voice was a furious echo, controlling, ordering.

The Captain raised his crossbow, one doused in oil, ablaze with fire.

"You still don't know?" He cackled. "You're a pathetic excuse for a Mistress, Mori."

Mori cracked her neck, then her shoulders, before a dozen arrows appeared in the air, following her command. She cried out, exhaustion clear in her posture as she ejected them towards Fian, he groaned, twisting as one caught his leg, the rest- somehow, missed. Fian dodged the arrows faster then any Hunter, any Human.

The disbelief on Mori's face was evident as Fian, the Captain of Hunters, arose from the ground, ripping the arrow from his leg, and observed as the skin immediately healed.

"What is this sorcery?"

"The rat, of course."

Arcane's heart dropped.

The Witch had aided them with her magic.

Mori was never the villain.

A hatred burned inside of Arcane, for herself- for her own decision. She had only worsened Mori's state, she had allowed herself to overthink, to succumb to the fear of death that came with an enemy living in her own home.

She had hurt Mori, and Mori had not done a single thing hurtful to her.

But her fury for the rat burns brighter.

She would kill them.

Slowly, painfully.

She did not care how much life it took from her, she pledged it.

13

Suavium

Arcane swiftly came to as soon as she realised her feet touched the hard surface of Mori's bedroom floors. Not only so, but the chilling touch of hands on her temples snapped her out of her heated trance. Her eyes began to adjust with the light of the sun through the window, the sun that glistened through the raining clouds- a brightness amongst the gloom.

Mori's hands shakily pulled away, and Arcane peered down through teary eyes to see the life that had drained from Mori's face, her lips were pale- eyes hazy, blind- as though she was so exhausted, she was falling in and out of consciousness. She tipped before catching herself on her feet.

Arcane panicked, her hands pressing into the wound at her side.

"Oh, Crow- I'm so sorry." She sobbed, she wrapped her arms shakily around Mori as she blinked the tears out of her eyes, pulling her into a bone crushing hug, breathing in the scent of her skin- feeling her skin on hers, cold, but alive, her heart breathing harshly into her chest.

The wound had swelled, blood dried and sticking to her skin as Mori straightened out of her haze at the touch of Arcane's fingers on her skin. Their bodies moulded perfectly, her hands moving into Mori's hair, nails digging into her skin.

"I- I'm so sorry," she whispered beneath her breath, eyes empty of tears. She had cried herself till she had no more to cry.

Mori moved into the caressing hold on her, relaxing into the taller figure, emitting warmth within the coldness of the room.

She had not been loved in such a way in a long time.

She hushes Arcane's fervour apologies, the regret oozing out of her like tears. Mori's hands caressing down her spine, sending chills through her body- forcing her to pull away. She feared she would do something she would regret, but it was not the intention of killing, Mori's lips were too kissable to stand so close, Arcane realised.

Her hands shook a thrill through her, soothed the inner demon screaming at her. If she were to get too comfortable, Arcane feared what her next move would be as Mori rested in her hold, her face a breath away.

"You have no reason to be sorry, Arcane."

"I threw you into your bed, your body literally snapped it in half." her eyes teared away from Crow, peering at the destroyed bed, a squeak parting from her lips. "Where are you going to sleep? Did I hurt you? Oh gosh the crack when you hit the bed was so deafening, I feel so bad-"

"Relax." Mori muttered. "I'm a Mistress, I heal."

"So? I hurt you," Arcane winced, her eyes roaming for injuries, but all she could see was the dried blood of her clothes.

"It'll only be a bruise."

"And with the snapping of my bed..." Mori shrugged exhaustedly. "I suppose I shall sleep with you, then. Is there room for two?"

Arcane halted, cheeks reddening- she peered to Mori with her thrumming, pulsing heart, who only smiled exhaustedly.

Mori sensed her surprise and continued gently. "The bed is an effortless repair," She peered at the still sleeping Ito upon the floor. "As is her, and the desk..." Mori clearly did not realise the desk was demolished, perhaps it hadn't processed till now, and the woman was gawking at the decay of the room.

Arcane grimaced.

Yes, she had destroyed her desk too.

"Does she...Know?"

"My memories are replaying in her head as she sleeps."

Arcane relaxed.

"I have hurt you beyond comprehension."

Mori was silent, she couldn't lie and say her words did not sting.

"Am I a monster to you?" She whispered, Arcane's words still replaying in her mind.

Arcane was too distracted by the exhausted details in the smaller woman's face to realize the bed was mending itself, nor that Ito's body had dissipated and curled the women into her bedroom, where she slept with her blankets pulled up to her chin, warm in slumber she had not received in weeks.

Arcane and Mori were left alone, standing in a room that began to mend itself together with magic, the breath of witchery wafting within the air, lighting up the stray candles with a white mist like fire that did not force the woman into a panic. The room was cool, the dim colours soothing their minds.

Arcane could not believe she wanted to kill her only a few hours ago.

"No, you aren't a monster to me."

Mori seemed as though her words did not stick yet. She peered away; eyes glazed over.

"I understand why you would see me as one. My mother was a heartless monster, I believed as I matured, I would never be like her, but my sister's death altered that principle I once had."

"Do heartless people love?"

Mori was silent, though she knew the answer.

"No, they do not. The heartless have no hearts to love with."

"Then answer this; Do you feel love, Crow?"

The breath left her lungs, Arcane's words replaying in their minds. Her touch was exhilarating, her body on fire at the simplest of touches, her heart hammered every time Arcane spared a glance in her direction. No matter how little, how weak, how ugly she found herself; Arcane found her eerily beautiful, her movement and mannerisms delicate, her authority powerful. She was perceived as lovelier in Arcane's eyes, and Mori admired that the woman did not see her as how her mother once did.

It made Mori feel as though for once in her sorry life, she was good enough for someone.

"I thought I loved you," Mori whispered the words out loud; mimicking what Arcane had said, the taller woman unexpectedly lost her voice, unable to fathom what Mori was going to say next. Her heart hammered in her chest, the sound soft in their ears if they were to listen close enough.

Mori sighed, content.

"I do love someone," she whispered, her eyes trailing Arcane's jaw, till her eyes trailed to meet the plump redness of her lips. "But from what I heard; my love is one-sided." She pulled away from Arcane's touch, watching her face struggle to hide it's features breaking.

Arcane lurched forwards, hands on her shoulders.

"I lied. About it all, I *promise*," she pulled her closer, urgently, observing as Mori resisted, uncertainty clouding her hooded eyes. The two women deterred between destroying the gap and completely widening it.

"I needed to hurt you, but I couldn't hurt you without lying. If I said you were vile and horrid, it would be a lie. If I were to say you were a monster, It would be a lie. You're pretty and compassionate; you have no evil or monstrousness in you."

"You saw me kill those Hunters!" Crow snapped, tears welled in her eyes, she was beyond exhausted- swaying as she stepped close. "Some were merely teenagers, my fury got the better of me, and now those boys are dead."

"They don't have remorse for us, Crow. You are no monster because you are remorseful," Arcane shoved her pointer finger into where her heart sat in her chest. "But them? They do not care who they kill, *they* are monsters."

"I just feel so horrible, I see their faces in my mind."

THE TRIPLE MOON | 189

"They helped kill Vera, Mori," At the name, Mori's face slackened, pain in her eyes as she blinked them away. "Do you think they had mercy assisting the death of a child?"

They stared at each other, silent.

"You care too much about how I feel," She muttered beneath her breath. "Makes my insides tingle."

Arcane's face broke in a beam and couldn't hold back her urges as she peered to those lips, imagining the intimacy of the two if only she were to take that one step closer, and close the gap that is stopping them from falling completely in love.

She reeled forwards, hand gripping Mori's collar, pulling her downwards in a bid to kiss. Her other hand gripped her waist, pulling her flush against her so they moulded into one another sensually, hip bones jutting and clashing.

The shorter girl's lips brushed Arcane's as she whispered.

"I was beginning to get impatient if you didn't kiss me any sooner."

She pressed her lips to Arcane's plump ones, understood the way she responded- a breath of shock, a second of faltering before she was kissing the woman back fervently.

Arcane's breath paused, her entire body froze at the caress of Mori's body against hers. The gears shattering in her head, her fingers dragging and gripped Mori's body, every inch of her, from her shoulders to her chest before she was grasping her hips and pulling her flush against her own body eagerly.

Arcane combusted at her touch, her lips dissolving the room around them- her lips chaste yet hungry all at once. She tasted metal and citrus, and with her lips moulding with hers- Arcane realized she had been starved from her touch for too long, from any contact in a long time. Her entire body buzzed, screaming to pull her closer as her nails dug into her hips, conscious of the woman's wound.

She could live off the taste of her for the rest of her life if she wanted to.

Mori's touch was like ecstasy as her fingers traced down the front of her blouse, and where it ended at her waist, her hands caressing the skin beneath her clothes. Her cold fingers alluding goosebumps along the skin, making her breath hitch at the cool, sensual touch that would not deter along her stomach.

Arcane pulled away for breath, observing the swollenness of Mori's lips, and the way the colour had come back into her cheeks, her crescent shaped eyes glistening as they peered up at her.

"That was nothing like I imagined." Arcane whispered beneath her breath, the pad of her thumb tracing her lips.

"I didn't impress you?"

"You do more than impress me."

Mori's breath caught in her throat.

"I never truly expected my emotions to be reprocessed by anyone."

Arcane's heart panged in dread.

Did she truly think of herself so low?

Arcane pulled Mori into her, and with a chaste kiss on the lips, the taller woman led her delicately onto the bed. She pulled herself away, disappearing into the bathroom to grab Mori's first aid kit before reappearing and sitting herself kneeling by the injured girl.

Mori peered down through downcast eyes, hazy and stunned as she watched with hawk-like eyes as Arcane began to clean the cuts along her legs, fanning her fingers along the bruises of her knees.

"When did you realise you liked me?" Mori mumbled sensually, observing as the woman began to wipe the alcohol wipes along her cuts. Mori did not flinch- her mind and soul consumed with one person and one person only as her fingers caressed down her legs as she cleaned.

Mori admired the way her long brunette hair framed her tan face, her jawline sharp- her wide eyes narrowed in concentration, voice and throat shaken at the mere thought of discomforting the wounded woman sitting above her.

Arcane tried not to peer to her thighs, or the way her skirt rode up, the cuts and bruises from being thrown into objects clear across her body, a cut of an arrow she merely missed sat stretched along her thigh, her skirt unable to cover it.

Arcane took a sharp breath, peering away.

"When I fell from that balcony, and you saved me despite never having met me before."

Mori furrowed her brows. "Truly?"

She shrugged. "Your touch was like electricity, I thought I was truly going to die that night," Arcane whispered, peering upwards through long lashes to meet Mori's intrigued face, the way her lips pursed- eyebrows furrowed. "But then you appeared, and you held me- caught me before I lost my life."

Mori gulped. "You only felt my body, you never saw me aside from a cloud of black fog."

"I realised I was dependant of you then, but when I truly realised you meant something to me more than any typical, ordinary person? It was when you forced Nipuna and I to leave you in that Forest, I was so terrified you would die, and It wasn't just because you are my Superior, it was because I had feelings for you."

Mori winced, Arcane was unsure if it was from her words, or from the way Arcane pressed the alcohol into the cut on her elbow before pulling away.

"Sorry-"

"No, no. It's fine."

Arcane stood, she gazed at the wound by Mori's waist, covered in blood, hidden away by her blouse and coat.

"We'll have to clean that, it'll need stitches."

Mori blinked, not processing what Arcane was implying.

"I need you to strip your clothes."

Mori jolted, and after a long silence of staring at one another, the woman broke the silence. "Oh, yes." She removed her coat, and unbuttoned her blood covered blouse. Her hands shook delicately.

The black-haired woman watched through hooded lids, exhaustion clear in those inky eyes, the way she could barely hold herself up on her elbows, onyx hair framing her face, clouding her vision.

Arcane proceeded to gently push the woman onto her back, her voice a soothing murmur against the sound of ruffling clothes, and the hoarse breathing of the half conscious woman as the adrenaline escaped her.

JESSE PIPER

"Try to stay awake a little longer," Arcane panicked. She knew how to stitch a wound, how to clean it, but she had no clue how to tell whether the arrows were poisonous, nor if she had any signs of a concussion. She needed to be cautious.

"Talk to me then," Mori whispered, staring to the ceiling as Arcane's fingers caressed her blood covered stomach, wiping the dried blood as delicately as she could from the wound. Mori winced, face averting before rolling back into that neutral stare.

"Of what?"

"Of you," Mori muttered. "You know, although I know your family name- you never truly told me about your family."

"It seems you know more than me, though." Arcane scoffed. Lips puckered into a strange scowl that Mori observed in a trance. An almost invisible raise of the corners of her blood-stained mouth.

"Please?"

Arcane relaxed as she wiped the alcohol, observing the way the woman's muscles tensed at her touch, quivered as the alcohol stung the wound.

"There were three of us, blood Sisters. Lan was the oldest, Aldora was the middle sister. Lan would've been twenty-seven next year, Aldora would've been twenty. They were always good to me; Lan was very musical- she enjoyed playing the piano."

There was a solemnness, sweetly pressed into each word.

"And Aldora?"

Her name hurt to be heard, but there was a tenderness in Mori's words that softened the agony.

"She was love obsessed," Arcane chuckled pensively, attention caught between stitching and the memories of Aldora's vigorous simper. "She used to write letters to this girl who lived in one of the villages not far from our home. It was quite romantic, but she was only human- and Aldora was a Witch in hiding."

"A forbidden love." Mori whispered.

Arcane nodded solemnly.

"I wish they could have run away somewhere, before the Hunter's found us."

"Unfortunately, a Witch cannot run from their demons for eternity." Mori tried to sit herself up after the stitches were completed, she groaned- but pushed through the pain to glance eye to eye with Arcane. A thrill pulsed through her veins, running down her spine.

She observed the way Arcane's eyes remained downcast, a lack of a smile on her lips.

Mori's fingers caressed her chin, lifting her face up to observe her dark brown eyes in a greater light. She found herself blinded by the beauty of those eyes, the way they softened at her touch.

"You couldn't have changed what happened that night, Arcane."

"You always know how I'm feeling, I don't know whether to love you or hate you for it."

"I'd rather you not hate me again, Arcane."

There was a pinch of regret and guilt that plastered on her face before it gradually dissipated as she pressed her lips to Mori's, a shiver running down her spine. She knew if she kept kissing her, allowing her hands to trail to the mess of her short hair, to caress her skin- she would not be able to stop either of them. She breathed into the kiss, Mori's name rolling off her tongue.

Her kiss was a form of an apology, an apology she had begged one hundred times.

"We cannot do this forever." Mori whispered with lips a breath away, her blood-stained fingers hooking a loose strand of hair away from her face, her touch ignited within Arcane. It was as though her touch was a cure, therapy for all the anguish she had succumbed to.

"Thank you," she whispered before standing herself up. "Do you need me to do anything else?"

"Yes."

Arcane waited, observing the swift second smile on Mori's lips.

"Lay with me."

In a blink of an eye, Arcane's body was pushed onto the bed by a magical force, and Mori had rolled her onto her side, swiping her finger along her skin, outlining the sharpness of her jaw and the plumpness of her swollen lips.

"Spring will get suspicious," Arcane muttered, curling into the warmth of the Mistresses' tired body. Mori pulled her close, her hand firm on her waist as her eyes drooped, breath soft as she mumbled.

"No, she won't."

There, Arcane dozed off in the warmth of Mori's embrace.

14

Porta Mortis

"I thought we would all be dead at this point," Ohno had muttered over the book cupped in her hands, circular glasses dipping off her nose. Arcane couldn't help the shiver that passed through her, the drilling of sobs in her mind, the memories of those bodies- keeping her awake at night.

She too thought everyone should have been dead by now, but she did not want to admit that.

A week had passed.

It was a whole week without a single death.

Every morning since the night she saw Mori's memory, she could not sleep. Her mind was clouded with conflict, the image of an army coming to kill them all. There was no comfort, not even coming from Mori, who had quietly and privately stated she would be working tirelessly to ensure that every level of protection was implemented.

Arcane would try to visit Mori, it was rare anyone could find her.

Arcane knew Nipuna had knowledge on where the woman was, but she had strictly stated her work could not be deterred, and that her application of magic onto the Haven would only alter how Mori acts.

196 | JESSE PIPER

"She's consumed with change," Nipuna sneered. *"She isn't the same right now; she hasn't slept in days. If I cannot make her sleep, neither can you. She's a Mistress, not a kid, not anymore."*

She had said it with a scowl, hands crossed indignantly over her chest; but Arcane could see through the grump's facade, those panicked eyes, she was restless- she despised not being able to help what was occurring. The more Mori worked on protecting the haven, strengthening the barriers, and incantations- the more sleepless she was becoming, the more drained she was.

This wasn't the only panic that was inducing her mind.

On the third day from whence they last kissed, Ohno had argued that they needed to evacuate.

Though Arcane knew better than that, and it seemed Spring agreed to.

Where would they go?

Everyone wanted them dead.

"To another island, we take a boat." She had chimed. Though the more she tried to strategies this plan, Arcane realised Ohno was losing her calm, losing her composure. It was not like her, not like her at all.

It petrified her.

She tried to distract herself with study, implementing her studies into her daily life. She turned to Ohno for advice as she practiced.

Though it seemed the closer the Hunters came, the less organised Ohno was in concealing her posture.

Arcane peered up from her reading on Necromancy- the imagery of the pages making her skin crawl, her mind breaking with strange abhorrent images. She was sick of the pages, overwhelmed by the words- but at least she was learning, slowly.

Her eyes caught Spring, who was attentively sipping her green tea before scanning her eyes to Ohno, who could similarly not concentrate on her reading- and sullenly slammed the book shut.

"Again, we could be doing more useful activities."

"Like?" Spring muttered as her nose breathed the scent of an ocean breeze. The heat softened her lips as she sipped from the teacup. She had been quieter than usual, it rubbed off on them all.

"Like patrolling the forest, giving Mori some support."

Arcane snapped her book shut. Her name created a thrill through her, she missed her comfort. She had visited Mori's room every single night, only one night there was a note- offering an apology, but still no Mori.

It's like Mori telling Arcane to stay with her as they slept was a way to make Arcane later forgive her for her lack of presence.

"Do you not remember what happened to Miu? To Vera? To all the girls they've found it the forest?"

Her name hurt to speak, a pang of gunfire going off within Arcane's body.

Ohno sighed, her voice cracking. "I…. That was a pathetic idea."

"What's going on with you, Ohno?" Arcane muttered, leaning closer in her chair, fingers caressing her own comfortingly. She feared the girl would snap her hands away like usual, but she allowed Arcane to have that single touch of comfort at their fingertips.

Spring cleared her throat.

"Usually you're quite composed." She whispered, a hand attentively holding onto her friend's shoulder.

"I cannot stay composed, not anymore."

Arcane furrowed her brows, listening.

"I've been dreaming of Sora every night, there's no comfort from knowing she's in that room- unprotected and so vulnerable."

So, it was Sora that was clouding her mind.

Arcane cleared her throat. "She hasn't recovered yet?"

"Her soul is still trapped somewhere, she hasn't reawakened. I tried to visit, but I couldn't undo the ward on the door," Ohno composed herself as Spring's hand fell away. She stood, grabbing her things. "I want you to help me, both of you."

Spring's eyes bulged out of her sockets, her hands almost knocking her tea across the library table they shared.

"Have you been talking to Takanashi?" Spring gasped. "Why would you break a ward?"

"Because I want to check on her, I have a bad feeling."

"If we break the ward, we are risking our positions here," Spring gushed as the two girls trailed the woman out of the library. The blonde's feet struggled to catch up as she huffed. "Imagine what Mistress Mori will say when she finds out we broke one of her wards!"

She was right, of course.

"Isn't Nipuna with Sora?"

Ohno peered over her shoulder at Arcane, her eyes brightened.

"I may be a little bit unorganized, but that does not mean I did not priorly arrange our plan."

"Our plan," Spring huffed, she peered up to Arcane, hands gripping her bicep and pulling close to her face to whisper. "I don't like this, Arcane."

"We are just checking on her, listen- There's a curfew, everyone will be in their rooms by now." Arcane tried to tell herself that, she realised she tried to see past the faults to make herself feel like panicked over the fact she was going against Mori's wishes to appease Ohno's nightmares.

She knew how it felt, though. The sleeplessness, the irrational fear of death as you sleep- the want to stay awake forever to avoid the demons within their dreams. Arcane knew it too well, to some extent- she wanted to help Ohno.

Perhaps visiting will silence the fears Ohno had.

Perhaps it would silence all their fears.

Spring only huffed, playing with the red bow on Arcane's wrist, smiling fondly as they halted by a corner, a domino effect occurring as Ohno stilled, Arcane and Spring colliding into each other.

It makes sense what Ohno's plan was.

Down the hall, Nipuna and Ito were in a heated argument, Ito's voice a croaked arrangement of insults as Nipuna stood by the entrance of Sora's isolated room, silent.

The vision made a smile crack on Arcane's face. Ito was trying so hard to make the woman crack, shatter, and break- but it seemed Nipuna was less than bothered by her presence, rather intrigued as she stood as a bodyguard in front of the door.

The girls hid behind the corner, waiting and listening.

"I asked a simple question," Ito blabbered on, stomping, and pointing aggressively. "If you're so incompetent to answer it then you're useless when it comes to guarding this bloody door."

Nipuna sighed, she seemed less than offended.

"I have every capability to answer your question, but I do not want to."

Ito groaned. "You're a proxy grub-fucking toe bag, you know that?"

Nipuna blanked, taken aback.

"A what?"

"A *PROXY GRUB FUCKING TOE- BAG.*" Ito's words slowly wailed; she placed every ounce of emphasis in each word. Arcane peered at Spring, who was bright red, looking more panicked for Nipuna's reaction than for the safety of Ito's life.

Nipuna sighed, exaggerated as she slowly undid her protective posture against the door. She peered down at Ito, scrutinizing.

"Mori was right."

Ito halted at the words.

"What?"

Nipuna was intelligent enough to know what screws to pull to destroy the structure, it seemed. A winning chuckle left her lips, confidently raising her lips into a sneering smile. She cocked her head to the side, menacingly like Ito would do, but this time Ito was abruptly not in the menacing mood.

"Oh, never mind," Nipuna edged closer, their heeled boots touched as she had to crane her long neck down to stare at Ito. "You just aren't worth the oxygen."

Ito sneered.

"And you are?"

Nipuna rolled her eyes.

"Why are you here?"

"Where is Mori!"

Nipuna scoffed. "You think I'll tell you after you called me a proxy grub fucking toe-bag?"

"Yes!"

Ohno peered to Arcane under her breath.

"Perhaps my plan fell through."

"Just wait, maybe?" Spring muttered.

Arcane shook her head, eying the two.

"They won't stop, not unless Ito does some damage."

She stood herself up, walked to the door with the scurried and panicked voice of the girls asking what she was doing. She ignored them, observing as the two women stopped their argument, expectantly watching as she stopped beside them.

"You wanted to know where Mori is?"

Ito snapped her head to Arcane, narrowing her eyes threateningly.

"Yes, little dove. Where is she?"

Arcane scoffed. "I heard a rumour that she's been in Nipuna's room."

Nipuna's face twisted into pure horror, and that's when Arcane realised, perhaps she wasn't even lying when she spurted the words-perhaps it was a coincidence Mori was in her room as they spoke. Nipuna immediately relaxed her face, smoothing her blazer.

"That's...Barbaric..."

Ito narrowed her eyes.

"As barbaric as your haircut?"

Nipuna sneered.

"You really did not just judge my hair, not with your mess."

Ito's hair was a mess. It was tattered and messy, half of it had been cut while the other half was left double the length and growing. Her bangs were another story, she had done them herself, and without a mirror.

Ito cackled.

"Fuck you."

"Fuck me?" Nipuna raised a thin eyebrow. "You do wish don't you,"

Arcane gave Ito a look, one Nipuna missed.

It was a secret, silent look that read.

'Do something.'

So, she did.

Ito lightly shoved the taller woman's shoulder, and as soft as it was- Nipuna winded her hand back and smacked her palm against the girl's face. A crack echoed, and Arcane stumbled back in shock.

Ito blinked.

Then, she bared her teeth and lurched onto the towering woman.

She clawed at her, and after a few seconds of Nipuna trying to get the fiend off her, the woman's magic threw Ito's figure to the ground. Ito tumbled, heaved in shock, and clawed at the floor as Nipuna dragged the girl by the legs.

"Watch the door," Nipuna sneered before disappearing down the hall with Ito throwing her hands around, insults spewing from her mouth.\The sound of her wails echoed throughout the halls, and as it silenced- Spring and Ohno caught Arcane's side.

"It took longer than I was expecting."

Spring shrugged at Ohno's words.

"I wasn't expecting it to work at all, if I'm being honest- but can we get a move on please? She'll be coming back if we don't do this quickly." the shorter girls peered to Arcane expectantly.

"What?"

Ohno scoffed, hands on her hips. "You're the only one who knows how to break wards."

Arcane furrowed her brows.

"I do?"

The girl shoved her circular glasses higher on her nose. "Neither of us can do it, so it's you."

Arcane huffed, pressing herself into the door, her palms hot against the deathly chill of the enchanted door. "If we get caught, you take the blame."

202 | JESSE PIPER

Arcane peered away, sight distracted on the door as her psalm dug into the wood, forehead pressed into the cold wooden details. She took a sharp breath, and with a gentler force than what she would usually implement- she hauled the door open, the creaking ricocheting throughout the hall, ringing in the Witches' ears.

Arcane ignored the strange silence of the room, it was eerie, devoid of life- of course. She should've expected death to linger, the stench wafting down her throat, welling her eyes- it hurt to breathe, like death on her doorstep, breathing down her neck menacingly. Too close.

There was a thick fog, misty and pale- depriving of the eyes. It choked down the throat, and as Arcane stumbled through the room, trying to loosen the fog- she realised there were two beds that sat eerie still beside each other.

Her stomach dropped, the dull sensation of dread pulsing through her. As Sora's soon to recover body sat still in her school uniform, a knife wound across her throat- Miu's bed was empty, though neatly placed, neatly preserved.

Arcane observed, ignorant to the quiet- grieving mutters between Spring and Ohno as they stood still, clearly unable to process their friend's dead body.

"She will come back," Arcane muttered. "Don't worry so much."

"It doesn't feel real," Spring whispered. "Despite how frustrating Miu was, Sora was always so sweet to everyone."

"Is, sweet. She won't be dead forever."

"But there's always a 'what if' to everything, Ohno. What if she doesn't come back at all?"

As Ohno began to ramble, the sense of being shocked through the body threw Arcane off, she straightened her figure, sensing it again- pulsing through her, close to her heart. The distant sound of voices occurred down the hall, then it hit her.

The aggressive clicking of heels on the wooden floorboards.

The air was hot now, harder to breathe in.

Mori was always watching.

Another hot pulse of electricity through her.

Oh...No...

Arcane reared back, gripping the two by the wrists.

OH.

NO.

"She's coming for us."

15

Subpoena

They'd been caught.
Expected.

It appears that electric shock pulsing through Arcane was the severity of how furious Mori was, and Arcane wouldn't question her fury- because the woman glowered down at the group as they all sat inelegantly in one of the private lounge rooms.

Arcane couldn't even look her in the eyes, and she could tell from Mori's glare that it only made her madder.

There was a thick silence in the room, the fire crackling in the distance- even though Arcane tried her hardest to ignore it. Through the menacing silence, the towering doors crashed open, Ito flying through them, rolling across the floor before heaving a sigh and lying limp on the rug.

Nipuna sauntered in, heels clicking before the doors slammed shut behind her, she stood by the door, glaring at the Witches beneath her, and the staggering Ito as she tried to seat herself in between Ohno and Arcane.

"Is this all of them?" Mori muttered, she stood rested against one of the tables, arms crossed aggressively over her chest, head dipped down in a terrifying glare that started making Spring tear up from beside them. Arcane peered away, too ashamed as Ito rested back into the chair, resting a long-bandaged arm around Arcane's shoulders.

Ito.

Ito….

You're just making it worse.

Arcane gave Ito a pleading look, but she only smirked in a cunning manner that told Arcane she knew what she was doing, and she was doing it intentionally.

"That's all of them," Nipuna gruffly sneered. *"low lives."*

Ohno gasped, gravely offended. She turned on Nipuna.

"That is the lowest of blows, Nipuna."

"You are a low blow," She peered down at them, as though they were the dust particles by her feet. "all of you."

Ohno's face twisted into fury, something that was quite extraordinary. She went to spit back, but Mori's face told the crowd there was no opposing her as she sneered, hand raised in warning.

"Silence."

The group quietened, aside from Spring wiping an anxious tear from her cheek- her chest heaving enough that Arcane could pick up on it from three seats away. Arcane observed the way her eyes would flicker to Nipuna, guilt clear in those wide blue eyes.

"What you four have done tonight has completely broken my trust and reliance on you. Against my orders, you broke my ward, disrupted Sora, and prompted a fist fight." Her voice echoed with vehement, eyes wide with a fire for carnage.

Quite frankly, the Mistresses switch from her usual deadpan expressions caused the girls to internally panic. Ohno couldn't fathom thew woman's ability to alter her face so swiftly.

Arcane heart split in two, had she realised what she truly would've done, she would not have helped them at all.

"I expected more from all of you," There was a stab in those words, as cold as ice. "I've been working tirelessly to ensure you are all safe, to make sure Sora comes back. If you truly cared for her safety, you wouldn't have done what you did."

THE TRIPLE MOON | 207

Ito went to speak, raising a hand- but Arcane's slap was as hard as thunder against her thigh, and the girl held in her cry as she dropped her hand and silenced herself, biting down on her tongue.

"What do you have to say for yourselves?" Mori muttered, she had been pacing, but moved back to recline into the table. Arcane analysed the way all her weight was put onto the side that wasn't injured, her face twisted distastefully, pain flashing in her eyes before it dissipated completely.

Arcane was silent as Ohno started the montage she had priorly planned for the occasion.

"I've been having nightmares," She started, abruptly vulnerable and unable to meet anyone's watchful eyes

"About Sora- they, I…"

She took a sharp breath.

"It's the same nightmare every time."

Arcane furrowed her brows- empathy drifting throughout her, she knew too well. Even now, nothing could stop her nightmares. They always lingered, like black shadows in the corner of her eyes, waiting at her bed for when she slept.

Arcane began watching as Mori's face flattened, devoid of emotion. It was a contradiction to her fury filled facade. She riveted now, waiting.

"It's all of us- Miu is there too…. But…We're in the forest. We're enjoying ourselves; we have a table with tea and food, it's like dinner," Ohno croaked, taking a breath. "But then there's arrows everywhere, and all I can see is Sora burning alive. Her screams are in my ears. I just…I had to see."

Mori's face slackened.

Ito nudged Arcane, giving her an incredulous look.

"Did she plan that too?" She whispered sensually into Arcane's ear. The taller woman only nudged her away with her elbow, shaking her head.

"Aika Ohno, why did you not address this with either me or Nipuna?"

Her whole name, Ohno winced at it- bitterness in her mouth. It was like being told off by her mother, but only worse.

"I didn't want to bother you..."

Mori huffed beneath her breath, contemplating.

"Spring," she started. She perked up, ringlets bouncing on her round shoulders. "Why did you accompany Ohno?"

"I..."

Silence.

"I don't know. She's my friend, I didn't want her to do something dangerous on her own," She whispered, tears in her eyes. "I'm so sorry Mistress, I'll never do it again."

"Both of you, leave. You too, Ito."

Ito groaned. "But I haven't told you why I did it!"

"If I'm honest, Ito. I don't care why you did it. All you did was agitate Nipuna and start a fist fight, and for that you're on cleaning duty."

Ito cried out dramatically as she was pulled out by Nipuna, slamming the door behind them.

Arcane peered up through the wisps of her brunette hair, caught in her eyes. She watched with a short breath as Mori sauntered to her, a stiffness in her posture as she stood over her, eyes narrowed.

"I cannot believe you." She muttered.

Nipuna crumbled into one of the single chairs, finding the conversation entertaining and Arcane tried to find the sound in her throat to reply. Arcane peered up, having to crane her neck from the lounge divan.

"I can explain."

"Can you?" Mori snapped. "Because I've mentally prepared myself for your excuses."

"Please, Mori-" Her outstretched hand was ignored as Mori pulled away, her back facing her. "Ohno came to me, she was desperate, she couldn't sleep. I felt awful if I didn't help her."

Silence.

"You know who else feels bad? Sora."

"Mori-"

Arcane cut herself off, realising the intimacy of saying her name without such a title added, when no other person had such a privilege aside from few. Her eyes peered at Nipuna, who was watching her with hawk-like eyes, unblinking.

"I don't want to accuse anyone- but there's a 'what if' always in my mind. What if they truly meant to kill Sora?"

Mori shook her head at Arcane's words.

"She's right," Nipuna muttered. "I don't want to agree, but what if Arcane wasn't there? Arcane is our eyes and ears to the people we cannot watch over. Your ability to astral project does not allow you to see everyone all at once."

"Ohno talked about her nightmare, what else did she tell you?" Mori muttered, turning to meet Arcane's observant stare.

"She said it made her uneasy, she panicked about Sora. I assume she thought what happened in her dream is what was going to happen to her. You can fault her for that, she was trying to help."

Nipuna gave Mori a stern look that Arcane could not understand.

"This isn't good." The towering woman muttered as she idly laid across the single chair, legs kicked into the air, her injury subsequently recovered.

"Arcane," Mori muttered. "Ohno came from a large Coven in Ina. They were known to birth Witches with the ability to dream of the future, they could see visions from the future, often muddled but still, they were always precise."

Arcane face paled, she stood- unable to keep herself grounded.

"Why did she not tell you?"

"She was only a child when she came to Venfic Island, she doesn't remember the Coven she was born to at all. She wouldn't know much of her Coven, even with books."

"So, she doesn't know?"

Mori and Nipuna glanced at each other, unsure.

"I think we all can agree to the fact she does not know, but she will have an idea of it." Nipuna cut in.

Mori nodded, unable to look up to meet Arcane's gaze, the lack of affection forced a bridge between them; one that Arcane wanted to break, just to touch her pale skin, just to feel her breath on her cheek.

"Nipuna," Mori cleared her throat, pulling away from Arcane-sauntering to the table, where there was a map. Nipuna dragged herself up, following- Arcane stayed behind, but close enough to see the designs across the table.

Close enough to see Mori's lanky fingers as they pressed across the layout, and the way her back tensed as she moved, her bone and muscle prodding from her white blouse, her head dipped down, absorbed into the material as Nipuna listened intently.

"Get the older girls on patrol, group patrol. Make sure you watch over Ohno, check up to see if she has any more nightmares. Please."

Nipuna nodded. "I'll get Beatrice on patrol down Sora's hall."

Mori nodded; mind caught in the gutter as she watched Nipuna leave.

It only left Arcane standing there, waiting- yearning for Mori's attention. She didn't care if she screamed in her face, or shattered her heart, she just wanted her attention, wanted her to look at her.

Arcane's hand reached out, caressing Mori's waist as she stood behind, waiting patiently for Mori to turn and look at her.

"I waited for you every day."

Mori was silent, hands outstretched over the map, head bowed down. Arcane pulled herself close, a breath away as her hand did not deter from its hold on her waist.

"And I thought of you every passing second," Mori whispered. "But this world is corrupt, and I have succumbed to trying to save it."

Arcane furrowed her brows.

"What are you trying to say?"

Mori took a sharp breath, shoulder's trembling.

"I was going to say we cannot remain intimate," The words shot through Arcane, and she took a broken breath as Mori twisted to meet her gaze, their chests touching as Mori rested against the table. "But I do not think I could survive without you."

Arcane relaxed.

"Don't…do that."

"I wanted to scare you," Mori muttered. "Revenge for going against my orders."

Arcane huffed.

"You make me realise how cruel love can be…"

Though Mori's face lacked emotion, one corner of her lip raised in admiration, eyes twinkling.

"And your persistence to have my attention distracts me from my work. We are even."

Arcane rolled her eyes, unable to stop herself from pecking Mori's forehead affectionately in a bid of goodbye.

"Please, once we leave this room; don't disappear for weeks on end."

"I cannot promise anything my love, you know that."

16

Mors Omnibus

The rain and snow had rolled in, like a blizzard- it was furious and unforgiving. The hail pelted against the bedroom window, leaving Arcane restless and unable to find comfort in her bed. She used to enjoy the cold weather, she used to bask in it, admire it.

Now, the evil of the world only forced her to seek the brightness within the dark alcove. She hated the dim sky, despised the empty halls- the things she found eerily comforting were now a terror to reside in. The lingering fear of death around every corner, she could no longer risk anything.

She rested into her blanket, toes curled as she sat posed by the window, face resting inches away as she observed the way the droplets of rain chased each other down the window, some gradually dissipating while others zoomed by, leaving their counterparts behind to disappear amongst the other droplets of rain.

The sound of rain deafened her senses, her body too exhausted to think, but too awake to sleep.

She peered to Spring, who was delicately curled into her blankets, and Ohno, who had fallen asleep with their glasses still propped on her face. From the dim light of the lantern, Arcane could see the tearstains on her cheeks, eyes painfully swollen as though she had cried herself to sleep, though Arcane was not sure- they had been asleep when she came back.

There was an abundance of empathy that oozed out of Arcane as she watched Ohno flinch in her sleep. She would do it every few minutes, face scrunched. Arcane knew too well, sensed it too well. Nightmares never truly left, even when they stop occurring- your mind never seems to erase them.

Arcane had thought finding comfort in a person would erase the terrors in her dreams, like what would happen in the romance books Aldora would read to her; but she was wrong, love wouldn't end terror, it would only soften the blow.

Ohno rolled, eyes blinking as her cold fingers sleepily tried to remove her glasses from her face. She looked worse for wear, peering up and trying to see the face in the dim light.

"Arcane?" Her voice was a chaste whisper against the rain pelting against the window.

"It's only me," was her reply.

Ohno relaxed her shoulders, yawning.

"I thought you were death itself," she tried to make humour of it as she rolled onto her side. Her soft words tried to lull herself back into sleep, too tired to stay awake- her mind half asleep and reeling from her nightmares.

Arcane tried to put a smile on her face, but it came across broken and sympathetic in the dark light- a grim smile that foretold the position they were in.

"No," Arcane huffed, delayed. "Perhaps you should try to go to bed again, I'll be awake in case you have another nightmare."

Ohno was silent for a long second, and Arcane went to turn back to the window when her voice came out in a tone riddled with uncertainty.

"We'll be okay, right?"

No.

Not with an army marching to kill us.

No.

Not with the enemy amongst us.

THE TRIPLE MOON | 215

She didn't want to see that face break; she didn't want the hope to drain from her.

"I'll make sure you're looked after, don't worry."

Ohno nodded into the pillow, glazed over eyes peering up at Arcane. She smiled, exhausted.

"Same goes for you. You're a good friend, you know?"

"You too, Ohno."

Arcane watched Ohno drift off into a dreamland. Her tense muscles are slackening after a long minute of silence and the sound of the storm quieting outside.

A loud echoing scream hit Arcane's ears, dulled by the horrendous rain and hail- but still there. Arcane's blood ran cold, heart hammering in her chest. She tried to peer through the rain and fog outside, but she could not see a single thing. She lurched out from her blanket, waking Ohno in the process as her foot found the girl's calf as she bound out the door and into the tenebrous hallway- it being consumed in darkness and an ominous cold that hit her bones.

Another scream shook the building, and Arcane ignored Ohno's panicked questions as she bound towards the sound, the harrowing, now dulling scream of what seemed to be a child. Arcane sprinted- ignorant of her ankles buckling.

The stench hit her before she had time to recover, her mind being consumed by the images of fire, of death- eyes, dead eyes- screaming, clawing in her eyes.

Arcane cried out, nails digging into her nose as she peered to the fire down the hall- a fire that was destroying the hall. Arcane stood with trembling legs, numbed to the little girls that sprinted past, escaping, to the older girls that were trying to put out the fire with their hydrokinesis, the water bursting from their hands in a bid to halt the fire.

Though as Arcane inched closer, panicked, she realised the fire was only increasing the more the power that was put into it, she watched- blinded by the brightness, her body numb from the memories, unable to do anything as the fire burst- catching on one of the Witches.

216 | JESSE PIPER

Arcane couldn't move as the girl shrivelled to the floor in screams, crying for help- not wanting to die alone.

Her friend faltered, turning to Arcane.

She had recognised her face, familiar amongst the older girls.

"You're Arcane, right?" She shook her shoulders. "What do we do?" She sobbed.

"It-" Arcane pinched herself, trying to drown the fire from her sight. She turned to the girl's black eyes, seeing someone else within them- and trying to calm herself, breathing. "This isn't normal fire, the more magic we put into putting it out, the bigger it will get."

There, that was the Arcane they needed.

Arcane reached out, grabbing a girl just as the fire crackled and reached for her.

"Tell everyone to evacuate. Do not touch the fire, do not try to blow it out."

The girl trembled, but nodded, tears brimmed in her eyes as she grabbed the other girls- relaying the message before leaving Arcane alone to watch as the fire only reached her at a more rapid pace. She stared into its redness, finding a face- imaging furious, gnashing teeth, and red eyes of the devil.

Arcane blinked, ignoring the stabbing agony as her sister's faces appeared in her vision, burnt, and decaying.

She took a solemn look at the dead witch's body before she took off- catching herself checking every room she came across on her way- praying the girls had urged each other awake.

The fire was hot on her heel, the heat echoing down the hall, catching on her, and twisting her mind. She turned down a hall, checking Beatrice's room, then Spring and Ohno's. Nothing. They had left, luckily enough, though now Arcane needed to escape.

Then, it hit her like a ton of bricks to the head.

She had to find Mori.

She didn't care if she was fine, but her heart urged her- screamed for her to.

She sprinted through another corridor, the heat hot on her skin- racing after her. It was almost as though this fire had a mind of its

THE TRIPLE MOON | 217

own, legs of its own. It was not the same fire she had watched burn down her home, it wasn't a hunter's fire. It was a witch's fire, alive and stemming from deep within, a magic connected to the soul, strived from the life of that very witch.

There was hatred, bubbling inside of Arcane- like the pits of hell. It kept her striving, kept her legs pumping- numbed her wretched ankle from snapping under her weight. She turned a corner, the fire rising into the roof, the heat blistering her skin, sweat dripping.

Ito had come out of her room- followed by a cowering Ohno wrapped around her. Shock plastered on their faces- though Ito controlled her fear into a rage that glimmered in that single calculating eye. Arcane grabbed onto her firm hand- pulling her along as the fire reached, urging to touch and devour them. Ito forced herself to keep up with Arcane speed as they tried to manoeuvre through the halls, Ohno gripping her hand in an iron hold though she was stumbling, eyes glazed over and straining to see.

Something was wrong.

Arcane turned around a corner, halting as Ohno bent over disorientated- blood spilling from her mouth as she wretched and hurled everything from inside her and across the wooden floorboards. It wreaked death as it sprayed onto Ito and Arcane's bare feet.

Arcane stumbled back at the sensation, Ito staring- petrified. She pulled Ohno up over her shoulder, trying to get her to run- trying to get her to push on despite the strangeness of her condition. Panic drained the life from Arcane's face, because Ohno was dying, right in front of her- and she could not do a single thing to slow it down as blood spilled from her mouth, skin deathly pale.

The fire only caught them, hot in their faces as it destroyed and consumed their home, the roof began to rumble, pieces falling, the structure collapsing beneath them as it scaled above them. Ito screamed; ears deafened from the cracking of the wood.

"Ohno! Ohno stand up. Stand up four eyes!" Ito pulled, and pulled- but Ohno only heaved more, stench consuming their senses, a deathly look on her face, her lack of glasses showing the redness consuming her eyes. Arcane recovered from the blood that had splattered on her, ignoring the way it sunk into her skin like a poison, lurching forwards and lifting the girl up with a levitating spell she had practiced with objects, but never on a witch.

Ohno's eyes rolled into the back of her head before she passed out, and dread rippled through her senses as she peered to Ito's trembling lips, terror in her eye.

"Come on," Arcane urged, pulling the girls with her, ignoring the hot tears that sprayed down her face, equivalent to the tears in Ito's eyes- brimming, and petrified. She had never truly been so expressive, never truly caring; this change truly showed the predicament.

They would die tonight, Arcane realised.

Truthfully, and if not today; it would be tomorrow.

Ohno's unconscious body trailed behind the sprinting figures, the girl's feet slipping as the blood caught the floorboards, but they continued- even past the mangled and dead bodies as the fire's consumption ate away at the structure. The roof fell, and the girls cried out as it merely missed them.

Arcane shoved Ito as it fell, an echoing crushing occurring as the girls tumbled to the ground- the force making them lose posture. The ceiling fell again, further, and beneath them- the sound of cries occurred. Arcane coughed up vomit by her side- her sight blinded through the smoke consuming their lungs. Ito was on her side, having been winded from the fall. She was trying to use her magic to slow down the speed of the smoke consuming them, but it did nothing- and the smoke blinded them completely from one another.

Arcane lost sense of where Ohno was, but the sound of her body convulsing was hot in her ear, as though it was her who was dying unknowingly as to why. Arcane crawled, through burning fire, her eyes only seeing the grey and red of fire and despair chasing her.

"Ito!" She cried, voice hoarse and silent against the roar of the fire as the building began to cave in around them. She would not stop calling for her, not stop crawling- a hand came into her vision. Moving, clawing towards her.

"Ito!" Arcane screamed, halting herself into Ito's figure, pulling her up despite the agony of her ribs- over one of her shoulders. She

THE TRIPLE MOON | 219

tried to search for Ohno, crying- sobbing, she could no longer hear, no longer sense of presence.

Ito tried to speak- but her tongue was tied as she heaved on the smoke stuck in her lungs.

The structure above them began to rattle.

Ito held tight onto Arcane, hands trembling as she inched her face close; close enough to see the little holes on her cheeks, presumably from piercings, and the intricate detail of the scar down her eye, and the way her lips trembled in a fear Arcane never expected to see in all her lifetime.

"Don't give up," Arcane sneered, heaving- observing how a dash of aching and fear flickered in her eye. "I have an idea- just please, don't give up on me." Arcane's hands fisted around her collar, shaking the shorter girl, panic eating her insides.

"I liked your company, Arcane." Ito whispered.

She had given up as Arcane began to rethink all the spells she had studied, all the times she had watched Mori teleport. Begging herself that she would not end up how her family did, that she would not let her new family down, no matter how many times she may fail.

Arcane ignored her as she channelled her fury into her fists, her eyes clenched tightly shut as she tried to concentrate over the fire raging for them.

"I wish you could've loved me how she loved you," Takanashi Ito whispered. "I liked to pretend I hated you, but I hated the fact you wouldn't love me." Her voice was overcome with the sound of wood snapping, and Arcane's mind reeled- unable to process her words, nor her hands as they trembled on her body. Their bodies twisted, flipped as the girls cried out- their bodies teleporting.

There was a split second as they stared into the blackness of nothing before their bodies were falling.

Nothing shielded them as their bodies collided into the snow that cascaded by the entrance of the haven. Arcane heaved, twisting, vomiting everything she had eaten, and after- she vomited nothing, dry heaves coming from her mouth, her body numbly lying in the snow.

She lurched up, searching- broken eyes unable to tear away as the Haven crumbled, leaving a decaying, cruel victory for their enemy. Arcane sobbed- but no tears descended her cheeks as torment stabbed through her, her ribs screaming for relief as her heart dreaded beating.

Everything.
Everything was lost.
Her friends were dead.
Her family was dead.
The children? The girls?
Dead.

Arcane turned, searching through the soft, drizzle of rain to find Ito stumbling from her place in the snow, knees caving, eyes wide as she searched through the snow for Ohno. Arcane sighed in relief, but a relief that could not silence the pain as she forced herself to stand, panicking to find her friends.

Through the fog, she realised, two bodies cradled in the snow.

Arcane sprinted, finding her knees buckling as she examined the way Nipuna cradled Ohno in her arms.

She dropped into the snow, ignorant of the cold that nipped at her skin, numbed her limbs. She stared, waiting for her chest to rise and deflate with every breath, but nothing happened.

Nipuna's head pulled away from resting against her forehead, there was a thin tear that slipped down her cheek, her eyes narrowed, empty as her wet hair framed her exhausted face. There was a sympathy in the way her eyes faltered from looking at Arcane's panicked features.

"She's gone…." Nipuna whispered, her hands pulling her figure closer into her chest, cradling her into her hold- as though she were a vulnerable piece of porcelain. Her gangling dark hand pressed to her neck, waiting, searching for a pulse.

There was no pulse, her face had paled enough to be blue, her lips tinted in a ghoulish green mingled with her blood, those inventive brown eyes had dissipated- the whiteness consuming them. Arcane crumbled, she couldn't bear to stay any longer, to watch her failures stare back at her, unwavering.

THE TRIPLE MOON | 221

She shouldn't have saved her.

She had promised.

Now, Ohno had one less life to live- and months of death ahead, who knows if she would come back?

Arcane's entire body shook in the snow, her body numbing- but she cared less. Aika Ohno was dead, the girl she had promised to protect, had died. She could've done more, she could've, her life was in her hands, Ohno was depending on her.

"Will she come back?"

Nipuna solemnly peered at Ohno's body, scanning.

"It will take months with the amount of poison in her body."

Poison?

"How- Did you just say poison?"

Nipuna nodded grimly, peering up through narrowed eyes. Her lanky fingers pressed to Ohno's slackened lips.

"There, the green? That isn't normal. I'm sure neither of us have seen a single body with such a colour," she continued. "And her breath smells like chemicals, like...ricin."

Arcane paled.

"She was vomiting blood, when Ito and I found her."

At the name, Arcane perked up- searching for Ito in the fog and finding her standing staunch beside a few of the older girls, some injured, blood stains in the snow, but alive.

Ito watched them from afar, eye unblinking as she stared to where Ohno's body was, but she did not dare come any closer, the blood of the girl on her hands.

"Whoever our enemy is, they're the one that poisoned Ohno."

"And…. Have you seen Mori? Or Sybil? Or Spring."

Nipuna huffed, dreadfully- there was conflict in those dark eyes.

"Mori had grabbed me just as the fire seized my room, but she was gone as soon as she was there. I assumed she panicked, trying to grab everyone as quickly as she could," She peered at the crumbling building, shocked that the fire's heat radiated enough to hit her skin from so far, clouded by the fog and the snow. There was an anxiety that riddled her body, and Arcane began to panic seeing one of the most composed people she knew fall apart.

"Mori could still be in there." Nipuna whispered, trying to control the eruption of her panicked emotions.

"Hey," Arcane reached, grabbing her collar, and forcing her attention to her soot-covered face, tear stained glittering her cheeks, a cut on her lip. "She's the Mistress, remember? She's okay."

Arcane wasn't sure whether she was trying to persuade Nipuna, or herself.

Nipuna nodded, though clearly disbelieving.

"She's more than capable, she was born for this. But...Her mother taught her that Mistresses fight alone, that Mori does not deserve help. She'll push herself over the edge, and she will not ask for help."

She was right.

Of course, she was.

Mori would kill herself because she's too selfless, not because she isn't powerful enough.

"And Sybil? Where is she?"

"She was ordered yesterday to evacuate a portion of the girls from the Haven, the children. She knew it would come, but not so soon. I...I don't know where the group is as of now, so I sent a raven with a note, telling her to not come back."

"Should we take the rest of the girls there?' Arcane waited, and watched as Nipuna shook her head, stubbornly.

"Mori told me we must not run, we must fight." Nipuna observed the way recognition appeared in Arcane's eyes, the way she could no longer hide her fear. "She agreed with what you believed, so I will too. You wanted to fight, so we must."

They sat in the snow, silent- waiting, before she solemnly shook her head.

The sound of an explosion went off, and the girls watched as one of the towers of the Haven crumbled, slamming into one of the others. It was a domino effect, watching as it fell. A dread overcoming Arcane as the ground shook at impact.

She stood, fisting her palms.

THE TRIPLE MOON | 223

The fury was bottling up, her vengeance was near.

"What do you want me to do?"

Nipuna peered up from her spot.

"Find the straggling girls in the forest, kill off what Hunters you find. I will prepare our attack. We are not defending, not anymore."

Finally,

Was all Arcane could think.

Finally, I will wreak havoc.

Finally...

I will kill them all.

Turn the pain into power.

Arcane always believed the key to surviving was to ensure her pain became her source of power. She knew very well she would not last in a world that wanted her dead unless she only fought back. If she had no want for vengeance, no want to overcome her family's demise, no want to destroy her oppressors' lives, she would be dead already.

She knew that.

The day she woke up to men leaning over her in a neighbouring village to where she once lived- if she had not reached into her soul and tried to embody her fury, she would be dead. If she was not furious enough; they would be alive, and her blood would scatter the alleyway. Her emotions and her magic came hand in hand, without it she was nothing.

Her magic controlled her- and without her vengeance for demise from her oppressors, she would be six feet under. She lived off her emotions, thrived from her pain.

She remembers the way she had smiled once their heads had disconnected from their necks, and the blood had splattered onto her skirts.

Now, she still has no remorse.

Her pain makes her powerful enough to kill an army of Hunters.

Her body shifted through the forest, swift enough she was unseen by a passing eye. Her feet picked up pace despite her ankle's protests, and the way her breath heaved through her chest. The further she ran, the more metallic taste was on her tongue, the more her heart hammered in her eyes, pulsing, thrumming with magic.

She teleported again- her stomach flipping and rolling, unable to stop the thrill that shot through her spine as she halted herself behind the enlarged base of a tree, the bark pressed into the back of her thin singlet shirt, the cold nibbling at her bare skin. She curled beside the stump, listening to the voices in the distance.

The snow no longer crunched with her bare feet- an incantation weaved into each step; her breath silent as a white mist parted from her paling lips. Though the cold was getting to her, nestling in her bones, her fury only numbed the pain.

The crunching of boots only closed in as their voices rang out. Their voices were boisterous, mocking- burlesque.

"Did you see the look on her face?" He chuckled, his head dipping back. He was a tall figure, dressed in the black and silver uniform of the Hunters. His crest, the face of a dragon. It was ironic, a creature poached for their magic and their body, almost extinct to humankind- used to represent the works of the Hunters, who did the exact same thing.

"The way she begged," The other figure muttered, all romantic. Arcane observed the way the blood dripped from his fingers, a splatter of blood by his cheek. Arcane blanched, listening to the crude cruelness of their words.

"She would've done anything to see another day. We could've used that to our advantage."

"As if we would be able to do that without being caught, that which is always watching us for Fian."

The words stumped Arcane, she narrowed her eyes, her brows furrowing uncomfortably on her forehead as she stood from her position, finding the courage to show herself.

She stalked out from the darkness, the lantern in one of the Hunter's hands illuminated her figure in the dark. They jolted, the lantern reaching out in his hands to pick up on her dirtied face. The other's breath left his lungs as he struggled to attach the arrow to his crossbow before firing.

Arcane took a sharp breath, slowing time as she swiftly dodged her head enough that the arrow sped past, hitting the tree behind her with an echoing crack that awoke the wildlife amongst them.

"What are your names?"

Arcane's voice was abnormal, like the voice of the wind on the back of their necks. Inhuman, and unsettling to their ears. One threateningly pointed his crossbow, brows knitted.

"You really think we answer to a Witch?"

Arcane cocked her head to the side, the breeze of icy wind like knives on her skin.

"You will," She muttered. Again, she repeated the words, a charm of truth twisting into her words.

One of the men gurgled for a second before composing. "Alba Duncote and Hisa Sato."

"Why does it matter?" One muttered, narrowing his eyes in the direction he wanted his arrow to hit.

The other replied.

"It doesn't, she'll be dead soon enough."

"How ironic," Arcane sneered. "Alba...The name means a new life."

The man gritted his teeth, dropping the lantern and fastening an arrow of oil before lighting it on fire.

"She babbles, the stupid bitch-"

They pulled their arrows, and Arcane took a sharp breath as time slowed. The drizzle of rain was like a snail as it passed, Arcane could see the detail of the rain drops as they went. Her hands outstretched and the movement of the arrows slowed in their pursuit towards killing her.

She lurched forwards, as the images of Mori doing the same thing plastered into her mind. The way her lanky fingers had spread, body balanced- and with every breath, the arrows would hit their victims. She recited the image of Mori's beautiful figure deflecting the arrows, and her own body followed.

With a cry, her muscles tensed with the magic thrumming through her, she forced the arrows back, they twisted and spun before lodging themselves in their head, a thud echoed in her ears, loud and clear as it silenced the forest.

Arcane shook, a breath of relief consuming her as she watched their bodies fall into the snow, a puddle of blood beside them, making the white snow a murky red. Arcane peered down at them, the fury unyielding as she stomped her foot into one of their chests, spitting on their face.

She left them following the trail of their boots in the snow, watching the blood that had come off them with every step. The nauseous scent of death coming closer and closer with each step, like flesh and skin burning down her throat. She struggled not to heave as the pattern of feet in the snow began to dissipate, and she found herself rounding on two still figures in the snow.

Arcane was expecting it, she had known they would be too far gone to save, long ago. Though the way they laid, hopelessly in the snow- the only comfort of their bodies beside one another shook tremors through Arcane's body. No tears fell, she had nothing left to cry with as she inched close, kneeling in the snow beside the two bodies as they held each other.

Their identities were destroyed from the fire that consumed their bodies, just as it did to all the other innocent witches across the island, across the land, across the oceans and kingdoms. Arcane could very well see how they had died- entangled, holding for dear life, and it hurt more than anything else; like someone stabbing her straight in the heart.

She feared she would end up just like them.

Their arms were holding one another, a desperate bid of comfort before their demise.

17

Proelium Incipit

The war was finally upon them. Like the tides closing in, the battle neared.

Nipuna led the astray of women through the folds of trees, she sensed the soldiers as they began their descent into chaos. Their voices distant, breaths short and feet crisp and crunching in the woman's ears. Their commands from afar were like sirens, and despite their want to flee, they could no longer do so. They were far too deep to turn away now, not when they no longer had their Haven, not when victory was near, hot on their tails, thrumming through their veins.

The Witches were haste as they dashed through the forest, magic hot in the air, consuming the wind. The elements were on their side, and the Hunters knew it.

Takanashi stood close beside Nipuna as they trekked through the snow, their magic able to keep them from freezing to death, their ears able to pick up on the slightest of sounds.

"They're close." Ito sneered beneath her breath, long nails prepared to claw at the eyeballs, if need be, her posture was animalistic as she stalked through the trees, her eye only able to see so much. Despite her lack of care for others, she prayed sticking to groups, for her sight was her own disadvantage against the oppressors littering the forest.

Nipuna sighed, mist parting from her thick lips.

"Very close," She muttered, crouching in the snow. The witches trailing behind followed, sinking into the darkness of the night. There was a lack of lanterns, lack of torches of bright magic, because the darkness was their advantage as they slinked through the shadows, observing the movement of the hunters ahead.

"We strike when I say so," Nipuna whispered, and the word carried through the air, hitting the women's ears.

The witches counted till it was countless the quantity of Hunters that appeared through the forest.

Nipuna took a sharp breath, observing the myriad of men carrying fire, ready to torture and kill the innocent.

Nipuna waited patiently, a stiff handheld up to silence the women waiting for her command, their shaky voices and hammering hearts loud in her ears. She feared the decision to fight was a wrongful one, that perhaps she did not deserve to lead the women who urgently looked up to her, but she realised; there was no going back, no choice for her to make.

Her parents had never taught her to fight, but they had taught her to be merciless.

Mori was unaccounted for, and despite the dread she sensed every time she thought of it, she knew as her closest companion, she had to replace the burden Mori carried. She could not dwell on whether she had burned alive in that fire, nor if she had left them all to fend for themselves, leaving on a boat, or if she was the witch that had betrayed them.

Nipuna waited; breath caught in her throat till they passed the mark she had made within her mind. She drew her hand down, and as the Coven swiftly carried through the wind, their enemy only a step away- Nipuna lurched forwards, hand outstretched as a waft of controlled wind swept the men off their feet like a hurricane.

Ito shifted, and with her moving body- sharp, knife-like icicles pierced hunters as their arrows shot to pierce sensitive skin. As quickly as it had begun, bodies were splattering, and the more screams and yells that echoed through the forest, the more soldiers

THE TRIPLE MOON | 229

appeared; only now appearing with fire bottles, and weapons as sharp as death's cunning grin.

The fire tore through them relentlessly, and the more the fire consumed them- cries echoing through the endless forest, the more hunters appeared, bearing gifts for death.

Through relentless fighting, Ito's sharp icicle narrowing missed a towering figure, tall and lean- with bright blue eyes. He was fast, faster than any normal hunter as the battle parted for him. He dodged every single obstacle as Ito stood close beside Nipuna, pretended to fight the figure as he inched closer.

Nipuna's magic spear missed his form, colliding with a hunter behind and impaling him across the snow forest.

The fire was hot on their skin now as it destroyed the life in its path- hot feminine screams in their ears as their Sisters fell- but they did not dare let a soldier live as they died. They made sure to take them down as they died,

It was sweltering, burning as the figure through the fight between magic and weapons, bodies falling in his path as he sauntered close, his two long swords unsheathed and prepared to puncture in his unfaltering hands. It seemed he was prepared as he swung, merely missing Ito's face as she stumbled back, baring her teeth.

"I'm going to cut your tongue." She howled, standing defensively with her fangs bared.

He chuckled, high- careless of the swords clashing beside him, merely missing his idle figure between the snow and fire consuming them all.

"Don't be so petty, little girl. I'll make sure you have no eyes before I kill you."

Nipuna stepped forwards, a cold relentlessness in those narrow eyes.

"What did it cost, doing this?"

He smiled, as cunning as a cat who had seized a mouse as their dinner.

"Witches are the bane of the world's existence."

Ito snarled, before she cackled mercilessly, reaching out as her claws took a swing out of his face.

He dodged it. Twisting his long sword and piercing the girl right through the chest.

Nipuna screamed as fire lit through the sword, consuming her figure.

The world flickered, red in her eyes.

There was a fury, an endless stream of fury that overcame her and ate her alive as she watched, helplessly as the enchanted sword pulled out with a gurgle and a splatter, and Ito's burning body quietly stumbled back before thumping into the snow.

No more sound came from her, a dullness in the air as the fire swarmed around them. Nipuna's eyes welled, her nails digging horribly into her fists, as she stared down at Takanashi Ito's limp body, barely identifiable.

Her eyes stared blankly up to the dark sky, as her body lay unmoving, blood coating the snow she lay upon. Her laughter had diminished, her soul parting from her body as the moonlight glared upon her figure, dead in the snow.

Takanashi Ito was gone.

Nothing but vengeance could bring her back from death.

"I'm going to kill you," Nipuna whispered, a seething, bone crunching fury drilled into her voice- it cracked as she tried to swallow, tried to breathe as she formed a longsword in her hands. Her hands shook, and she realised she would not win as the man only grew in height as he sauntered closer, careless as he stepped over Ito's lifeless body.

He only laughed, a careless- cruel laugh that shook Nipuna's body, made her heart shrivel up inside her as her lungs struggled to breath in the air amongst them. As she peered through him. Fury through her veins, she prayed for a way to win this war, a way to live without fear of death in every corner and every moment of her pathetic life.

She lurched forwards as he did, and as his second sword aimed for her stomach, close- too close within the confinements of slowed time- a black mist burst behind, and through that darkness, was narrow- black eyes, veins allow her cheeks as her teeth bared with fangs of death and carnage.

THE TRIPLE MOON | 231

Nipuna merely dodged the swords as they thumped into the snow, and Nipuna stared- aghast as Mori's lanky hand ripped from inside of him, a splattering loud echo of bones snapping as her hand went through his ribs, a heart held in her hands as his body followed his weapons, falling face first into the snow.

Blood dripped from her hands mercilessly as the heart still pumped in her blood covered hands.

There was a fury in her eyes that matched Nipuna's as she threw the heart into the snow- carelessly as a snarl purred from her lips. Her eyes faltered as Ito's body lay, before she turned- only more furious, her black mist beginning to slip within the mouths and noses of soldiers, choking them ruthlessly as they tried to maim and kill.

Bodies fell like rain, and Nipuna only watched, unable to comprehend the death scattered along the forest as it began to quieten, and only was left were them, and a few scattered, injured Witches who had been able to last within the slaughter.

"I'm sorry," Nipuna sobbed, falling into Mori's hands, crumbling to the floor. "I watched it happen, I couldn't- I didn't-"

Mori's blood covered hands rubbed caressingly along her hair, along her ear and down her back. Hushing her, Mori's voice was a chaste difference to the darkness of her eyes, the blackness rimming her eyes, and the blood covering her hands.

"I'm so proud of you, Nipuna."

They sat there, numb within the snow as bodies littered the ground, fire only simmering with the soft rain that descended upon them, wetting their hair- their clothes becoming drenched.

Nipuna felt the sensation of wetness on her shoulder as tears leaked down Mori's cheeks, her eyes strained at the remains of Takanashi Ito in the snow.

"We cannot stay in embrace forever, Nipu."

Nipu.

She remembers like it was yesterday, when they were children, safe within the confinements of adult women protecting them. Now? They were the protectors for the new generation, barely surviving slaughter.

Crow Mori cupped her best friend's face in her hands.

"I need you to take the remaining witches to where Sybil resides. You know where I trust?"

Nipuna nodded, but there was sheer reluctance in those eyes that made Mori smile, grimly.

"There are more, you must go now."

"I'm not leaving you, not again."

Her voice was hard, stubborn as always as Mori's long fingers brushed through her short boyish hair.

"That's an order, Nipuna. I cannot risk losing you too, losing Takanashi and all the other witches is hard enough."

Her voice broke, and Nipuna realised Mori was not as heartless as she pretended to be.

"Please?" She whispered, begging as her lips trembled. "You know I cannot lose you too."

"And what if I lose you?" Nipuna sneered. "Do you care how I would feel?"

"I'm more than capable of looking after myself."

"No," Nipuna sneered. "You aren't capable, your mother was right, Crow. So, stop playing hero, come with us!"

Mori stared into those narrow brown eyes, waiting- a lack of emotion in those blackened eyes.

Nipuna knew she was waiting for a change of words, perhaps a change of heart- but Nipuna would not give it to her. Mori was both selfish and selfless, so selfless she became selfless. She was careless with her life, careless with Nipuna's already broken heart.

Nipuna would not lose any more Sisters.

Mori could not see the seriousness of parting ways so soon, not even when another battalion was coming as reinforcement, preparing to destroy their lives, destroy their existence and their livelihood.

Nipuna's eyes narrowed as she observed the sympathy in them but could not halt the woman as she dissipated in a black mist.

18

Meminerunt Omnia Amantes

Arcane sat in the snow, dreading the more dead souls she would find, taken away by the moons light shining down upon them, just like it had with her sister- but that did not make it any easier to watch, only more used to the image of the life leaving them. Arcane swallowed the bile in her throat as she stood, unable to peer away from their bodies.

She had not found a single living witch, not yet- at least.

She feared she would find Beatrice's body.

Or Spring's.

Or Crow's.

She feared it enough that she did not stop searching, even when the moon began to disappear, the sun likely to begin rising as time came, even when she had found and killed enough Hunters to bathe in a river of their blood.

Even with every kill, it would not quelch her vengeance, she only yearned for more.

Begging only made it better, but in the end- the pain would not falter inside of her, buried deep.

Her hands were withered, her figure exhausted from having to fight alone for so long.

Arcane listened as the crunching of feet as it echoed further away, she straightened- her shoulders tensing as she inched through the snow, her bare feet covered in blood, her nails stained with red, her muscles strained from the fighting.

She followed the sound of quiet sobbing till she came to a figure, golden blonde hair in warm ringlets, her plump figure curled over in the snow as she sobbed, the sound echoing as Arcane peered to a limp figure in her arms.

"Spring!" She called lurching forwards. Hot ears in her eyes, ready to fall.

Spring wobbled up, pulling away from the body, she wore the school uniform she fell asleep in- covered in blood and dirt, ripped, and decaying from war. Her face was blotched with tears, her blue eyes dark and emptier than usual.

Arcane knew she had those eyes too, but it was an uncommon, fearful look on Spring's face.

Arcane ran to her, engulfing her in her shaking, painful arms. Tears streamed down her cheeks, a throbbing ache echoing throughout her body, and out her mouth as cries wracked her body. The shock had only just set in, the Haven was destroyed, and the little to no leftover girls were being hunted, ruthlessly within the woods they hid in.

Arcane held relentlessly, tight- she didn't want to lose her.

Arcane barely recognised the fact that it took Spring an increasingly longer than usual time to wrap her arms around her figure. Her hands skimmed the girl's ripped blouse but did not dare touch her skin.

"I was so worried I lost you, forever."

Arcane's voice was hoarse, overcome with the nagging sensation that death was close behind them. Spring was, oddly silent, breath shaky. Arcane recognised the choking of her breath in her lungs as she pulled away.

Arcane's eyes faltered to body sprayed out across the snow, assuming it to be one of the Witches, but the more she fluttered her eyes to it, she realised it was not a Witch's body.

"Are you okay? You weren't hurt, were you?" Her voice slowed as she furrowed her eyes, struggling to look away from the dead body. One more masculine the most, and further away- Arcane caught Beatrice's dead body, lulling by a tree, eyes bloodshot and wide.

Arcane tried to breath, trying to distract herself with the detail in Spring's face.

Spring's eyes were glazed over, as though she were holding back tears- though was strong enough to breath them away peacefully. She twisted her lips into a thin line, almost as though she were deliberating something.

"I'm glad you're alive," she muttered, reaching to pull Arcane back into an embrace, but did not pursue it. Her fingers skimmed the skin of Arcane's hands, though they halted before she could hold onto them.

Arcane couldn't comprehend her strange behaviour, the way she feared touching her, feared pulling her into another embrace. It was as though the battle had completely played with her senses; she had perhaps lost her mind to grief.

Arcane leaned to grab her hands, but Spring snapped away as though retaliating.

"Hey…. Are you okay?"

Spring nodded, clearing her throat.

"I'm glad you're alive," she took a sharp controlled breath before she spoke again.

"I don't know how I'd bear seeing someone else kill you."

Arcane furrowed her brows, tongue unable to piece together words.

"What?" she breathed,

Spring took a shuddering breath.

"I'm sorry, Arcane."

"You- what-" Arcane stepped back, bewildered. Her lips parted in a silent breath of question as her fingers shook with adrenaline, her heart hammering within her head, along every inch of her body as she tried to understand what Spring was saying.

"But power must come with sacrifice. I didn't want to kill Beatrice, but she realised it was me, she almost warned you." Her eyes glazed as she peered over her shoulder at Beatrice's dead body.

Arcane couldn't breathe, dreading this was some sort of sick joke.

Spring leapt forwards, a long knife- shining within the light of the rising sun sliced through the air, raised menacingly towards Arcane's body, her blonde curls whipping in front of her face, a deranged look in those innocent blue eyes.

There was a second where time stopped, and Arcane was stunned to a halt.

Her closest companion was the one who had betrayed her.

Spring Lee.

Spring Lee you monster.

You were the rat, the whole time.

I trusted you.

That's when Arcane realised.

It made sense.

The red bows she had gifted to everyone- making them promise to always wear it, the nights she visited Beatrice, the strange disappearances that connected to the greenhouse, the poisonous plants she grew.

Her eyes were downcast bitterly, those sweet lips twisting into a furious and greedy baring of teeth. Her eyes, aimed at Arcane. Though rather than looking her straight in the eyes, her glazed over eyes stared to the place she needed to stab Arcane.

She glared right at Arcane's heart.

The erratic beating that allowed Arcane's body to survive, Arcane could not move as her friend planned to kill her, just like she had with everyone else. Arcane knew she had the magic to stop Spring, but what would living do?

The sense of betrayal was too overpowering above anything else. What was the point in living once the most lovable person became the spawn of evil doings.

Arcane cried out as the knife's tip grazed through her blouse and against her chest, though within a matter of seconds, she was swept across her feet, slammed into the ground as a swirl of black overcame them. A burst of black magic shoved Arcane away- she twisted against the snow ground, knocking into the base of a tree.

She crawled, heaving, and holding her side as she struggled to stand. She was beyond winded as her ribs screamed and her muscles ached, struggling to find the will to stand as her sight was blinded by the black mist cascading over them.

Mori.

Where is Mori?

Through tangled hair, blood, sweat and tears- she observed as Mori dived from where Arcane once stood beside Spring. Though Spring was no longer where she once stood, Mori had thrown Spring across the forest, her body knocked into a towering tree leaving her staggering from the snow, magic wafting in the air as fury glimmered in her bloodthirsty eyes.

Spring lurched for the bloodied knife, picking it up in her quivering hands.

Mori threw herself into Arcane, and as rapidly as she appeared, the two were disorientated and teleported through the black mist of magic till it swept them to an empty clearing through the forest.

The black mist began to subside with the abrupt silence of the night, the forest trees idly singing with the wind as Arcane took a few seconds to breath, she stared to the sky- the eerie colour of the sunrise above.

The ringing in Arcane's ears began to subside, her breathing-relaxed though her heart still hammered against her rib cage.

"You always seem to be there to save the day," Arcane heaved, breath heavy and hoarse= the pain in her ribs did not subside.

"Don't you... *Mori?*" Her head lolled, turning to where Mori had fallen into the snow, though to Arcane's unsettling discovery- Mori was struggling to breath, unresponsive to her words as blood sunk into the snow.

She stumbled up, ignoring the screaming of her limbs and bones as she pulled Mori's curled form into her lap, her fingers shakily brushing away the shaggy hair from her face.

Her breath was more than an *'I'm winded and hurting and exhausted'* it was a *'I'm dying.'*

It was the same breathing her sister made as she died by her side. Dread overcame Arcane.

The brunette's eyes peered down as Mori struggled to breath, through shaky breath and parting lips; blood began to drip from her mouth, slipping down her neck idly as she lay curled in Arcane's warm lap.

"Where are you hurt, Mori?"

The shaky breathing became overwhelming as Arcane began to search Mori's body, her fingers skimming her skin.

"MORI!"

At the overwhelming yell, Mori twisted out of her curl- vividly overcome with agony. She struggled to sit upright, using Arcane's chest as a wall to hold herself up on as she moved her hands from where they pressed into her stomach, a gnashing wound that spilled blood across her blouse.

"Just- just a cut."

"Let me see," Arcane begged, agony clear in her voice as her hands quivered as they held Mori's figure. It was a booming sort of urgency Mori had never heard before, and she peered up through grim eyes to observe the wreck in which was Arcane Amunet.

Those eyes, those damaged and aching eyes.

Mori knew she did not deserve the pain she would soon endure.

She shakily pulled her hands from her stomach, blood instantly exuded from her injury- her hands covered in the thick red substance of blood, it only spread like quickfire, staining her blouse.

There was a second where Mori peered into her hands and realised it was too late.

Arcane quivered.

"No," She sobbed, unable to breathe.

Arcane's voice was hoarse, overcome with grief as Mori's figure began to weaken, using her chest as a crutch as her head nestled into her shoulder, struggling to stop the blood with their shaking hands.

"Hey, it'll be fine- Mistresses would have hundreds of lives, they would have to- they're the most powerful members of the Coven. We can just find you-"

Arcane's voice began to trail off as she observed the sorrow in Crow Mori's inky black eyes.

"I only have one life, Arcane."

Silence.

Her heart shattered, hard- brutally.

Then, like the crackling of lightning hitting the earth, Arcane's hands shoved harder into the wound, tears streaming down her cheeks despite how hard she tried to stop herself from sobbing and quivering at the sight of Mori's form nestled and weak against her.

Everything was crumbling around her.

"We can fix this; I can fix this. I know how to stitch I- I just need-"

"Arcane." Mori whispered.

Mori's hands- weak, and shaky, held onto Arcane, blocking her from trying to stop the blood flow, trying in any way to stop the prevailed death awaiting her lover. Although Mori couldn't bear to see her in such a state, there was nothing that could prevent such a destiny.

"We can no longer restore what has already transpired."

"Why did you do it?" Arcane sobbed. "Why did you have to come and save me? Why could you not just let me die?" Her last words were boisterous, shattering the silence of the forest amongst them. Mori's head began to loll as her body reclined into Arcane, she peered up through emptied eyes- though there was a shimmer of pity as she peered at Arcane.

"There are no limits when it comes to you, I promised myself I would do anything to keep you alive, even if it means killing myself."

Sobs wracked Arcane's body as she pulled Mori close, unable to tear her eyes away.

"Why do you have to be the sacrifice? Why couldn't it have been me?"

Arcane's breath against her face was a cool reminder of the comfort Arcane provided as she rested in her embrace. Arcane's tears began to fall onto Mori's pale face, like raindrops- it soothed Mori's skin.

"I would never let you be the sacrifice; you know that."

"Why didn't you just let me die?" Arcane sobbed.

"I took the risk of death, for you." Mori's voice began to loll, began to quieten- hoarse in her throat as blood began to clog her mouth. Her bloodied fingers rose to cup Arcane's jaw, her fingers skimming the bottom of her lips as it trembled.

"Loving you is killing me," Arcane sneered beneath her breath- faces overcome with a grief that transcended throughout her body like fire. She wasn't just betrayed by Spring Lee; she was betrayed by Mori. "I *cannot* do this without you."

Arcane should be dying, not her.

The pain on Crow Mori's sickly pale face was hard to fathom, blood dripping from her lips like the sand of an hourglass.

"How mournful, We were the right people, at the wrong time."

Arcane shook her head, struggling to speak through the grief, her throat closed, only able to listen to Crow's voice, broken and faint in her ear.

"Death will never reduce the love I have for you. We were the right people, perhaps in another world we will have the right time."

Mori's blinking slowly lulled, her head rolling back without the muscles holding it up. Her heart stilled against Arcane's thumping chest, her heart shattering into millions of pieces she knew she would never be able to rebuild.

The silence was agonizing, like a pin drop within the stairway to death.

Her breathing had ultimately stopped as a teardrop fell upon her cheek.

She was dead.

She was dead.

Arcane screamed, hoarse- filled with hatred.

"I'm going to kill you, Spring Lee."

19

Dolor In Ira

"I'm going to kill you, Arcane Amunet."

Spring's voice was calloused.

Not like herself.

Her face had increasingly paled, eyes wide as she beseeched- urgent and craving victory, but unable to truly fathom the fact she had not been able to kill the one girl she had waited so long to eliminate.

She hadn't won her victory yet, Arcane was one of the people she had promised to grasp in her fingers. The necromancy within the Amunet blood would only strengthen her, and she knew she could not abandon her plans now.

Not even when the Mistress was dead, not even now that Spring could sense Mori's soul, thrumming inside of her. Her black magic had given her a high- an endless elation that overcame Spring, made her see the world in a refined simplicity, and her body colder, more withstanding of carrying the black magic Mori once retained.

Spring smiled cunningly down at her hands, sensing the way her fingers tingle, getting used to the ecstasy of Mori's soul being provided to her.

Spring stood to her full height, her bones cracking and splintering; the length of power within altering her body to a taller, more domineering height. Her fingers lengthened, and she watched in an addicted trance as her nails spread into claws.

She sighed, content.

There was a lack of remorse that came from this game of hide and seek. Once, Spring had wept and sobbed at the bodies she had maimed and burned, their faces etched into her mind as she slept.

But Now?

The souls she devoured, the power she earned removed all sense of human interaction from her. She could not love, could not *feel*. There was barely any sense of regret as she urged herself to stab her enchanted knife through Arcane's heart, nor when she poisoned Ohno with her tea.

Now, it was Arcane's turn.

Her biggest enemy was dead, and now all that was left was the little fiend that trailed her like a lost puppy.

Spring sauntered through the forest, Fian's heart in her hands. It no longer beat, the blood dried in her hands, warm like gloves. Although she lacked remorse, her fury did not falter.

"I knew you and your fruitless army would be useless," Her sneered beneath her breath, squeezing the heart indignantly in her hands as she sauntered through the snow, blood trailing her as she halted to observe the wreckage of what once was her home.

She prayed that Nipuna had withered up, decaying to fire - just as Ohno should've.

She imagined their dead bodies, and a strange sense of content ran through her veins as Takanashi Ito's body had been found earlier through her trek of the battle-ridden forest. No one truly knew how long she had waited for the day to happen when Ito had her last breath.

Spring scowled at the memory of them as children, a twelve-year-old Ito being praised for her magic despite the effects it had on the ten-year-old Spring Lee, the fact that despite Ito's strange existence, she still received more love from the Coven then Spring ever had. She always earned more attention from the Mori family, no matter how hard Sporing tried; she was a lost cause, merely a speck of dust in their eyes.

Not to mention Nipuna, who publicly humiliated her, over and over, rejected her, belittling her, perceiving her as less then. Spring found content at the imagining of Nipuna's dead body, despite once loving her- death was inevitable, and Spring adored dishing it out to her Sisters.

Spring couldn't forget Miu Hino's face from a distance, the way it scrunched up in pain, sobs wracking her body as tears streamed down her face. A face Spring always assumed was emotionless unless tormenting. At least now, Sora would live with her sister, together in death.

Mori's death? It was the most satisfying, an unintended death that left the woman craving for more. Crow Mori's death awoke a darkness crueller than hell inside of Spring, her black magic now thrumming inside her veins. Spring had wished she'd killed the woman long ago, but to kill the woman was like trying to catch smoke in a net.

There was not a single tinge of remorse Spring sensed as she felt her blade run straight through the woman's flesh., hearing her breath catch before she ran away, tail between her legs and into her black smoke.

Aika Ohno was another story, she was one of the less fortunate, less deserving ones of death. Just like Arcane.

Poor, little Arcane.

The only one remaining.

Spring was very aware of the incantation that was silencing Arcane as she sauntered towards the woman, inching closer through the forest, blood covered feet sunken into the snow.

Her eyes burned holes through Springs' back.

It would be ignorant to say Spring could not feel her agony and fury radiating off her from so far.

"You underestimate me."

Spring's voice was cold, not what it once was as she peered at Arcane over her shoulder, observing the quivering of her knees, the fisted palms, the blood that covered her body. Crow Mori's blood covered her body, Spring could smell the black magic on her blood, the magic she now had possession of, the previous owner dead, bled out into the snow.

Spring still had not adjusted to the glimmer of Mori's existence within her, nor all the other girls she had killed, within her- distant in her head, felt through her skin, their emotions stammering in the back of her head like sobbing.

Arcane inched closer through the snow, her figure more demeaning with each step, the stench of magic wafted into the air as the wind began to rise, a whiplash against the face as they struggled to stand, the wind was like a hurricane, and Sporing could not stop the tempted smile on her face.

She had waited for a real fight, and at last, it was here.

Her eyes were ablaze in a fury Spring could not fathom, and only snickered at.

"Did you bury her body, then?"

Spring found humour in the way Arcane's lips twisted into a scowl, eyes flickering in pain.

"No," Arcane sneered. "I promised myself I would end you before I let her rest."

Spring stretched her shoulders, the sound of cracked echoing as she stood over Arcane, a wicked smile tipped on her lips. The magic had altered her form, made her bigger, more powerful. A sense of dread hit Arcane, as she tried to process how she could possibly beat what once was her friend, but only now stands as a monster of the peace, a betrayer, a rat of all things.

"She won't ever rest with that mindset," Spring chuckled, high and bright. As though she had not killed hundreds of Witches, her friends, Arcane's lover, The Mistress of their Coven. Spring peered down at Arcane with an avid stare as she swept her hands up, and the roots beneath the ground stretched out, reaching up into the sky and looming overhead, waiting to pounce on Arcane.

Arcane ground her teeth.

"You underestimate me, Spring."

THE TRIPLE MOON | 245

Spring's laughter echoed through the commanding gust of wind, halt and fog beginning to shadow her vision as her hands outstretched maniacally, the roots coming down to strike.

The profound sound of collision and cries echoed through the rumbling clouds, and Spring observed- a sneer painted her lips as a protective abjuration wrapped around Arcane. The hits did not take, and only rebounded with a thump and squeal of the snake like roots.

Arcane used Spring's faltering as an advantage and with every strike of the roots. She began to panic from the amount of power the roots had as they cracked at the protective shield and twisted her hands to make long sharp daggers with the stream of hail slamming down upon them.

Long, human sized daggers were formed from hail, as sharp as a spear as they spliced through roots, impaling them, but unable to completely halt their motives.

Arcane knew where to hit this time.

Her hand outstretched with a cry, and all the swords of hail she had used to fend off the roots whizzed through the air in a split second, too swift to be seen as they aimed to hit Spring's figure.

Spring caught it a second before it hit, she punched the air, and a chunk of the earth took the hit before her body did.

Arcane faltered at the inhumane speed, a speed even a witch could not follow.

She could only try to shield her hands over her face as Spring shoved the piece of earth straight back at her. Arcane heard the crack of the shield shattering before the piece of earth slammed into her, throwing her across the snow, and leaving her numb- unable to fathom where she was exactly as her head spun, her mind reeling, her ribs screaming in agony as she fought to stand herself up. Her hands shook, as a small cry left her lips, she couldn't move, it hurt so much- to breath, to think, to feel.

She knew then that she was doomed.

Her ribs were broken, her sight blurred- head heavy as her muscles quivered from beneath her.

She peered up through wet wisps of hair to find Spring teleporting through a black smoke, standing domineeringly above, her foot shoving down against her back, slamming her body back into the snow, her ribs aching as they cracked, her skin numb from the cold.

Arcane cried out, the fury overwhelming her-seeping through her bones as she watched Spring handle Mori's magic so effortlessly, the magic she had taken, along with the pinch of her soul and the remaining life she took. Crow Mori's murderer stood above, her boot sunk into Arcane's back, and she couldn't take much more of it.

"Just give up, Arcane."

Arcane shook her head as she clenched her teeth against her cheeks, a sting radiating through her mouth as blood oozed in her mouth. She spat into the snow, shoving her weight against Spring's heeled shoes as she tried to stand, pushing her strength against the domineering power above.

"I don't just give up," Arcane heaved, wheezing. "You should know better than to assume I would let you live."

Spring cackled, devoid of any sense of humanity as she twisted her heel into Arcane's back, hearing the crack of ribs, the shivering and clenching of Arcane's face.

"There is no point living anymore, Arcane."

Spring sneered menacingly, and it was a foreign gesture on her sweet face.

"Mori's dead, Ohno is dead, Ito is dead, all those girls are dead, they are never coming back. You have nothing left to live for, Arcane- so why do you still fight?"

Spring's facade mocked a pout, peering down through the heavy gust of wind and hail with puppy dog eyes, ones she had used to her advantage for so very long, without any consequences for her actions.

Arcane grinded her teeth, struggling to fight the weight on top of her, pain searing through every inch of her body, making her see black dots, her body beginning to numb against the red snow.

"You-" she heaved blood, choking. "-Underestimate me."

"Do I?" Spring cackled. "- As I can see, you're dying here, underneath me. You're losing, Arcane."

Silence as a sword made of raging fire shifted in her hands, it was negligent to the hail peltering, to the thunderous clouds looming above. The fire only brightened with each rain drop that hit it, and Arcane's death loomed over her.

"Just let me kill you."

She didn't want to die.

The wind began to sweep so hard, Spring faltered, her body unexpected of the speed the wind spewed. She furrowed her brows as a crackling of thunder echoed across the Island like a calling, a grim ringing of the bell that calls upon midnight.

Spring observed the way Arcane's eyes rolled to the back of her head, blood dripping menacingly from her nose. With Spring's faltering, Arcane used the last of her strength to shove against her enemy. She faltered back, sword raised as Arcane remained struggling to stand, though now- her body's power was not directed within itself but controlling the skies.

Lighting struck the ground, the earth and snow exploded with an echo, blinding Spring- she faltered, the fire ablaze in her hands, yet she was negligent to such a danger as her teeth grinded, she blinked-struggling to find Arcane through the fog and lightning that began to throw itself against the ground, merely missing each time.

Spring whipped around in an arising of panic, conscious of the distant sound of feet sinking through snow as Arcane was now missing from her bloodied position on the floor. The weather began to blind, Spring's threats and curses disappearing through the sound deafening to the ears.

"Give up Arcane! You cannot kill me, not now!"

The voice was inhuman, a whisper in Arcane's ears as she hid within the whiteness of the blizzard that she forced down upon Spring. Her emotions began to rain from her the more she put her energy into her magic, the agony, thumping in her heart dulling- Mori's will to live still forced her to remain alive, instead of meeting her in death.

Her fingers numbed, breath catching as she watched the fire brighten through the blizzard, and Spring's figure came to view, sauntering in her direction, the wind parting for her with each step, her ringlets blown out into a mess of crimped hair, her face twisted into a dark scowl, her eyes peering in an unforgiving promise of death with each step.

"Why?" Arcane whispered.

"Why!" Spring cackled. "Power! I have hundreds of lives, magic beyond anyone's control. I will kill you, and it will be the most painful demise I have given."

"More painful than Vera? The nine-year-old girl you burned to death?"

Arcane's voice oozed with a fury that only empowered the storm's strength.

Arcane struggled to see the guilt in her blue eyes.

There was none as she clenched her teeth, stomping closer.

Arcane's eyes rolled back, her entire body numbing as she surged her magic energy into the lightning that struck from the war of clouds above. Spring shoved a root to block the attack, but the lightning was so overpowering it struck through the roots, hitting her, and throwing her back across the snow, she shook before screaming, struggling to stand as blood oozed from her face.

"The next one will kill you."

"It will do no such thing," Spring bared her teeth, standing on quivering legs. She spat the blood from her mouth, cracking her shoulders perilously.

Arcane sneered. Her legs ached; her body overcome with a sense of exhaustion.

She was sick and tired of listening.

Arcane controlled her fury- bottling it inside of her quivering body, her companions pained faces in her vision as she struck an enlarged, abnormal lightning from the sky. It crackled the air, blinding her vision completely as her ears rang like bells, hot in her mind- unable to process the crack of lightning that snapped the earth in two.

The ground shook, earth falling- Arcane lurched back, too exhausted to fight as she stumbled into the snow. The wind caught her, resting her gently beside the large fissure that began to destroy the ground, taking anything in its path.

Arcane observed through blinded- blurred eyes as Spring barely saved herself from the endless pit of death that Arcane had created. She stumbled, catching herself on the edge and regaining herself on the other side of the humongous crack in the ground.

The echoing sound of screams were in her ears, she tried to calm herself- her mind playing tricks on her as she twisted to peer down the endless crack of blackness, her body almost tumbling off the side, too numbed to do anything as she lay limp, peering down.

She did not see blackness.

Deep within the fissure she had created was a world of turmoil, death at every wake, screaming, sobbing- and howls of despair echoed from down the endless hole. She knew she was hallucinating; the fire distantly looming, the towers and kingdoms, black like coal within the fire. There was a whole world of death beneath her, her mind was in a complete fright, and Arcane was battling to establish between reality and fiction. Arcane's stomach twisted, her mind reeling at the strangeness her mind was providing her with.

Arcane peer up through the fog and storm to find Spring on the other side of the fissure. There was a large distance keeping them apart now, it would give Arcane time to recover, Spring's deathly glare, and sauntering progress only showing the less time she had with each passing second as the woman crept closer and closer.

Spring rose from the ground like death itself, a fury beseeching her as the wind began to follow her command. She began to levitate, using the wind as steppingstones as she began to cross the fissure. With each step, her laughter was louder in Arcane's ears.

She couldn't find the muscles to run as she lay, watching and waiting as the woman she once trusted crossed the fissure through thin air, prepared to end her life, end her suffering with each step. She had a menacing smile upon her tinted lips as a sword of fire appeared by her side.

Arcane knew the elements were of bias to her, she had recognised it ever since the lightning directly struck her enemy, ever since it supported her in creating the fissure across the earth, taking her energy and emotions as compensation.

"I'll make your life easier, Arcane."

Arcane called upon the wind with a cry, her arm barely outstretched as the storm fell from the blonde woman's grasp. The brunette watched as Spring cried out, barely catching the other side of the fissure as her hand pulled Arcane down with her.

Arcane's entire body flipped, her hands catching the edge just in time before they both fell through the fracture of the earth.

"What have you done?" Spring shrieked.

Arcane gazed below them, entire body aching, her wrist almost snapping at the power she had to hold on so well and for so long. Spring hung unwilling to let go of the girl's wrist as she dangled below, hands clammy as she held for dear life.

She would die, but she would bring Arcane down with her.

Arcane did not reply, which only fuelled Spring's panic as she peered down below.

Arcane assumed it was a hallucination, magic- exhaustion, trauma and grief playing with her mind. Though she was wrong, the fear on Spring's face told her otherwise, the fire, the kingdom and screams below were real.

"You opened up the portal to death. You'll kill us both."

Arcane didn't care, not anymore.

Arcane grinned through a blood-stained face, her teeth caked in blood.

Her fury and grief had opened the portal to death, and Arcane only needed to do one little move to end her enemy's life.

"I thought you said you cannot die?"

Spring's nails dug into Arcane's wrists as she bared her teeth.

"There is something worse than death, Arcane- and you invited it to us."

"Not to us," Arcane whispered. She smirked, menacingly. "To You."

Arcane kicked her foot as hard as she could into Spring's bloodied face, and she screamed at the crack of her nose. The blonde Witch choked on her blood as she tried to breath, too exhausted, too disoriented to catch herself with her magic as she lost her clawing grip on Arcane, falling down the hole with a hazy, quivering scream that echoed through the fissure and into Arcane's ears.

There was no regret as Arcane grinned, watching her body disappear completely.

20

Cum Laude

Nipuna had found Arcane's body a week later.

She was neither dead nor alive once Nipuna had discovered her, nestled into herself- hypothermic in the snow, with crows lingering, waiting to eat a carcass.

It took six months for Arcane's soul to come back to her body. For those gruelling, empty months of sitting in a void blackness- mind distantly replaying the memories, Arcane's body remained hidden in the abandoned village across the island, hidden within an overgrown forest.

"Now I only have seven lives, and no will to live." She sneered, kicking a fallen piece of stone from the remains of the palace amongst them. She ignored the stinging in her feet, the way her eyes drooped from exhaustion as the group searched for the remains of their Sisters. She would push on, despite how tired she was.

There was a solemn grimness in the air, stifling and hard to ignore with each body in the rumble, or heirloom or child's toy or belonging they would find. With every discovery, was only more sorrow.

Arcane observed as Nipuna lifted a frame from the rubble, she dusted it off- gazed at it before breaking away to look at Arcane with an intrigued stare. Her hair had grown out slightly, dead ends sticking out, her eyes as usual, were grazed in disinterest unless prompted.

She was thinner than usual, though- they all were.

"We'll find a way out of this."

Arcane gulped.

"I cannot see us surviving at that village for much longer, Nipuna."

She bristled slightly, before shrugging.

"We must bury the bodies before we leave."

That at least, was a mutual agreement.

Though the idea of burying her loved ones forced a strange discomfort to overwhelm her. She did not admit it, although she didn't need to, Nipuna translated silence as though it were a language. She was a skilled Empath, she knew people better then they knew themselves, most of the time.

"It's a strange, empty feeling. Though it must be done."

Arcane was silent as she watched Nipuna peer back at the frame, her eyes softening the longer she stared.

"What is that?"

Arcane walked till she leaned around Nipuna's towering figure, catching the image.

It was a photo of the Coven, her Sisters.

"Mori gifted Sybil a picture frame that was enchanted," She began, her finger caressed a face, she leaned closer- and Nipuna allowed her to have a closer look as she continued in a soft mumble. "It would add Sisters Sybil loved, it would change and alter every year."

"Do you see?" Nipuna muttered. "Miu and Sora." They stood side by side at the back of the photo, hand in hand. Miu had a coerced smile, Sora was curled into her sister- a genuine smile on her face. "It makes it accurate to who we are, Sora always forced Miu to smile in pictures."

Nipuna moved her finger, pressing it to the blonde woman, who sat on the corner on a chair, further away from the others. "Spring used to be in the middle, beside Ohno," Nipuna's lips pulled into a scowl, a hateful one. "We all loved her, and the frame can tell what she has done, she is fading away from Sybil's loving memory."

Arcane wished she was in the picture, hoped perhaps Sybil adored her as much as she longed for, cherished her as much as she needed and craved. Mori had left her heart shattered, she just wanted to know she was still loved, even if it wasn't Crow Mori who said it.

Arcane peered closer at the picture; Ohno stood beside Nipuna and Sybil, her fingers caught sliding her glasses up her nose, as Nipuna stood still, arms crossed and disinterested. Sybil had a gleefully gum-less smile, her hands curled around her skirt, long hair caught in her eyes.

Arcane couldn't hold back the forlorn raise of her lips, eyes welling as at the front of the frame sat three figures. First was herself, a strange look in her eyes, thin lipped, but her chair had sat earnestly close to Mori, and if Arcane looked close enough, her pinkie touched Mori's thigh in the picture.

Mori sat close beside her, and although she did not smile, there was a twinkle of pride in her eyes as Takanashi Ito sat beside her right. sunk into her chair. She had a wicked- Ito like smirk on her lips, her skirt awkwardly raised high across her thighs, blouse unbuttoned too many.

Arcane sighed, excruciatingly.

"She'll want this back."

Nipuna nodded.

"We all will," There was a grim frown on Nipuna's face as she gently took back the frame.

"I don't know what to do, Arcane. Mori passed this power down to me, but our Sisters will never be satisfied with what I can do, compared to what Crow used to do for us all. I'm not as powerful as she was, not as peaceful, not as gracious or dedicated. I'm hot headed, and I get lazy- while she was always working, she sacrificed sleep for *us*."

"You already have done that for us, Nipuna."

"A few nights of hard work is nothing compared to what she did for us."

Arcane waited, listening.

256 | JESSE PIPER

She could tell Nipuna was evaluating her emotions, by the way she side eyed her.

"I don't want sympathy." She continued. "I just want her back."

Arcane peered away, finding interest in the pile of rocks as she began to kick them to see how far they could fly.

"Ohno is smart, she can help us if we decide to leave this island, if we want to migrate to INDUSTCOR, but Mori? Her name is renowned, she would have links, her magic would protect every single one of us, she could look after us," Nipuna snapped, hands tugging at her shirt despite the cold, she was overwhelmingly hot in the tattered uniform. "None of us can do it without her, you know that."

"What do you expect me to do? You say you want her back like we can just wait patiently, and she'll magically appear." This time, Arcane snapped. "*She's dead,* She's dead and she's not coming back."

Tears welled, she snapped her eyes shut, numb as she stood still-unable to look at Nipuna.

"Maybe we're better off just dying on this island."

"You don't believe that I know you better than that."

Arcane gulped back the gravelling pain in her throat as she tried to talk.

"I wish she wasn't gone; I wish I was in her place; it would've made everything simple. It's my fault she's gone, if I had just not loved her, she would never have sacrificed herself. But the past is the past, Nipuna, *she's gone.*"

Nipuna was silent before her eyebrows furrowed, distractedly staring off to the afternoon sky.

Arcane spoke, but the lanky woman cut her off with a raised finger in her direction.

"Shut up for a second."

Arcane frowned.

"You're a Amunet."

"Yes?"

Nipuna gave a withering look, one that looked as though what Nipuna was saying was obvious. As though Arcane was too dim headed to understand. Arcane only scoffed, crossing her arms. Ever since she had woken up, her body struggled to agree with her mind, she knew it would take time- but right now it felt as though she walked in another person's body, a foreign body.

Ohno would say the same if she still wasn't dead.

"Your ancestors encompass Necromancy."

Arcane scoffed, narrowing her eyes.

"You think I haven't tried!" She snapped. "I don't know how to do it."

"You could learn."

"What if I bring her back, and she is a living corpse? What good is she?"

Nipuna scoffed. "I know more about Necromancy than you do, and you're a Amunet?" Under her breath she scoffed. "What a fraud."

"I heard you."

Nipuna ignored the woman, stretching before safely placing the frame within a large pocket inside her jacket.

"If you want them alive, you give one of your lives. Same basics to killing a witch, you get their lives, if you kill a witch, you get their single life, if you burn one, you get them all."

"I'll try again. I guess."

"You will," Nipuna snapped. "I don't care if you won't risk a single life to bring her back, I'll make you."

Arcane sneered.

"You act like I wouldn't die for any of my Sisters."

"So, you would take a life to bring her back?"

"I would give every single one of my lives to bring her back."

CPSIA information can be obtained
at www.ICGtesting.com
Printed in the USA
LVHW110542220322
714058LV00005B/59/J